Werewolves of

Stoney Creek

From the Files of the Department of the

Arcane

By: S.C. Houff
405 Buchanan Street

Richlands, VA 24641
schouffwrites@gmail.com

Fall Rituals

©2021 S. C. Houff

Self-published edition 2021
ISBN 736738504
ISBN-13: 978-1-7367385-0-4

Cover design: S. C. Houff
Original Art: Marissa Letterio
Grammarmancy: Rebekah McGrady

SUPER AWESOME THANKS GO TO...

THE GRAMMARMANCER, BEKKAH, WHO MAKES
ME LOOK GOOD.
TO YOU, THE FAN WHO KEEPS BUYING
TO MRS. WILEY WHO HAD TAUGHT ME HOW TO
WRITE
TO HAL WHO KEEPS HANGING OUT....FOR
WHATEVER REASON.

OFFERED IN TRIBUTE TO MARILYN BANKS
CARROLL

WE HELD TIGHT TO OUR LOVED ONES AND WE HELD ON
TO THE PROMISE
AND WE SCRAPED OUR MEAGER LIVING HAND TO
MOUTH
WE PRAYED TO WHAT WOULD HAVE US, EVERY
DOUBTING JOHN THOMAS
SPREADING THROUGH THE APPALACHIA EVER SOUTH
SPREAD THROUGH APPALACHIA EVER SOUTH
-DRIVE BY TRUCKERS
"EVER SOUTH"

1.

Dusk painted the autumn sky an imperial violet, slowly pulling a blanket of inky black speckled with dancing white stars over the mountain. At that time, Dan officially stopped fiddling with the radio. They had run out of podcasts and music hours ago and he needed something, anything, to keep himself awake. He had to give up on that hunt. This far into the mountains, all he could find was country music or the radio preachers screaming about salvation. Even with darkness settling over the high mountain road, it shouldn't be particularly dangerous, but this was the only road through the county. He wasn't worried about hitting another car; at that time of the night there were things that he was terrified of far more than other motorists. There were logging flatbed trucks and coal trucks that would be trying to make good time. Dan had seen <u>Final Destination</u> one too many times. He had no desire to die in that way. Yet not even that was his specific fear tonight; he was more worried about what might be waiting for them at the bottom of the mountain. The base of the mountain was a favorite spot for the county sheriff's office to speed trap and Dan was determined not to be pulled over. They had an ounce and half of grass and two very large mason jars full of moonshine. Dan knew that there was no possible way a traffic stop could end well for him. He didn't want to get arrested and if anyone would be, it would be him and not Mike. Mike would charm his way out of it and Dan would end up with the contraband. The biggest slight was that Dan didn't even want it in his car in the first place.

But like the man said, you can't always get what you want.

He wasn't going to pretend that the booze and drugs weren't things that he'd loved at one time. Dan had partied hard in his teens and twenties. Now that his twenties were fading, it was less important to him. He hadn't smoked weed in years and the heavy drinking had faded away when he'd landed the office job along with a promotion out of the cubicle farm at the insurance company. He had earned that through his hard work, and he was so close to throwing it all away the second he started the car for this trip. It was only now that he had started to realize that. The excitement of adventure had created an element of poor life choices. Dan could only hope that he wouldn't pay for his irresponsibility of allowing Mike to bring drugs and illegal drinks on his way back. He had to remind himself that Dan himself didn't buy anything. He could take pride in the fact that he didn't buy any of it. Of course, he wasn't sure that Mike had paid for it either. He might have gotten their party supplies, as Mike called it, through a weird network of bartering for something that made sure he didn't have to pay. It was either that or he charmed someone into giving him the stuff. That wouldn't surprise Dan. Mike was the kind of social Sherpa that knew everyone and had few people that hated him. He would miss that sort of magic. On the other side of the mountains, adulthood was waiting for them.

Or, at least, it was waiting for Dan.

Dan's nose crinkled at the earthy smell of pot that wafted over to the driver's side. In a misguided attempt to sooth Dan's paranoia, Mike was smoking the last of the weed so that it wouldn't be with them when they got back home. That was what Dan was going to want to believe as opposed to what it was really about. It had nothing to do with Dan and everything to do with Mike's mother. Mike on and off lived with his parents. If Mike's parents -- especially his mother -- found out that there was weed in the car, he would catch all sorts of hell for it. Mike could control the narrative about how he was just around pot and not smoking. Joe Sr., Mike's father, wouldn't believe it. His faith in Mike was shook ages ago but Juanita would wholeheartedly seize upon any plausible deniability her son offered, however half-assed.

That was all that mattered to Mike.

Dan tried to force the thoughts out of his head and focus back on the road that stretched out before him glowing in his high beams. He could have asked Mike to drive but there was no chance of that. Mike drove too fast and that was a danger. Of course, that would also mean that he would have to give up to a secret truth: Dan loved long car drives. It was a nice moment that could allow him to pretend that he was doing something else. He could pretend that he was following in the same steps as Kerouac or something out of

Easy Rider. Those stories had tragic ends. Dan was about ready to end this one too.

All good things usually had to end.

Dan wasn't planning to end his life, not really. He was starting a new phase of his life and that was enough to keep him alert. At the end of this road was something he was excited about. Not that he was 100% ready to walk into that new life. As much as he was excited, it was nerve wracking. Part of him wanted to be able to turn back time and start this trip all over and live in that festival scene. He wouldn't have to hurt his friend and they could just be aging hippies. Quickly, he knew that was just a stupid idea. It was a fantasy world and Dan had to live in the real world.

Well, thought Dan, *I live there. Mike still lived in high school.*

Dan couldn't figure out where that thought came from -- maybe because Mike lived at home. There wasn't anything wrong with living with your parents. Dan had moved back for a little bit after he graduated from college as he tried to figure out what his life was going to be. Mike was different when it came to living with his parents. There was simply no desire in Mike to ever change his life to make himself into an adult. Dan hadn't fully realized that until this trip.

It was because of Tucker.

Tucker was a friend of theirs from the old days. He was about a year ahead of them when they met him in high school. Tucker was pretty cool back then because he was the cool college kid who came back to hang out with High School Friends. He was also the one who would buy them alcohol when they hung out over the summer. Tucker had dropped out of college at some point and was working part time for a big box retail store. It had been a long time since they had seen Tucker. It was amazing that they were able to meet up with him at the concert.

He wasn't exactly the Tucker they remembered.

Tucker hadn't come alone when he met up with them. He'd brought his wife who seemed to be okay with Tucker being Tucker. He was a happy man who was staying at home with their beloved two-year-old. He'd married a very wealthy woman who was working hard at a good paying job. While talking to Tucker about his life, Dan had a wretched epiphany: Tucker had gotten his life together, so what was holding Mike back? Dan knew the answer to that question.

Mike.

Dan wasn't really someone who believed that it was always one person's fault when it came to their lot in life but then there was Mike. As far as he could tell, Mike was pretty happy being a teenager no matter how old he was. Dan found it strangely depressing that Mike was never embarrassed by his immature life.

Mike had a lot to be embarrassed about.

Dan looked over at Mike. He was snoring at that point which was strangely different from his usual M.O. of filling the car with constant talking. Dan couldn't think of a time that Mike wasn't running his mouth, but it was a defense. Mike couldn't stand silence. There had to be a reason for this hatred. Dan wondered if Mike didn't want to be alone with his thoughts because he might have realized hard facts about himself. Maybe if Mike was alone with his thoughts, he'd realize how dependent he was on mother and how unhealthy that relationship was.

Mike was the traumatic death away of Juanita from becoming Ed Gein.

In the last few years, Mike had been repeatedly bailed out of trouble by his mother. They never spoke about it in the family but it was something that hung over everyone. Juanita had a favorite and it was Mike. She'd deny it, of course. Juanita would deny everything with a laugh and say that she loved all her children equally. Everyone who came into contact with that family knew that it was a lie. She had a special place in her heart for her youngest son and this had afforded him a level of exploitation. Dan knew that he couldn't blame Mike for this dynamic. Juanita felt more at ease with Mike. The oldest of the three was too weird for Juanita to fully understand

and Laura was decidedly Daddy's little girl. Mike exploited this bond so that he could get what he needed. They were co-dependent. At the end of things it would be mommy and Mikey.

No wonder he stayed an overgrown infant.

All of these thoughts swam around in Dan's head as his nose twisted at the scent of the pot smoke before he tried to break himself from his reverie. He was doing mental exercises trying to turn Mike into a bad guy and he knew why. He was going to have to make a choice at the end of this trip. If he was angry at his best friend since preschool, it would make that choice so much easier for Dan. It wasn't really a choice at that point. Dan knew that he was going to give up his wilder existence. He was starting to move on to the next part of his life. He was going to be an adult and it would affect Mike. He had tried to tell Mike this before the trip home started.

"You know," Dan had said as they pulled away from the campsite, "I'm going to miss this."

"Yea, that party was pretty dope," Mike had replied. "But dude, there will be other shows."

Dan didn't have the heart to tell him that he was wrong. It wasn't on purpose, but Dan had been lying to Mike for a long time about two things.

The first thing seemed dumb to Dan. He had been dating a girl named Brittany for several years and they had since broken up. Dan hadn't quite figured out why he didn't tell Mike about Brittany. It would have been something that would have made the second part of his news easier. Mike hated her and would have been thrilled to know this important piece of information. It would, however, meant that he would have to explain why he'd broken up with Brittany. It would have gotten back to Mike's little sister Laura. Laura and Brittany hated each other, and it all came to a head when they had gotten into a fight. Dan broke up with Brittany after it. It was then that he realized that the reason he hadn't told Mike was because he would have to mention to Mike why he'd broken up with Brittany

Dan had been dating Laura for the last six months.

It might have seemed weird. Dan had known Mike's little sister for almost as long as he'd known Mike. She'd been a pretty good friend to Dan as well as Mike and they were close. That relationship was exactly what made Brittany hate Laura. She was jealous of the relationship that she and Dan had. It was this jealousy that had caused the fight that had ended his relationship with Brittany. Well, that and finding Laura half dressed in the bedroom that he shared with Brittany. It was long over but there was a complication to this.

Laura.

Laura didn't want Mike to know that she was dating Dan. Mike had often scared off boyfriends and made her romantic life difficult. Dan could respect that but, it was well beyond that. Because Mike was friends with lots of people, she had forbidden Dan to tell anyone about them. Dan had started out okay with this secret relationship. Brittany had been dramatic and public and with Laura it was all very low key. It was refreshing at first, but now it was starting to wear on him. Dan liked her too much to keep it hidden from the world. He knew quite a bit about Laura, and he loved her. He wanted to show that off to the world.

He wanted to go out on dates with the woman he loved.

That was the thing that was keeping him from going out on the town with Laura. There was no chance that he could just walk into a bar or a restaurant and Mike would not know. It would end poorly. He had worked up the nerve to tell Mike that he'd broken up with Brittany before they left town. It was a terrible idea. Mike had figured that he could use that as an excuse to party harder; Dan knew that he couldn't say anything else to him. The music festival had been a whirlwind of booze, drugs and Mike trying to pick up skinny blondes with headdresses. Dan knew that it was time to tell Mike before it was too late.

He was going to marry Laura.

Dan had everything planned for this. He had to break his rule about not telling people about this relationship. Dan was sort of old fashioned. It wouldn't be fitting to ask to marry his girlfriend without telling her parents. He had asked permission. Juanita didn't say anything. She simply made a little "hmph" noise and then privately started to budget for the wedding on a scrap of a piece of paper. Joe Sr, on the other hand, quietly listened to Dan and then let out a loud laugh.

"About damn time," he'd told Dan.

After Dan had gotten his permission, he started to sit down and make every step of this plan. He'd book a hotel room for a long weekend in Boston for the two of them. Laura had gotten the time off from work. Dan had already gotten tickets for the Boston Philharmonic. He would walk her down to Merton. He was proud of that, since it had taken almost the length of their relationship to get reservations. At Merton, it would be time. He would tell Laura what she meant to him and then ask her to marry him. He knew that she could say no and if she did, that would be fine. Laura was practical and if she wasn't ready to be married then it would be only a matter of time. He really hoped that wouldn't be the case.

He wanted her to say yes.

He had to say something to Mike before that. He was about to say it then but he stopped. It caught in his throat like a lump. It wasn't the time and there would be time enough later.

Dan was going to enjoy the last few moments of the road trip.

Just as they turned around the base of the mountain, the radio crackled alive with a loud version of Cream's cover of *Crossroad Blues*. By the thud that opened the glove box and the high pitched scream, Dan knew that Mike was awake. His pudgy arms flew over his head as he convulsed with startled body language. Silence washed back over the car before Dan erupted in loud laughter that stared at the bottom of his stomach. Mike narrowed his eyes at Dan to stop his mocking laughter. When he didn't the only warning that he got was:

"You fucking suck."

Mike brought his large hand down and started slapping on Dan. It wasn't exactly like that was able to stop Dan from laughing. Dan turned to try to keep the slaps from hitting him. He put his hand up. There was nothing that Mike could have said to stop him from laughing him, well, except:

"Holy shit! Look out!"

Dan looked over long enough to see the shadow of a figure in the middle of the road. His eyes went wide as he looked at the shadow. He couldn't make sense of what he was seeing for a moment before he realized what he was looking at in the middle of the road was a person.

Dan saw a woman.

Her hair was long and braided back. She wore a simple dress that looked like it was somewhere outside of this century. For a moment he thought that she was a ghost but that didn't stop him from trying to not hit the woman. Dan tried to hit the break in order to not run her down, but for whatever reason he couldn't hit it hard enough to stop. It was too late. The fender of the SUV hit the woman forcing her under the car. Dan skidded the Jeep to a stop. He glanced back to see if the woman was okay. He was about to open the door when he felt something pull the car up from behind. Dan looked at Mike with a swallow. Before he was able to make a plan to get help, the SUV was tossed over the side of a high bank. They screamed at each other as it rolled end over end down the hill before it hit a tree.

Then, it was silent.

At the top of the bank, the woman looked down at the SUV. She could grab the people in the car, but she knew that wasn't her job. She would have to tell her boys where they could find them. It was the road though. She knew that there would be more cars along by dawn and people would be looking for them. That wasn't something that she would be able to explain, if it meant that there would be more outsiders on the mountain. Pa would have to know about this, but she would go home first. She hesitated for a moment. If this was a good hunting place, then Pa would need to know that. She turned to a tree, pulling a knife out of her apron. She slowly carved the letters in the tree. She nodded at the simply carved letters of: CRO.

This was theirs.

2.

There was a metallic clank as the front left tire hit a pothole on the country road. The whole right side of the state-owned van bounced up and down violently. Huston Whelan suppressed an explosive swear as his chest compressed against the straps of his seat belt and his testicles felt like they were trying to retreat into his stomach. He gave a weird snarly look at the back of Officer Barry Brown's head. He was hoping that the man could be smart enough to avoid the potholes. For the most part, he could be relied upon to avoid road hazards, but they were now past the sign that said "End of State Maintenance" which meant that all bets were off. The roads that were paved at this point were going to be ignored for as long as they could be. For now, the gods of the country roads would take up offerings of balding tires, popped hubcaps, and off-kilter alignments until summer. That seemed so far away from this cold day in fall.

These days seemed to be going on forever.

Huston didn't have time to recover from the shock of hitting the potholes before his form was forced into the bulletproof glass of the side window as Officer Brown took the curve of the mountain road too fast. All Huston wanted was to throw a punch at the back of his head to tell him that it was too damn fast and if he didn't watch what he was doing, he was going to get them all killed. Huston thought better of it. It was good policy to not attack the man who was driving the car. More so than that, he couldn't blame Barry. Barry wasn't meant for the jail life. He was too dumb to be able to get a good job. If he had been alive twenty years ago, he would have worked in the factories. Those were gone now to somewhere in China or Cambodia. Prisons weren't the best places to work. The time that Huston had been in jail, he'd seen lots of people who had come through who had been burned out. Sometimes the only way that you feel better for a while is riding down the twisted road as fast as you can like there's nothing to worry about. Huston was right there with him.

If it wasn't going to be weird, he would have stuck his head out the window and let his tongue flap in the wind.

Of course, Oswaldo didn't agree with either Huston or Officer Barry. He was white knuckled holding on to the seat looking like he was going to be dead in the next thirty seconds. Huston, honestly, felt sad for him. Oswaldo, or Wally as they were calling him, was from somewhere around Nashville and had clearly never had the joy of riding too fast around gravelly switchbacks. Huston slapped him on the back hard.

"You okay there, hoss?" Huston asked with an exaggerated drawl.

"No!" Wally screamed at him. "How are you okay?"

"You get used to it."

Oswaldo scoffed at Huston in utter disbelief. Oswaldo was never going to be comfortable. That was his problem handling his time in prison. The thing that got Huston through this life was holding on to the little differences in the schedule. When you have nothing but free time, you try to find something that makes life easy. If you didn't find something to distract yourself, the boredom would kill you. When he'd done his first term in prison, he didn't have anything to do. It had made him violent and worse. It was why he was determined this time around that he was going to make it out. He was going to be an adult. He was too old to be stupid.

Of course, there were so few people suited to be a death porter.

Death porters were inmates at the jail who would help move a body from the scene of their death to the coroner's office. It was a new job in the county. Before he had retired, old Roy did the whole thing. He would go to pronounce the body, load it up and then take it back to the hospital to do the autopsy. Roy had retired however, and the county didn't think they could hire anyone else to do that kind of multitasking. You didn't have to pay prisoners like you did a medical doctor though. They'd gone through quite a few people before settling on Huston and Oswaldo. Oswaldo liked the idea of getting out of the jail even if he had a weak stomach. Huston wanted to get out of his cell too, but he had a stronger stomach. Dead amadan never bothered him. They were on the other side of the veil and probably killed by someone he knew. Wouldn't surprise him, after all.

They weren't kin.

If you thought that Huston was a mundane person who was living in this fantastical world, I'm afraid I have some bad news for you.

He was not.

Huston Whelan was a natural born predator. It had been borne in his blood from a long history. His father was a predator as was his father before him. He had married a bride who was a predator just like him. He didn't know anyone that he was closely related to who wasn't a predator. It was the point of having a pack. Huston was greatly proud of calling himself a member of the *conry*. They were a proud people who had always straddled the two lives of humanity and the woods. It was because of this life that made the last days before his release start to make him concerned.

Huston had never been out on his own.

Huston's life had started in a large pack with lots of brothers, sisters and cousins. They had spread up the spine of the mountains of Appalachia and they had roamed from the tip of Georgia and up to parts of Western Virginia. His branch of the family had settled in East Tennessee. It was a charmed life and would have continued to be charmed if he had been able to keep his marriage together. It was hard to be married to a *conry* princess.

Maybe it was their fault.

He hadn't chosen to be betrothed to her. It was a smart choice to marry someone from the Hounds of *Deisi Muman* (Last great kings of Ireland in their mind) to the Pack of the Crowe Black Wolves. Them Crowe Boys, as they were called by everyone in the county, had become the most powerful pack in three states. It was better that he accepted the marriage. It wasn't that he didn't know her. Huston had run with the younger members of the Crowes. So, he knew her. God, she was gorgeous back then. She was probably beautiful now, but he couldn't remember what she looked like except when he thought about her as she was back then. They were young when he met her. She was younger than him by at least four years. He had been introduced to this stunningly beautiful girl with dark black hair and pale skin. What did her mother claim it to be? She always said that the Crowes were Black Irish. She would mention that when the Spanish Armada crashed on the shores of Ireland, they gave them a welcome into their homes and you had these pale blue eyes on black haired girls. She wasn't real Irish. She wasn't full-blooded *conry* that was for sure. She had one eye that was a different color than the other. She was some sort of half-breed but that didn't matter. It was important that it worked. After the agreement was set, Huston tried to learn everything about her. They did grow closer. She fell in love with him.

He was horny.

During his first stretch in prison, Huston thought about where things went wrong with her. He wondered if he could travel back in time, would he tell his younger self to just walk away from her and let that girl be. That didn't las very long. Everything would have happened the same way because, well, he knew that he was right. He had done exactly what he was meant to do. He had enjoyed her company and sowed the seed for the next generation. She became pregnant. She was the one who was worried about that. She had begged for him to let her get an abortion and not tell her parents. That wasn't going to happen. He had told her father. Prince David hadn't been happy about them laying before they were married but was happy that they were going to do the right thing. She wasn't as happy about it. She didn't want to be married. She'd had plans of rejecting the pack. She had tried to explain it.

"You don't get it, Huston," she'd said. "There is more to life than the hollow."

He had hit her when she started saying things like that. It was the first time that he hit her, but it wouldn't be the last. What Huston learned from that was that his child bride was highly intelligent and willful. That was fine and good when it turned out to be a fight against an enemy but not in a marriage. He hit her often when she wanted to do something. She wanted to finish high school, he tried to beat that out of her. She didn't need an education. They had a small pup and would need to be taking care of their small pack. She eventually relented and got her GED when he was gone. That was what he would have changed if he learned how to time travel. She had learned how to sneak out and finish her high school education. He hadn't known that until she was in her second semester of community college. She would take their daughter with her to class. He accepted that for the time being. She was busy taking care of their child. It meant that he had to take care of his wife and child.

He was bad at that.

A hundred years ago, his people had made their money from the stills that they had hidden in the woods and then running the fruits of their labor into town for a profit. Hell, they did that fifty years ago, but no one wanted shine anymore. Pack cooking had to become more educated and smarter and there was something that his cousins knew how to make, and they could make a lot of money.

They knew how to cook meth.

Huston had been good at it from the start. He had always had a good eye for cooking, and it did translate to cooking meth.

There was an axiom that comes with this sort of work: people who cook meth shouldn't do meth because it's the second batch that explodes on you. Huston had started taking meth so that he would be able to cook more. Soon, Huston was far more interested in taking meth than cooking it. When he started stealing from his grandmother, he was turned out by his pack. You could steal, kill or hurt outsiders but you didn't hurt family. Huston was convinced that's when he was caught and given three years in jail. He thought he could handle this and grow up.

Then, she betrayed him.

The turning point was at the end of his second year of his sentence. He was clean for the better part of a year and was looking forward to a life outside of prison. He would have to repay the honor of his family but that would come in due time. All of this stopped when the sheriff's department served him with a notice of divorce. It seemed that in the eighteen months that he was in prison, she had finished her degree and had gotten a job to support herself and the kid. Huston was willing to take blame for what he did to put her in that position. If he'd been a better man, then that wouldn't have happened. This was far more than that. She should have only had to work until he came home and resumed his place. She was willing to break off their bound marriage and, somehow, she had gotten permission from the elders to file for this. Huston could only feel one thing from all of this.

He was furious.

He had been betrayed by his family and her. He could understand that his family would allow this because, honestly, he'd done some terrible things to them. He deserved that but she was different. She should have been under him and she was supposed to be bound to him for life. He knew that it had been the job she was holding. Someone had got into her ear during that and convinced her to leave him. There had to be someone who had gotten into her ear. He knew who it was.

It was *him*.

There had been someone who had been sniffing around her since her high school days. Huston had hated him for a long time. It had started with him being an *amadan* that wanted his girl. Now he was worse than that. He wasn't just an outsider. He suspected that she was under the influence of someone who was a *jake*. There were few things worse than running with an outsider, but an outsider who was a cop? That was the ultimate betrayal to Huston. For the last few years of his life in prison he had focused on what he was going to do when he got out. He would have probably forgotten it if he'd not been released early. When he got out, Huston immediately walked out of prison and back to his home. He didn't find the *jake* there, but he had found her.

He beat her within an inch of her life.

Huston knew that he would have killed her if someone hadn't stopped him. He couldn't quite remember but it might have been the *jake* or her brother who pulled him off. There was no mistaking that he was going back to jail. It was done then. He was shunned by his pack. He was ignored by her pack and there was nowhere else to go. Huston knew that he was done here. When he got out this time, he was going to be gone.

He needed to get the hell out of East Tennessee.

There was no way that he could have ever asked anyone for help, but he did get the blessing of his mother to go up north. He had a cousin that ran with the pack of the Sons of Sirius. He wasn't looking forward to being in a non-familial pack, but it was better than nothing. There was something about running in the wild without fear of hiding that seemed like a dream after the life he'd spent in prison.

He couldn't wait.

"I hope you boys have strong stomachs," Officer Barry said casually like he had a wedge of chewing tobacco in his jaw. He did, but he was having too much fun with this. "Dad says the one they found looks like spoiled hamburger meat."

Huston stared at Officer Barry almost too nonplussed at that statement. It was Officer Barry's hope that he'd make someone look green from the idea of dead bodies. Huston didn't flinch. He'd seen enough death to be numb to it by this point. Oswaldo made some sort of noise that might have been a whine for him. It was the black humor to make things easier for someone when they had to move a dead body. Humans needed to find a way to reassure themselves when facing their own mortality.

"We got another drunk sleepin' on the tracks?" Huston asked as casually as he was told about the dead.

"Ain't near the tracks," Officer Barry replied. "Off the main road. Might be a bear or something with the body that mutilated."

A jolt went through Huston that made him perk up at Officer Barry words. It was that key phrase of "bear attack" that clicked in his brain. Officer Barry's dad was the coroner of the county. If he was calling it a bear attack, then he could only think that meant one thing. There was something else.

For those of you who don't know, bears are generally docile creatures who don't attack. If you leave bears alone, they generally leave you alone. Hence the old adage is never get between a mother bear and her cub. That could have been the problem except that it was fall. There shouldn't be any cubs around, let alone any mothers that would be protecting them. He knew exactly what a bear attack meant in this part of the world. Some *amadan* died at the hands of something that no one could understand. Huston knew what that meant normally.

Bear attack was always a label that was applied to werewolf attacks.

A lot of thoughts went through Huston's head almost immediately. Could some poor bastard have been killed by one of his kind? There hadn't been blatant human hunting for more than thirty years. If there was something hunting humans, then it meant that the thinly held treaties that kept people together in the hollows were starting to come undone. If that was the case, then he wasn't sure if he should be going to New England. It could also have been something less likely than werewolves. There were vampires in the woods somewhere as well as other things. If that was the case, then the next people who would be at the scene would be the Department of the Arcane. She worked for the Department of the Arcane. That was more upsetting than anything. Could he even look at her? For all he knew, he would do something to her at the scene. He could feel her neck snap in his claws and the heat of bathing in her blood.

He was still angry at his ex-wife.

Huston came back to reality when he finally felt the van lurch into park on the wide side of the road. That would be the only way to make sure that the winding road was clear. Officer Barry turned to look at the pair of convicts in the back. He gave them a dopey grin.

"Bodies are at the bottom of the hill," he announced gleefully. "Hope y'all brought your walking shoes.

They walked down the steep hill to make their way towards the scene. Huston guided the gurney through the dead leaves as he looked around. He felt his brow furrow as he listened quietly. His second stint in prison gave him this time as death's end porter. In that time, he had been to more crime scenes than he could count and there was always something there: noise. Even out in the middle of nowhere, crime scenes had a ton of sounds. It was the sound of radios buzzing and the casual talk of men who were charged with finding out what happened. Even if it was far away from where Huston was walking, there should be sounder than that. Huston couldn't hear the sounds of the forest. Then, Huston smelled it.

He smelled death.

It wasn't fresh death, the kind of smell that you smell at a scene. This was old death that had been living for years in the ground and dug up mixed with old soil and thoughts forgotten for centuries. Huston could feel a thick mat of grey fur rise on his back. He looked around as his teeth bared and he fought back a snarl. He wanted to try the painful and quick shift into his large wolf form so that he could run.

Something was there with them and it was watching him.

Huston could feel cold ancient eyes watching their every move. If they had the same sense of smell he did, they could smell his lupine blood and he would be first. He had to be a threat. They had to leave before all three of them lost their lives.

"Inmate," barked Officer Brown, surprising Huston. He thought that maybe Barry felt it too. He never called anyone "inmate" unless he was pissed. "Where do you think you're going?"

Huston suddenly realized that Barry was mad at him because he wasn't moving. He was still on the hill looking at Officer Barry and Oswaldo as he blinked at them. He should have told him then but he wasn't sure how to express himself. He wouldn't regret it later.

"We've got to get out of here," Huston stammered. "There's something that ain't right about this."

"Whelan, get down here now!"

"You don't understand, there is something evil out here and we've got to go. Get better support."

"Whelan don't be a pu-"

Before Officer Barry could finish that statement, he was gone. What Huston saw was a blur of black, brown, and bone white and he was gone. Then, suddenly Oswaldo was also gone, only leaving a high-pitched scream as he was pulled into shaking leaves. Huston didn't wait to see what happened to him. He started running tugging off his safety orange before letting out a painful wail as he bounded off into the woods on all fours.

3.

The bedroom that Jodell Crowe and her husband shared was both dark and cool enough in the morning that all she wanted was to stay wrapped in the blankets and not move. She was still in her bed watching the large windows as pre-dawn was burning into a warm grey that she knew would raise a fog just above the ground to usher in a kind blue day. She wanted to think of today as a Sunday. There was an ease that came from this morning that felt relaxed like a Sunday. Logically, she knew that it wasn't Sunday as she rolled over to her side and burrowed into a small pile of pillows that she had made into a nest. If this had been a Sunday, she would have been up on her feet demanding Rowan get up and get dressed because they would be late for church. It would have been met by complaints of how Rowan didn't want to go to church while Bill Jr. would be walking with his mother trying to use his four-year-old logic to explain why it was okay to wear his Halloween costume to church. Jodell would lightly curse her mother-in-law for her part in this new wrinkle in Sunday morning routine. It had started around the beginning of September when Bill Jr. saw <u>Godspell</u> with his grandmother and her church group. While he didn't fully understand what he was seeing, what he did understand was that "Jesus wore a Superman t-shirt" and since then, this was going to be a fight that she had to deal with every Sunday. She would win this battle and overcome Rowan's new fourth grade atheism and they would all be heading to church where she would be greeted by the angry expression on the face of her mother-in-law. Jodell would smile trying to make things better. She didn't like going to church herself. There was something about Christianity being the faith that had shunned her ancestors and made her life hard.

She still had some inherited resentment towards it.

Her mother-in-law was convinced that she was raising her children in the mountain paganism that had been here long before people tried to bring Jesus to these mountains. Jodell had tried hard to let that go and pretend that she wasn't a part of that long forgotten past. She knew that it didn't work.

She would never be good enough for Darlene Harris.

In the time of her marriage to Bill, Jodell hadn't exactly lived up to what Darlene thought a wife should be for her only son. It wasn't that she hated Jodell outright. Someone like Darlene didn't believe in hating people. That was not something that her one true God did. She could disapprove of Jodell in lots of different ways, however. Everything that Jodell did had been analyzed and graded by Darlene's personal scoring method. She knew that she was being judged as a wife and mother. It was stressful for Jodell, but Bill had never really cared about his mother's approval. If that hadn't been the case, then he wouldn't have signed up for the Marines when he graduated from high school. He definitely wouldn't have taken a job as a sheriff's deputy when he came back. It was something that Jodell had learned from an earlier point of her life only to marry into it later. It was the sort of constant trauma that she hadn't been able to shake, and she knew that it would never be gone. She would have to learn to accept that the world had people like Darlene. Today wasn't going to be the day she had to worry about her in-laws though. Today was Saturday.

Jodell had other judgmental people to worry about.

No matter how she had ignored this day, she knew that it was all coming to this one thing. She had pretended as long as she could, but here it was and that brought the flood of fears back. She didn't want to borrow trouble before she needed to, but she knew trouble was there aplenty. The looks of her uncles, aunts and cousins as she walked her young family towards them. Her second marriage that hadn't been blessed by the ancestors. The outsider that she married would be shunned, and -- even worse -- she knew that by this point they would have known about him being a cop. Jodell didn't want to acknowledge this problem. She rolled back over and pulled a blanket over her head. It was rare that she got to lay in like this. For Jodell it was simply decadent to be lying in bed like she had nothing to do.

It wouldn't last but she was going to relish every second.

What a shame, she thought, that Bill didn't appreciate the luxury of lying in bed on a weekend day. Jodell wanted to be wrapped in the tired warm body of someone who had about fifty pounds on her and leaning over her while he quietly snored. She didn't know how many mornings she'd sat in the blackness of night listening to him snore softly as she curled next to him. Of course, she realized that if he was still in bed it would mean that Rowan and Bill, Jr would be alone in the house and nothing good could come of that scenario and that Bill was sick. She had never known him to ever stay in bed past six AM. It had to be something that was beaten out of him somewhere in the time that he left Watertown. She wouldn't have him any other way. Bill was a morning person and she loved it about him. It meant that he understood that she preferred to stay in bed as long as she could. He was letting her relish her one vice. It was something that you did on special days. Today was a very special day.

It was the first day in months that both she and Bill had a weekend off together.

To clear her mind, Jodell let herself fantasize about what her day would be like if they just stayed home. She could see it perfectly. She would lounge in bed for most of the morning while Bill would make breakfast. It was something that he did any time he had a weekend morning or holiday off. If she was lucky, he would bring her breakfast while she was in bed. She could see them loafing around the house until boredom won. Then, they would finally decide to leave. She could see them going on a drive down to Johnson City for the day. She and Rowan would go to the mall while the boys would go somewhere to run around either downtown or at Rocky Mount. Bill Jr. loved going there to see the sheep. It could all be possible if it wasn't for the fact that it was Formal Day.

Formal Day was Jodell's least favorite day of the year.

Formal Day was a family holiday honoring one of the oldest ancestors. It commemorated the visit of the King of the Moons and the Lord of Night Eldtha bringing down his prized children, the Fomrians. It was said that he came down in his glittering silver ship to bless his children with the Mark of Cuchulian. Those who had the blessing would be given the family legacy. It was the time for everyone to come home. It had been the way ever since the first Crowe settled on the grassy shore of the creek back in 1782. The Crowes had lived there since the land had been given as a trade for service and loyalty to General Washington. The Battle of Kings Mountain might not have been as successful if it hadn't been for the werewolves who fought along with the patriots. Over the years, celebrating Formal Day had only grown in importance to the family. This new emphasis had started when her great-grandfather brought his new bride back to the Cove.

Kirk Allen Crowe was the weird one in the pack. He'd been the first one to not be able to commune with the earth to grow anything good and didn't care to hunt. He was still loyal to the pack, which was why he'd thought about running the bootlegging, until his youngest cousins were murdered in a revenge plot against their father. Mob war wasn't something that he was willing to put his family through. Kirk instead became educated. After that, he met Emma. Emma O'Connell had been educated quite well on the East Coast and had come across the mountains at the urging of the deaconess to bring some sort of civility to the untamed mountain folk. They had married and continued to teach over the border in North Carolina. Jodell was certain that the hand cart that Kirk and Emma had owned to get to work had been found by at least one of Them Crowe Boys.

The Hand Cart was the most important part of her Family Tradition.

According to legend, it was on the Day of Fomrians when the future unfolded before Kirk. On their way over the mountain, riding the rails with their handcart, they heard the low whine of the train whistle. This was a moment of panic that Kirk knew too well. The trellis over the gorge had only one set of tracks. They were not going to be fast enough. Kirk knew what he had to do in order to save not only himself, but his Emma. It was a strange day for Kirk. Kirk, unlike his other family members, had never gone through the change. So, when he used all his great lupine strength, he threw the hand cart off the trellis and into the creek below. When he emerged from the water with Emma, he could smell fear and blood. There was no mistaking the stinging pain that arched through her leg. She knew that her leg was open to the bone. In a quickened heartbeat of Emma, a large black wolf started to leap towards her. Emma let out a scream as she backed up and he lunged at her. Emma found herself whispering a prayer to a god that she didn't know existed to her. It was an old god that her family had worshiped in the old country. She hoped that he would listen.

The gods of her ancestors were listening.

When Kirk forced his teeth into her flesh, Emma let out a loud roar as her body shook. She felt something that she hadn't felt before that day. A large claw came down and ripped Kirk from her as she bared suddenly large teeth. No one knows how long they fought or whatever happened after but at the end of it, they rested on the rocks next to the creek. She settled against him and they knew. Kirk had been hiding this part of his life, but now it was time to come back. They were both *conry*: the last kings of Ossory. They knew that there were so few of them left in the world that going forward, it was time to honor the traditions of their people. And it spread. Their generations were blessed with the blood Prince Meori who flew across the sky in his boat of the moon. There were some who never changed. Jodell was one of them. She ran the rocks and never became a wolf. That wasn't the thing that was bothering her this morning, but she was bothered, nonetheless.

Jodell wasn't looking forward to this day.

The last time she had been to Formal Day was before she had gone through the divorce from her first husband. That had been painful. There were a few that knew what exactly happened to her. She could trust her mother or Lord Byron to protect her. She knew that it wasn't enough. Jodell could remember walking with Rowan on her hip and being stared at by everyone as she walked into the farmhouse. She couldn't go back to that. She had brought so much shame on everyone. It was more difficult now and she knew what made things uncomfortable for her.

She couldn't face the pack back then, and so she just didn't. She had rejected her heritage.

It had been an easy choice. She was halfway there when she was denied the blessing that her brother and her cousins had. She was only half accepting of the arranged marriage, but it was better than being with her family. Then, she had the divorce and that was the worst thing that she had ever done. She had long ignored this part of her life, but it came down before she knew what was happening. She let out a sigh. She was going to suck up the humiliation to do this one thing because of love.

She was going to do this one thing because Bill asked her to.

Jodell knew that it was only a matter of time before she was going back to the family. It wasn't because of the birth of Bill Jr. It was Bill Sr. Jodell knew that Bill had the largest family that she'd ever seen outside of a wolf pack. It was his conry values that made her like him. Family came first for Bill and it was a shame that he hadn't been introduced to her family. He'd met her mother and interacted with Vaughn, but it wasn't really the family that she knew. He wanted to see this family and she knew it was only a matter of time. Jodell wondered how much longer she could delay her fate.

At least, she thought, *for five more minutes.*

She knew that it was selfish, but Jodell was going to enjoy every second of her alone time. It was precious and limited. Soon, it would be lost, and she could be bound by the commitments of her life. If it wasn't the responsibility of being one of Those Crowe Boys, it would be something more pressing. She knew that it would only be a matter of minutes before one of the children would end up running in to disrupt the silence. No sooner than the thought crossed her mind, she heard the heavy feet of a toddler pounding down hardwood floor towards her bedroom. Jodell braced herself for a child to bust into her room. That moment was forestalled by the warm voice of Bill from the hall.

"You wake your momma up and Ro will lick the bowl by herself."

Silence echoed for a moment before the heavy footsteps of a small child ran back down the hallway. Jodell sat up as the door cracked open. She licked her lips as Bill's square face peeked through the door with a soft smirk. She pulled a sheet up looking at his serious gray eyes.

"You owe me," Bill whispered to her with a strange hiss. "It's going to get weird later."

Jodell couldn't help but laugh at him with his threat. The door creaked open showing him standing in her doorway with a wry grin. Bill was up to no good.

"Oh?" She purred. "Are you planning on locking the kids in the basement?"

"Well, I do have the keys to the office. I could get the animal control cages."

"Does that mean we ain't going to the Cove?"

She watched as his shoulders dropped angrily at her words. She made a face as she watched him build up for the same fight they had been having for the last week.

"You do not want to know what I had to do to get this day off," Bill started.

"I know…but…"

"But what, Jo? What are you afraid of?"

"Another incident like the one at Cowboys."

Bill regretted telling Jodell about the incident at Cowboy's, as it was now her weapon to keep this day from happening. Cowboy's was the only bar out in the county and it wasn't uncommon for the Sheriff's Department to be called out there for any manner of problems. It wasn't always a major issue but this one had been different. Bill and his partner were called out to Cowboy's to find out that the complaint was Vaughn. Jodell wasn't sure what Vaughn had done to have the police called but by the time Bill had gotten there he was angry. Bill was good enough to know that he couldn't take Vaughn in. It didn't mean that Vaughn wasn't spitting bile at him.

"Don't touch me, *amadan*!" he had screamed at Bill. "You made my sister a whore!"

To Bill's credit, he didn't punch Vaughn. Bill had been on duty and wasn't about to punch a man in cuffs while he was on duty. It was also better for Bill. Had he thrown a punch, Vaughn would have gone full on wolf and attacked him. Vaughn would have gotten away with it too. Cowboy's was a *conry* friendly bar.

"Well," said Bill as he closed the distance between himself and the bed. She felt his retired army weight on her body as she wrapped her arms around his neck. She made a content face catching his scent. "What is the worst that could happen?"

"Vaughn rips out your throat and leaves you to the buzzards."

That was true. The worst thing that could happen to him. A frown crossed his face.

"I don't think he'll do that until I challenge for a place in the pack."

Jodell let go of his neck and turned away. She couldn't bear the sight of him in that moment. This was going to be the thing that calmed everything down. He was going to ask for a spot in the pack. She didn't want that. Part of her liked Bill not wanting to be a part of that life. She then heard a grunt of frustration pass out of his nose.

"Especially if you are going to do that," she explained with a snarl. "Why would you do that?"

"You know why."

Jodell was on the verge of telling him exactly why she thought it was a stupid idea. He didn't need to prove anything to her or her family. She loved Bill. He was the father of her children no matter what her family thought. She was about to tell him that when the door burst open violently. Jodell and Bill sat up and looked into the large brown eyes of Bill Jr.

"You said to not wake up momma," Bill Jr said suspiciously.

"You are correct," Bill said. It was clear to him that his son took after him. "I did say that."

"Oh, okay." Bill Jr. paused as he remembered why he came to this room. "Rowan did something bad."

"What did she do?" asked Jodell.

"Oh, she let Mr. Arlis into the kitchen."

If Jodell had one good reason to go out to the Cove, it was to avoid being called into work. The Department of the Arcane field office was staffed meagerly. If something happened, she would be called to go check it out. There was no greater hell than spending a

Saturday in a trailer park on a Bigfoot sighting. He couldn't help it. Bigfoot was just looking for a better cell phone signal. Jodell rolled out of bed reluctantly.

"I'll take care of it," she growled.

4.

Norvita Patel had been dreaming a lot more lately. She knew that dreams weren't just dreams or, at least, they weren't for people like her. The dreams of psychics had important messages and she had to find them. The problem was that she couldn't find a reason for these dreams. Norvita knew that these were signs that would point out her next path. Until it was clear, she wasn't enjoying these dreams. Norvita liked having visions because it meant she was doing something and that she was starting to head in a direction, but the longer this kept going, she couldn't find any path.

Her dream started as always in a way that she hated. Norvita would be walking towards a thick-looking forest. She knew that there were forests that surrounded parts of Gaiman Heights, and it was her least favorite place to go when it came to anything involved with the Department. The Sons of Sirius, a nomadic werewolf pack, often camped in the woods and they were the most civil. There were lots of monsters living in the woods and they weren't exactly friendly when it came to the Department. Norvita was also going to ignore that this was the same place where she had seen and felt true loss. Marcia had died in the woods. Karl fell there too. If she never went into the woods ever again, she'd be happy.

But Norvita knew that she couldn't have nice things.

She was walking up to the woods and stood at the mouth of an ominous tunnel of greenery. Whatever was in the woods, she had to fight it and Norvita knew that she would be the only person who would be able to fight it. She cast her eyes up to the black night sky asking someone, anyone, who would be able to help her, to maybe prevent her from going into the woods. As if it was her answer, the stars started to blink out one by one as the moon slowly disappeared. Whatever she had to face, she couldn't hesitate. Norvita knew that she would have to combat it. She carefully set down the bag that she had slung across her back. Norvita started to dig into her bag. The first thing that she did was pull her hair back into a tight ponytail. She knew better than to keep her hair down when she was heading into a fight. Next, she pulled out a set of black mala beads. She had to have those beads around her neck. They surely provided some protection for her from the more negative emotions and impressions. She sighed as she started to wrap a bright red scarf around her ponytail and her head. Norvita squared her shoulders. She couldn't wait any longer.

She had to go in.

Norvita took one step into the woods as she looked around. She couldn't see anything that was going to threaten her. She quickly switched on her flashlight as she walked along. She cast her light up along the canopy. The trees were dead and that wasn't surprising. If anything, it was comforting with that and the sensation that she was sensing while there. If there had been a vibrant living forest surrounding that feeling, then she would be very upset. She continued her steps as a wind picked up her pace. With the dry leaves, it sounded like a dry sarcastic laugh. Norvita ignored it quietly as she kept walking along.

Suddenly, she felt something reach up for her. Norvita hesitated as thick thorns pull around her ankle. Then she felt her body hit dirty ground. Another long thin thorn scraped down along her body. She struggled as she tried to pull herself out of the tearing restraints. Norvita then stopped. She scowled as her mind went into a spiritual place. Norvita's lips parted as the soft sound of a prayer passed her lips. Quickly, a light shuttered over Norvita's body burning away the vines. Norvita stood up and brushed dirt off of herself.

"Yea," she said, spitting. "That's what I thought."

The trees shook in defiance at Norvita's words. She scowled at the trees as she stood up and started walking in a direction that she had picked before entering the woods. She ignored the fact that tops of the trees were starting to pull towards each other, blacking out of the sky. That would matter if this was even a dream that had some kind of sky and yet there was nothing there. She shook her head as she went on. This was nothing to make her mind change. She knew that she might have been desensitized to the idea of frightening trees. After all, she was a child born after 1986. She was fully aware of the sort of Empire Strikes Back vibe that these trees would have. She almost expected to see Darth Vader appear and then turn into her dark double. She was just going to ignore that. Of course, Norvita didn't want to admit to how many times she'd really seen Star Wars.

She'd seen all of them a lot.

She wasn't scared of the forest. She just was finding this all very trying. There were apparently only so many categories to the imagery that her visions could show her before she found all of it very boring. This was the most boring thing that she'd seen in a long time. It was cliched and that bothered her. She kept walking as she let out a loud petulant groan. She could do with more originality when it came to her psychic visions. Her flashlight started to flicker. Norvita stopped walking just before she stood in the middle of the forest. Having learned the best way to fix a flashlight was to smack the side of it, she did this. Then it became steady and Norvita focused the light forward.

Norvita immediately regretted her actions.

The light around her started to dance off the branches of the trees surrounding her and then it fell on the bodies dangling from the trees. Norvita cringed as she let her eyes and flashlight make inspection easier. They were dead and they had been there for quite some time. Norvita kind of hated that she knew this, but she could get a fairly good idea of how long a body had been hanging from a quick look at it. She and Karl had been a part of a case when a minor group of hunters were hanging witches or people who they thought were witches.

"It's a bad way to go," Karl had told her. "If the neck doesn't break, it takes a long time to strangle to death."

Karl did that often without thinking about what effect it would have on the mental state of those around him. Karl knew a lot of horrifying and weird shit and that was why he did his job so well. She had thought that was all there was to it at the time in the middle of this case. The longer she thought about it though, she began to understand that was really a sign about how much Karl was scared. He didn't like the idea that someone was relishing the murder of people regardless of who they are. He had no sympathy for those who torture people.

The people that she was staring at had been tortured.

Their eyes were wide and pushing out from the sockets as they looked sightlessly down at her. The lips were parted and blue with tongues dangling out of the corner of their mouths. Norvita didn't take time to see if they were the faces that she knew on any of these people. She couldn't look at them at all. There was no benefit from seeing these bodies at all. She wanted to move on because she didn't need to see more death. It wasn't like it was a major symbol in visions or anything.

Right?

Norvita ignored that out as she started to walk in a different direction. She tried to ignore the pained feeling in her stomach. She wanted to also completely ignore that she wanted to walk away from just about everything. Before she could regain her composure, her feet stubbed against something. Norvita was confused more than anything as her eyes stared up at what seemed to be a grand white marble staircase. Norvita pushed the light up the long steps to see where it led.

Nowhere.

These stairs stood in the middle of nothing and there was nothing beyond them. Maybe Norvita should be jarred by this but this was really nothing new. As a little girl, Norvita had been forced into the Girl Scouts and there were always adventures into the

Patterson National Forest. Patterson had once been a high-class neighborhood before the Great Depression. When the houses became too expensive to be maintained they had been abandoned. Over time, nature had started to reclaim everything. It left weird things in the middle of the forest and the strange sort of images that included things like the staircases to nowhere. For a moment, Norvita felt her head being filled with the ideas from strange creepy pasta about the stories of people who just disappear when they walk upstairs to nowhere. She knew that she shouldn't do that based on her anxiety. This was a vision. She had no other choice.

She was going up those stairs.

It seemed to take forever to get up the stairs. This was another thing that seemed to be a theme in her visions. She hated the climbing-forever stairs. Once she had gotten to the top, she stopped. There was nothing there that she could see. That was when she felt someone, or something push her forward. Norvita stumbled into a strange place.

It was a weird sort of wax museum. She had been to these places before. She had been to the Madame Tussauds Waxworks on a trip to the United Kingdom or that was she could remember it being. The truth is that Madame Tussauds had done most of the waxwork for the National Trust through England. Replaying this moment of her childhood had become difficult to tell whether she'd ever stepped inside the building or not. It didn't matter but what did was the expectation of finding thins far more upsetting. The faces of the figures were tortured like this was some sort of bad horror movie. This was what she expected to see when she saw the sign above her head for the auditorium. She knew that she didn't have a choice at that point but to follow the vision to its conclusion. She walked into the auditorium. Norvita walked down an aisle before she sat down and looked up at the stage.

There was a low mechanical sound that seemed to be propelling a strange platform forward. Before Norvita, there was a scene that she might have actually seen before. There were four people tied to a stake. The man at the forefront had his head pulled up towards the sky. The tinny sound of a soundtracked howl echoed through the empty auditorium. On closer inspection, she could see the wax figure of the man had large fangs drawn out. The flames below the people tied to the stake were bright blue that flashed with a light that she'd definitely seen before. That was the energy of the nexus. Around the pyre were Puritans looking pleased with themselves. Behind them, she could see the violent face of a wild-eyed Prudence Goodchild who would later kill everyone in Harmony. The lights went down on the scene. It came back up to tear at her.

The next scene was an apartment that she had long ago erased from her developing brain. She didn't want to remember this place or what had happened in this apartment and yet it was there. She saw a man standing next to a crib that was probably where a small child was supposed to be sleeping. He looked strangely handsome with a long scar down the side of his face that was broken up over his eye. If she could remember him in her waking life it would hurt more, but he was gone and that was just perfectly fine. Behind him, there were a pair of feet and legs laying in the particularly awkward way that she knew belonged to a dead body. She couldn't see the face of the woman and she didn't need to know who it was. If this was what she thought, then that was her mother. This was confirmed when she saw the policeman.

She saw Karl.

He was younger than Norvita had ever seen him be. His square face was still handsome even with the thick plastic glasses that were somehow fashionable in the early nineties. She had not seen him in that uniform in a very long time. She knew that he wore it, but it was so long ago that it didn't seem like she had ever seen it. She'd forgotten that he'd had brown hair at one time. His gun was drawn as he stared at the man. The soundtrack was full of screaming and a baby screaming. Norvita flinched quietly.

"Stop!" it screamed. "Police."

Norvita turned away from the scene with her mouth covered. She knew what would come next. Karl would kill her father and then carry her around until her grandparents arrived to take her out of his arms and that was it. She was going to be with Karl for the rest of her life.

No, she was bound to Karl for the rest of his life.

She was going to lose him after that. He wouldn't be able to keep himself from succumbing to his demonic possession. It was only a matter of time before Karl fell. She had hoped that she could have kept him from falling, but she should have known better than that. He was going to be a devil and then it was all over. She still loved Karl and that made things far too painful.

Norvita wiped the tears off her face.

"You aren't showing me anything that I haven't seen!" she yelled loudly to no one. "This vision is stupid."

When you expel some sort of angry comment out into the universe it does make you feel just a little bit better about your life. For the thirty seconds before she realized that she was falling, Norvita was quite pleased with herself. She had time to let out a surprised scream as she fell through the sky before she found herself hitting the floor. She kept her eyes shut as she sat on the ground. She was almost certain that she was going to find herself back in the forest where she'd started this vision. If that were the case, then she was going to start screaming. There was just no point in being in the woods like that. After a long time, Norvita allowed herself to open her eyes. She was in a field. Norvita stood up and looked around. As far as she could tell, there were woods, but they were far away. She furrowed her brow as she saw a figure moving through the woods. Norvita squinted her eyes looking over at the figure. She couldn't see anything that she understood. Antlers tore through the overhanging vines and she could see what she thought was a skull. The creature stopped in its path and turned its dead face towards her. Norvita felt a wave of fear go through her. She started to back up as it moved towards her. Norvita didn't stay to watch, she ran away from the woods. She wasn't sure if she was being chased, but it didn't seem to matter. Just as she was starting to run, she saw a great figure running into the woods. She wasn't sure what it was, but it was bellowing violently as it ran.

Wolf?

No, Norvita was sure it was a bear.

Novita never stopped running until she realized that her feet were starting to slow down. She looked down and made a face as she realized that black blood was starting to pool around her feet. It was a blacker than black that she had ever seen. Norvita tried to keep her pace up as she made to keep running, but she was suddenly pulled down. Norvita rolled over to her back. She swallowed. As the black started to pool around her, a figure began to rise to loom over her. She could see its bone white face. It smiled down at her.

That horrible smile.

She tried to scream but didn't have a chance to do so before the Grinning Shadow lunged at her with a loud snarl.

Norvita hit the floor of her bedroom as she suddenly woke up. She looked over as Mischief, her beloved and spoiled cat, bounced away and then trotted off towards her bathroom. She must have another pixie infestation in her bathroom. She sat up with a furrowed brow. She would have to leave a key for Leah to come feed Mischief and keep the windows closed.

As much as she hated to, she had a plane to catch.

5.

The fall sky stared down through the branches hitting the red and orange leaves dance like fire in the breeze. It made the world feel cool but not quite like the fall that ushered winter into the mountains. Paul could remember his grandmother talking about this being an Indian Summer. It was warm and dry and somehow right in the middle of October. Paul wasn't sure that it was racist, but he knew at least one thing: it wouldn't last. It would be winter soon enough and he had to make the most of the fair weather while he could. He had loaded up his backpack that morning and put the boys in the truck. There was no good that came from this day, if he wasn't out on the Wolf Falls. He was always better off hiking. Paul loved the trails.

It was in his blood.

Paul didn't know how long his family had walked the woods. His grandfather had never wanted to leave the woods. That was why his grandfather worked on the trail when it was still the train ride that went from their hometown almost all the way over to Roanoke. Still, he wandered in the forest like he was the only one on the mountain. He knew that there was a way to follow this trail on to the backbone of the Appalachian Trail. He dreamed of hiking the whole two-thousand miles down the spine of his beloved mountains. It wouldn't be today, but some day. He figured when his brother got out after doing his twenty, they'd walk it out. Today it would be going to Wolf Falls.

The hike out to Wolf Falls was nowhere near as long as the Appalachian Trail or as difficult. It was a wide trail that had places to walk off to either camp or fish or both. It was popular in the summer but a day like this there wouldn't be anyone on the trail. You didn't go there for just a day hike unless you were from around there. It was well worth it for some quiet and peace.

The boys loved the trail.

Paul had two of them. His oldest was Beau. Paul was given Beau when Nate left town under duress. Beau was a Newfoundlander and was too big to travel with his human to the base. He loved Beau, who had turned out to be far more mellow than a spoiled big dog should have been. He trotted beside Paul quietly like they were old friends. Paul didn't need to keep him on a leash, which was great. He had to fight with Jackson about this.

Domestic dogs have very few wild relatives, but one of them is the gray wolf. It is believed by evolutionary biologists that thousands of years ago these two species diverged from a single common ancestor. Wolves became really great hunters and dogs, well, it's the survival of the friendliest. Paul could always see that in Beau. Beau could have his moments of being a wild dog. Then there was Jackson.

Paul was convinced that the only way that Jackson was descended from wolves was if the dumbest of his wild ancestors had somehow made it with a throw pillow. He was dumber than a sack of hammers and was pulling on his leash, determined to find something to smell. He was far too excited to be moving in anything like a cohesive direction and desperately wanted to be into everything at once. Paul knew that it was his age. Jackson was barely out of puppyhood and was probably not quite as mature as Beau. Beau was older and better trained. He'd get Jackson trained when he was old enough. Of course, he'd have to make sure it was okay. Jackson wasn't really his dog.

Jackson was Missy's dog.

Missy had wanted a dog that could be "theirs" and she'd picked out this adorable idiot. She liked his face and Jackson *was* cute. Paul liked Jackson and this was convenient because he basically had to. Jackson lived with Paul. Paul took care of Jackson. Missy would come over and see her dog and it would be all about the pair of them. Missy loved Jackson.

Paul loved Missy.

Melissa Street had been the love of Paul's life for as long as he could remember. He had met her in kindergarten. He didn't start dating her until they were in high school. Missy was now in her senior year of college and they were still together. No matter what had changed, Paul was still with his prom queen. He wasn't sure if Missy was as dumb as Jackson or just loyal like Beau.

Paul wanted to believe that she was loyal. He worried that she was dumb. He wouldn't deny that Missy wasn't quite the conventional definition of smart, but Paul believed he knew what dumb was and that wasn't Missy. Paul couldn't judge though.

He wasn't too smart either.

Paul had always known that he wasn't academically inclined and that was pretty obvious to him early on during his career. He wasn't a good student and that wasn't really a problem. Neither of his parents were good at school so it wasn't a push. Paul was probably going to be working in the auto shop that his father and uncles had built up with his great-uncle. That was where Paul took flight. He had spent almost every day of his young life in the shop, and he knew every piston and bolt in the world that would go into a car. Paul could see what his future was and knew what he needed to do to keep it going. He did vocational classes in high school to be certified to work on cars. He also did sixteen months out at the community college so that he could also run the books. Paul was going to take the shop when his dad retired. He was good at it and had added business. Paul had learned how to service the luxury cars of the snowbirds who came down to Abingdon in the summer. He was ready for his path. Missy was still working it out. She would be shaping the minds and carving the pathways for the future with America's school children.

It might not be a good idea.

It didn't surprise Paul that she went to college for a liberal arts degree. It was the sort of thing that you did when you didn't know what else to do after high school. She found her way to the small liberal college an hour's drive away which often accepted local students. She wasn't a great student, but she had at least found where she could fit. Missy was going to be a teacher. She had been focusing her path on teaching high school. She'd had a beloved history teacher that she was desperate to emulate. Paul thought Missy would be better off teaching something like elementary or pre-school. It was harder to ruin a life when they were younger. They were almost adults when she got them at high school, if she got them. Paul was confident this wasn't going to be a permanent state of employment. Paul was more than confident that her passion for teaching would last if she remained without a child. Once she got pregnant, Missy probably would quit her job and become a full time stay at home mom. She'd end up selling Pampered Chef or something to their neighbors or what have you after that. She'd talked about homemaking since her second semester of sophomore year.

Missy was with him in the woods today walking almost three large steps in front of him and the boys. He kept his eyes trained on her as they walked through the woods. The trail out to Wolf Falls had lots of side paths and they weren't always friendly things that you found at the end of those paths. Missy could easily get lost and hurt or worse. He kept his eyes on the back of her shirt and shorts quietly watching her. If he lost her, he thought, he could always find her by the sound of her voice.

Missy was always talking to him about something.

Paul was sure that this had to be something that came from her childhood. Missy had been given up by her teenaged mother to be raised by her grandparents. Her aunts and uncles were grown but had yet to have their own children and they showered her with all the attention and if they didn't, she would just talk nonstop until she got that attention. Living with someone meant accepting the weird shit that they did.

Some of that was listening to Missy telling the same story over and over.

Missy was telling him about her wedding plans yet again. It didn't surprise Paul at all. She had been obsessing about the planning for almost two years. Paul had also tried to tell himself that his aggravation was just because he hated listening to her talk about this. It wasn't the man's place to care about the wedding itself but that was a lie. Paul was as excited to get married as she was, and he wasn't allowed to be a part of the wedding planning. It hadn't been an easy task for her to get all the right things for this wedding. Today, she was telling him about the hassle of finding the right venue for the wedding theme. Missy was planning the wedding based on Margaret Mitchell's 1936 classic *Gone with the Wind*. It had yet to fall out of favor in their part of the world. As long as people proudly fly the stars and bars, *Gone with the Wind* would still be very fashionable.

Missy was upset today about the venue. Her first pick had been the Blackmore Estate. It was the largest local plantation estate and perfect for the wedding. The problem was that the Blackmore Estate had caught on fire and burned down in the summer. The tragedy had come with no indication that the plantation would ever be restored to its full glory. Now with her first choice gone, she was searching for a new place close by. There was the Penn House in Abingdon or Black House in Blacksburg. She didn't want to go any further than either one of those. Anything past that radius was too far.

"I'm sorry," said Paul.

"It's not your fault, unless your soul is the reincarnation of the souls of one of Sherman's troops."

Paul wasn't exactly sure which was more upsetting: that Missy believed in reincarnation or that she thought that Sherman's march to the sea had gone through East Tennessee. That wasn't the case. The mountains had been more supportive of the Union. How could she not know that?

Paul was almost certain that was even in _Gone with the Wind_.

Paul had opened his mouth but stopped. If he corrected her, then she'd get mad at him because she was the educated one. She'd storm away from him and then get lost. She might be fine and end up somewhere like on a trail next to the creek, but it wasn't smart to be alone. Paul knew that.

He'd seen the wolves.

* * * * *

When Paul was a young boy, he'd gone on a hike with his brother and grandfather. He'd wandered off and found himself on a trail that led to the waterfall and creek that was next to the railroad trellis. He'd heard the stories of the wolves that roamed back there but didn't believe them until he was there.

One by one, figures moved out from the woods and stood around him. He looked up and watched them move into a pack. Paul froze. Thousands of yellow eyes staring down at him. At first, he thought of them as wolves. They were shaped like wolves but there was something wrong with them. He'd seen wolves before at the wolf sanctuary at Bay's Mountain, but these were bigger than those -- bigger than normal and black. Paul hadn't been sure he'd seen them until the bright yellow eyes were clear, but their fur was blackest color he'd ever seen. Each one of those black wolves stared down at him like towering shadowy nightmares. That was unnerving to young Paul.

"What are they waiting for?" Paul asked himself.

"They're waiting for me to tell 'em to attack."

Paul looked around until he saw a figure walk slowly down the hill. One of the wolves was walking towards him and staring at him. He sniffed thoroughly before he walked around Paul and then stopped.

"Not today, boy," said the wolf. "One day I might not be so forgiving."

* * * * *

Paul wasn't sure if what he remembered was real, but he was always scared of the woods. It was a strange fact that the memory should resurface as he walked through the woods. He was thinking about it when he felt something in the woods watching him. Paul looked around and saw the leaves move. He tried to shake that off until he looked down. Jack had decided that he was going to sit as he looked up at him. His large ears pointed up as he looked around. His tale dropped before he looked at Paul. He was being less brave than Beau.

Beau stood with his head down, buzzing a low growl. The fur on the back of heck stood up as he growled and then let out a low bark. Paul felt it too. There was something that made him nervous about this whole situation. Then a raw pungent smell filled his nose.

It was time to go.

"Missy," Paul called. "Baby, I think we need to head home."

Silence.

"Melissa?"

Missy was gone.

6.

Jodell had taken her time to get herself together before she walked into her kitchen to find Arliss Thursday sitting at her kitchen table like this was his home. Jodell tried awfully hard to not be angry. Mr. Thursday was not a welcome visitor in her home. Admittedly, she'd far rather have him spontaneously appear than Mr. Trumper if given the choice between them. As outsiders, it was hard to have them in any home, but Mr. Thursday was preferred. He was more likeable than Mr. Trumper. Mr. Thursday was a good ole boy from somewhere in West Texas. With that and being from a good hunter family, meant that most of the people around here likely would deal with a member of the Department of the Arcane like him. They didn't like Mr. Trumper. Mr. Trumper was out of place first with his fine British accent that had been carefully crafted and he was clean.

In fact, Mr. Trumper was too clean.

Jodell watched the taller man quietly before she looked down. Rowan stood before her mother, eyes wide as she shook her head, her mouth opening and closing like a dumb fish.

"I didn't mean to," she whispered.

Jodell offered Rowan a soft smile as she leaned down and squeezed her shoulder.

"I know," she whispered to her before clearing her throat. "Go get ready. We need to get gone in a little bit."

Rowan had never run so fast out of the kitchen. Jodell made a face. She wasn't sure if she was okay with her daughter following her directions. Then again, she might be smart enough to know that a Hunter was something she should avoid. She knew the smell of brimstone and human ash. Considering how much wolf Rowan had in her, she probably could smell it. Jodell shook her head as she went to the coffee percolator while she glanced back at Mr. Thursday. He watched her with a head turned to one side. She continued looking at him as she stirred her coffee, blending the sugar and milk.

"Ah didn't mean ta upset your day." Mr. Thursday said in his thick Southern Texas drawl. She didn't know what she hated more about him, the smell of death and ash that was present on him as a hunter or his lazy accent.

"Little late for that," Jodell snapped back. "If you're about to tell me that I need to be at the office, I asked for the day off."

"Still plannin' on goin' out then? Good." Mr. Thursday said. "I don't hafta make you."

"Excuse me?"

"I need you to go out. So, I don't have to lie to Ed later."

"That's it?" Jodell's disappointment at this anticlimax was mingled with annoyance at the way he was able to drag the word "lie" into two syllables.

"No, I wouldn'ta come down here all this way for that."

He paused as his lower lip curled for a moment. He was avoiding the real point. If he didn't tell her what it was, she was going to make him. She hated when people thought she was fragile.

"Didja know Huston was on a work release program?"

Jodell covered her snarling with a long swig of her coffee. She knew that he was on work release. They had to ask her before he could do it. She didn't bear Huston much ill will as long as he stayed away from her.

"Yea, his lawyer told me. Why? Did someone finally shoot his mangy ass?"

"Don't know." He paused, looking at her. "We can't find him."

Jodell felt her heart stop. She couldn't handle the idea of someone losing Huston and today of all days. Her heartbeat quicker. She wanted to tell the kids to get their things and run. Bill needed to have his gun ready.

And he better have some silver bullets.

"I've got a unit from the Department looking for him," said Mr. Thursday. "I ain't about to let someone from the mundane side go looking for him. He done somethin' to get out; he ain't goin'ta be kept in their jails. I'll send him off to Iron Keep. I don't give a shit if he did something that wasn't magical."

Jodell felt a smile threaten to cross her face. Iron Keep Correctional Facility was somewhere out in the mountains between Kentucky and Virginia. It's where they sent tribunal-convicted citizens that lived behind the veil. She'd never understood why they didn't send Huston there in the first place.

"You think he killed someone?" she finally asked.

"Honestly, Jodell, we don't know. We can't find a body, which isn't werewolf behavior. I'm asking for the home office to send down the Patel girl because somethin' don't feel raight."

"Don't feel right?"

"Somethin's in the woods, I don' know if it's Huston or his pack or somethin' else."

"If it's his pack, they won't stop until they get me."

"I know. I never ask you for anythin' but please, go on to your kin. Don' be a hero, but if it's his pack, they'll shuras-hell think twice a crossin' Them Crowe Boys."

She didn't want to admit it, but he was right. It was suicide for him to try to come down on her family. Jodell sighed, knowing she had no other choice but to go out to the Cove.

7.

Mid-morning was wearing on when Huston's calves started to ache with each pad of his quick trotting through the woods. He hadn't stopped running since he'd left the crime scene. He wondered if Officer Barry and Oswaldo were still alive. He also didn't care. He needed to keep going. He knew that he had a lot of speed when it came to running in his full powerful wolf form, but that was taxing. He could only spend so much strength when transforming outside of the lunar cycle. It was possible, but it took a lot of focus and energy. It was going to drain him sooner rather than later. Huston knew that he would have to keep it up, however. He didn't know what was behind him. He started to pad more slowly. No matter how tired he was, there was no reason to switch back into his human form. If he found someone out in the woods, it was probably better for them to see a large wolf than a naked person. He wasn't sure if there would be anyone in the woods.

Hikers, maybe?

It wouldn't be that hard to find someone. When the leaves started turning there were all sorts of strange people out in the woods. This close to trails, he could be safe from people who would shoot him. Then sickening reality hit him. There was almost every chance that there was a terrible thing behind him. There was something out in the woods that would just kill whoever he was running from or to anyway. He had to believe that in some way because otherwise what happened to Oswaldo and Officer Barry would be unexplainable. It also meant that there was exactly no one else to help Huston. Anyone else who encountered him would be either killed or worse. Whatever was in the woods was looking to hunt and that meant anything that got into its way as a meal would be taken down in a heartbeat. Huston wasn't sure what he could do except just run from whatever was in the woods with him.

Whatever?

Whoever.

Huston had to accept that whatever was in the woods was a human or something like that. Some sentient being. Even if that wasn't true, he needed to think of them as people as opposed to things. You could fight a person and you could kill it. A thing couldn't die and that meant that there was no reason to keep going. You couldn't fight it off. You could outrun a whoever, but maybe not whatever. He had to keep running.

He just needed to keep running.

His plan had started getting to him. He wasn't just tired but he was also getting thirsty. His mouth was open, his tongue dropping out, swaying as he panted like he was tired. He was hot and he knew what that meant. He was tired and hot. Wolves didn't sweat. Much like dogs, they panted to release heat from their body. That could only mean one thing if he didn't stop soon. He could get dehydrated, and he could start slowing and then become a threat to anyone who crossed his path. Huston slowed his run as he thought quietly about what he needed to do to survive. He could easily ignore the need for food in his body. It wasn't the first time that he'd felt the painful pangs of hunger. He could catch a rabbit or a small dog later. That was going to worsen the need for a drink. He was going to start to get sick if he didn't find a place to rest and drink some water. It was all less important than putting space between himself and whatever was in the woods.

Whatever?

Whoever.

It wasn't too much longer after that, Huston decided that no matter what was coming, he needed to take a moment to breathe. You could allow yourself to get too tired to keep going. That ended with him falling over and dying or getting caught. While at the moment, being dead before someone could kill him was preferred, there was no immediate reason that his death shouldn't be delayed. He focused his nose to the ground as he followed the scent. Soon enough his tail started moving fast with excitement.

There was a creek near him.

He could smell the water. Creek water smelled cold and fresh to Huston and it was the best smell in the world. He paused once again as he lumbered towards the creek. He wasn't sure if he bent down or collapsed by the bed of the creek, but soon his muzzle and dry tongue were in it, hungrily lapping at the water. If he had been in the state of the mind where he could have thought about what this must look like, he could almost imagine the people in prison who talked about how disgusting it must be to drink water that hadn't been treated. He didn't care at that point. He was dealing with his survival.

Dysentery was the least of his worries.

Huston found himself sitting by the creek bringing his massive head down between his front paws with a soft sigh. His eyes drifted with light amounts of desperate slumber. Oswaldo and Officer Bobby were dead by this point. He hadn't stopped to think about what he needed to do next. The smart thing was to run and keep running. After all, he knew that he couldn't fight anything off without a pack. Lone wolves died off if they didn't have a pack that ran with them. Where was he going to find that? He couldn't imagine going to his kin to tell them what had happened. He had dishonored them by agreeing to the divorce. He could always go to his ex-wife's. Would Them Crowe Boys even listen to him? They would listen to him better than his pack. The next thing he would have to do was get to them alive and not be taken by whoever was in the woods.

Whatever?

Whoever.

Whatever.

Huston woke with a start, unsure of how long he had been asleep. As his entire body ached with weary pain, he rose to his paws and looked around. He tried to figure out where the things that were hunting him were. He sniffed the air and ground with caution only to realize that he had no idea how to track it. The smell of decay and death hung too close to his nose for him to figure out whether or not they were around him. Running had done nothing to protect him. Huston was going to have to figure out how to survive beyond running. That meant that Huston was going to have to start thinking of a brilliant plan to outmaneuver whoever (whatever) was in the woods.

Well, he thought, *I'm fucked.*

He was not one to plan. If he was capable of any sort of decent planning, then he wouldn't have been in the situation that he was in at that moment. He wouldn't be running the woods, scared for his life and burdened with the obligation of still protecting the secrets he'd been raised with. Huston could at least see where this was going to go if he didn't warn someone. There would be outsiders in the woods investigating his absence which would be bad enough on its own, but it would certainly lead to them being killed in the woods. If it wasn't done by the thing in the woods, it would be by some other person who wanted to be left alone. Huston might have felt guilty at some point for the blood that would be on his hands, but that wasn't what stopped him from simply putting as much distance between himself and the whole wretched area. He didn't want to bring more dishonor to himself and his family. As of right now, he could live with all the things that he'd done but exposing the world that he'd protected since he was aware of it would just bring more shame. This had to end quickly or with a warning. Huston looked around looking for a direction. He had to find the Crowe homestead. Huston looked up at the trees. They had started becoming obscured behind fast moving clouds as he started to trot along. If he followed the creek, it would lead him where he wanted to go. It would either go towards the Crowe house or, at least, to the roads. He would have to tell someone about this place and whoever was in the woods.

Whoever?

Whatever.

There was no reason that he should even think about whatever was in the woods as a person. Its seeming sentience wasn't a reason to think that it was alive. All the evidence that he knew of pointed to it probably being something dead and Huston didn't want to think about what that really meant. He started to trot along as if there was nothing going on.

Huston never would figure out when he stepped into the wolf trap.

Huston would continue to go through this over some time and still not quite manage to place the sequence of events. The very last thing that he could remember was seeing her. As Huston was walking down the path of the woods, he saw her. She was standing by the creek bed and working on some fabric on the creek. He watched her as he slowly approached. Huston wasn't sure that she was real. Her hair was strangely long and braided back. He wasn't sure if it was going to be black or brown or gray. She wore a dress that Huston hadn't seen on this side of the century. He listened to her hum as he got closer. He wasn't sure how to begin the interaction, but he needed to do something as he trotted for her.

That was when he felt the snap of a metal trap.

Huston let out a howl as steel tore into his flesh. He tumbled forward and then smelled her. If he thought she was out of place before, it became clear as he smelled death on her. She looked down at him and she turned her head to one side. She then walked away from him. She knew what it meant. She reached up and started to carve three letters into the side of a tree. Huston saw them as they were torn into the bark:

CRO.

She looked up at the sky and then let out a loud howl. It was a few seconds before the tree shook with the sound of ATVs. She looked down at him as men approached.

(Editor's Note: Due to the difficulty of translation, we've taken it upon ourselves to translate the dialogue from this point forward.

Granted, we used the same translators as we did for the Crowe dialogue, so some licenses have been taken.)

"Garoul?" asked the tallest man, looking at her.

The girl shrugged as she looked down at Huston.

"Smells like one." she said. "Pa's gonna need to look at it."

The tallest man nodded before he picked up Huston and started to walk away.

8.

For a second, they thought that the music was buffering before it became clear that there was no cell phone service. This was discovered by Bill who had picked up his smartphone and stared at the face of the phone. He turned to the back seat with a fake, pouting scowl for the kids. It was the same face that Bill, Jr. made when he was trying to manipulate a situation that he wanted to go to his favor, and it didn't work for him. That always got a laugh from Rowan who wasn't happy about the lack of Blue Oyster Cult in her car ride. As he picked up his phone to show them both the spinning of the app and the "No Service" message, Jodell knew in a second, she was going to be thrown under the bus. It was always a strange thing for her to realize that their parenting seemed to be like their interrogation style: Good Cop/Bad Cop. Jodell was always the bad cop. She wasn't sure she liked that.

"I know, kids," he said to her. "Your momma's kin live out in the middle of nowhere."

Rowan's laugh at Bill's words cut at Jodell. She was going to be defensive of her hometown and heading out into the Cove. She might not have liked it and she might have said the same sort of thing to Bill over the years, but this was hers to make fun of. It was her family to be critical of. That was what she tried to convey to Bill as she turned her scowl on him with her bright eyes flashing. Bill

60

blinked with a soft smile trying to smooth it out. Then, there was a silence. She was angry at Bill. It wasn't like his family was any better. Sure, his parents were all high and mighty about their family and where they were living in town, but his grandmother lived out in the middle of nowhere and didn't have city water. Yes, the Cove *was* isolated -- that was because it had to be.

The Cove was a holy place.

The new age types can talk about ley lines and how there are types of rocks that are in the ground that hold on to a holy sort of magic that lives in old earth. Jodell didn't know if that was true about the Cove but it was just as special as Mecca or the Holy See or Jerusalem. When the first Crowes had crossed the mountains and settled in the Cove, they asked for the blessing of their old gods. It had given them much wealth and good favor from the Prince of the Full Moon. It was where they buried their dead, binding their souls to her place. She had been born out at the Cove and baptized in the creek. She had been given her name by her great-grandmother. It wasn't a place that she wanted made fun of by anyone, least of all by Bill. Then, it hit her. She didn't believe in the strange faith of her forefathers. She was hurt by Bill's words for only one reason.

She was embarrassed.

Bill cleared his throat, picking up on Jodell's discomfort.

"That don't mean it don't deserve respect," Bill continued. "Your momma was born out here."

"Really?" Rowan stared wide at the back of her mother's head. The idea of Jodell ever being a child, much less a baby, was odd for her.

"Yup, sure was," Jodell said brightly. "So was my daddy and his mother. Crowes been out here for a long time."

"We ain't!" Bill Jr. protested. "This is the first time we've been out here."

Jodell wanted to dispute Bill Jr. quickly, but he was right. They had never gone out to the Cove as a family. She thought about it the last time that she went out there was after she and Bill had eloped to Pigeon Forge. She had driven out to the house and then stopped. She'd turned around when she saw family out on the lawn. She wasn't sure if they'd seen her that day, but she knew deep down now that they did. As she remembered it, there were thousands of eyes looking at her. She had never gotten out of the car. Instead, she'd driven past the house. She found the parking lot for the trailhead and then she'd driven away. It had taken a long time for her to get the courage to try it again.

She was fighting the urge to run.

Mr. Thursday's coffee stop that morning had started to put her on edge. No, that wasn't true. She was worrying about this day for the weeks before this when Bill had told her that they were going out there. Mr. Thursday had pushed her over the edge and down the side of a cliff that fell into a massive pool of terror. It became physically real when she thought about the idea of Huston running around in the woods. As she drove, the incidents of her marriage to him went through her head. She wanted to counter every bad memory with a better memory. Surely there were good times when she was with Huston. No, there was never a good time. Her heart pounded adrenaline through her body. Jodell wanted nothing more than to pull over and throw up.

"Mama." Rowan quietly interrupted Jodell's thoughts. "Why are we going out there?"

"It's a special day for my family," Jodell explained with a strained smile.

"Yea," Rowan thought about it for a long time before she looked up. "But we ain't really a part of that family."

Jodell's heart stopped immediately in her throat. She didn't look back at Rowan to answer her question. This was something that she had done to her children. She might have been embarrassed by her family, but they were family. She had allowed her shame over the divorce and embarrassment of the rural faith that might seem strange to most people to deny her children access to their inheritance. The Crowes may not have any sort of money, but they had a rich heritage. A great deal of sadness came over Jodell as she drove her family vehicle up the side of a mountain.

Jodell was ashamed of everything that she'd ever done.

She was ashamed of the primitive faith that she'd been raised on. She was embarrassed that she didn't stay with Huston no matter of how bad it got with him. Then, instead of staying a single mother and relying on her family to help her raise a child she'd decided to leave with Bill and get married. Maybe she still spoke to her mother, but mothers were supposed to love their children regardless of what they do. She could only imagine what the extended family would think of their wayward child. She didn't know if she wanted them to welcome her. She wanted them to hate her and shun her away from the family. It would mean that there was a hard truth that she could ignore until being around her family.

She would rather be shunned than admit that she was different from the rest of the Crowes.

Jodell didn't want to talk about the fact that she'd never been able to *athru* or change like the rest of the pack. It was terrible to realize that she went through the Pilgrimage to the Trellis and somehow, she had never been pushed to the otherside. That was the hell of things. Most *morrcan*, the members of werewolf packs that didn't turn into werewolf form, often died from the Pilgrimage. She did the trip and there was nothing there. She knew that she would never be allowed to be a part of the Wild Hunt if it was ever called by the pack. She would be told to sit at home with the women and children. She would rather not be a part of that family who didn't want her as she was. So, she had been shunning them instead and that's where they were now. The one thing that Jodell was embarrassed and ashamed about was a simple fact that she had been ignoring for all this time.

Jodell had been passing for *amadan*.

It hadn't been hard when she married Bill. Darlene was not going to allow her oldest son to be married to some hillbilly pagan trash. Jodell had let her railroad her life almost gladly. She had become a member of the Methodist Church and had been baptized.

She did all the right things and joined the right clubs including the Garden Club and the DAR. Jodell even altered what she looked like to hide her strange human appearance. It took a lot of money to strip the black out of her hair and she covered up the wrong-colored eye with a colored contact lens. It was a life that was absent of her true self.

What if the kids went through *anthru*?

It was all gone when Jodell saw the end of state maintenance marked by a sign and heard the crunch of gravel under wheels. She knew there was a sharp twist in the road before it flattened out into a path that went over a poorly taken care of road. She saw an abandoned white church standing sadly where it had been put up some time ago. It had been slowly reclaimed by long vines of ivy and overrun by long stalks of tall grass. The parishioners had long moved into town and away from the well-intentioned building that had been erected during the Second Great Awakening. They had civilized the wild mountain folk who wanted to be civilized and now it was a relic that would be slowly absorbed into the landscape. What was the line that the Christians said, of dust were ye made and dust ye shall be? She felt her lip get mangled by her teeth as she gnawed at her intangible anxiety. She glanced back at Bill as she turned down a familiar road.

Bill offered her a smile as he looked at her pensive face.

"Are you going to ask me again?" he said to her.

"No," Jodell squeaked at him. They both knew that she was lying. "But if you don't want to…"

"Jo, baby," he said in that smooth voice that he'd used to convince her to do anything. "I think I should embrace your family like you did with mine. This is how we do that."

Much like Napoleon at Waterloo, Jodell was fighting a losing battle with her own Duke of Wellington. He would have pulled back long ago if he didn't want to do this, but once committed, this was Bill. He was good at being all sorts of stubborn. She knew that it was going to be all over. It was only a matter of a few seconds before the inevitable occurred.

They were there.

She saw the farmhouse rising over an orphaned field. She wasn't sure how it had been built or when, but she was certain that the second story had been added later as the family grew over the years. There were generations of cousins sitting on the porch and along the yard. They slowly stopped doing what they were doing as they watched Jodell's Jeep turn into the long driveway. She saw them start to stalk towards the Jeep in a suspicious posture.

"Is this going to be safe?" Bill whispered.

"I've got it," Jodell said with a growl.

After parking the Jeep, Jodell slid out of the driver's seat. She met the eyes of each one of her kin as the social tension was pulled taut and then subsided as they started back to whatever thing they had been doing -- except for one. He sat on the stone porch that was connected to the kitchen. She wasn't surprised to see him dressed in ripped jeans and a tight t-shirt like he was Mathew McConaughey in Dazed and Confused. He'd tried to project that image for so long, he probably believed it by now. He pushed his curly black hair out of his face as he took a long drag. He dropped down from the porch, landing on his feet. He pulled the cigarette from his lips as he stalked towards Jodell. She crossed her arms across her chest and looked up at him flatly.

"Hey, baby sister," he said carefully.

"Vaughn," she said sharply.

Vaughn smiled at her as she looked up at him. She liked her brother, but this moment was nothing about liking him. This was all about being as strong as he expected her to be. She watched him pick his head up and sniff the air. His smile turned into a sharp snarl showing rows of pointed teeth.

"I smell your *amadan* boy scout here," Vaughn growled.

"I'm amazed that you can smell anything smoking them Cheap-os," Jodell retorted.

"If he steps out of that car, I'll-"

"You'll what?" Jodell growled back. "Sic your boyfriend on him?"

"I ain't got a boyfriend."

"Oh no? You weren't attached to the hip with Huston until the pack married me to him? Shit, Vaughn, he was more your husband that I was ever his wife."

"What's that *Cul Tona* got to do with this?"

"Don't try me here Vaughn. I damn well know that you're the one who got him out of jail. You did this for the day of all days to just do this. What do you think was going to happen?"

"Huston got out of jail?" Vaughn asked quickly. He stepped closer to her. "He ain't talk to you yet?"

"No," she said quietly. "My boss came and told me. If you..."

"I'd let you rip my throat out for putting him before my family. He nearly killed you, I ain't letting him near this family."

Saturday was for embarrassment and shame. Vaughn had never really stopped talking to her even after the divorce. She knew that it had been tense. Briefly, Jodell wondered if it had been her that had created the awkward feelings between herself and her older brother. Still, she had to know if Vaughn was going to be a problem. Vaughn took a step back brushing a hand through his hair as he started to almost pace. If there was someone upset by all of this, it was Vaughn.

"I'll get some of our cousins, we'll go see if we can sniff him out in the woods." Vaughn said so quickly it sounded like he was barking.

"Ain't no thing," Jodell said. "He's probably at his mom's house in the camp. Department of the Arcane will handle it."

Vaughn stopped, giving her a strangely irritated face. She knew that it wasn't something that he wanted to hear. Of course, he wanted to go off and be a hero, but slowly, he was accepting that there were other ways of handling any sort of wrong.

"Fine, at least you came out here," Vaughn said. "He won't put a finger on you or the kids. Not unless it gets detached from him."

Vaughn stopped quickly as he looked up. Jodell watched his face change as she heard blades of grass breaking under footsteps behind her. She looked at Vaughn and put her finger up to her lips and told him to be quiet. She hadn't mentioned any of her new facts to Bill, let alone the kids. Instead, he let out a low growl at Bill.

"You ain't welcome here, Barney," Vaughn said with a hard growl.

"I'm here with my wife," Bill answered defensively. Jodell didn't like this any more than her earlier conversation.

"That's what you say, but you don't get to parade her around like she's your whore."

Vaughn had found the pressure point to hurt Bill. Jodell tried to convince herself that this was being done for some sort of greater good but Jodell couldn't quite see it as Bill pushed past Jodell to stand with his large shoulders squared, staring down at Vaughn.

"You gonna do something about me being here, pup?" asked Bill in his best bad cop voice.

"Count Ralph Vaughn Crowe!" yelled a voice from the kitchen. "You leave him alone before you forfeit your rights at the Running of the Rocks."

Vaughn pulled his lips apart to show his teeth as he let out another snarl and then slunk away from Bill and Jodell. Jodell watched as Bill breathed angrily. Jodell put her hand on his back trying to get him to relax. She silently waited for something to break the tension.

That would be Bill Jr.'s cue.

"Grandma!" screamed Bill Jr. as he ran up the steps of the back porch.

Rowan dashed right behind him as they embraced their grandmother. Bill's shoulders relaxed as he watched. This whole thing was a bad idea but, at the very least, there were people who were going to be her ally out here and there was always going to be her mother. Jodell didn't know a single person who didn't like her mother.

"Timey!" squealed her mother as she bent down to embrace her grandchildren. "I could eat you up! Oh!"

"Rachel," Bill said slowly. "Good to see you."

"William." Rachel said sweetly. "You came too. Well, I'm happy to see you. Why don't you take them down to the creek so they can play with their cousins before they make you go run the rocks?"

Bill smiled as he thought about it. There was no reason that his children wouldn't need some sort of pressure release. He nodded to Bill Jr. and Rowan, who almost ran towards the creek. Jodell glanced back up her mother, who stood on the edge of the porch with her hands on her hips. There was some sort of problem that they would have to deal with, but not right now.

Rachel let out a huff.

"I need a drink," she said. "You?"

"I've heard worse ideas."

9.

Missy had thought that she'd passed out, but she really just went black for a few seconds. When she came back, she felt the inside of her mouth was dry to the point where her tongue was stuck to the roof of her mouth. She bit down trying to get some sort of moisture in her mouth only to find a rough piece of material forced between her lips. She wondered if she was screaming earlier. There was a chance that she had been because Missy was always incredibly good at screaming. She twisted around as she gained her bearings. Missy couldn't figure something.

What was going on in her world?

The last thing that she could remember was that she had been walking in the woods with Paul and the dogs. She had been talking to him about the wedding and she couldn't exactly remember what happened after that, but she suspected that it was terrible.

Missy tried to turn her head around to see if she could figure out where she was. All she could see was the blue sky staring back down at her through twisting black limbs zooming above her. Her hands twitched as she tried to determine her location. She could see nothing that told her anything about where she was or where she was going. Missy gave up as she failed to find anything that gave her a clue. She choked back a sob then as a crushing reality came to her. She'd been kidnapped and as a female living in the last thirty years, she knew that the likelihood of her survival was dwindling as she kept going farther from the site of her disappearance. She could only believe that Paul had been killed, otherwise she couldn't have been taken. Missy wanted to cry.

It wasn't fair. She had a lot of other things to do with her life.

A dry lurch came out of her mouth as she tried to push forth a scream while jerking in her bonds. Her feet started to kick on the side of the box that she realized she was contained in. There was a moment while someone got quiet as the motion stopped. Missy held her breath feeling someone look over her. Missy turned her head uncomfortably again to look up at a shadow looming over her. She couldn't see his face.

"Ease up, hurtling," he said, softly brushing a hand through her hair like he was petting a dog. "Bein' a fuss ain't gonna help you none."

She wondered for a moment if she was losing her mind, listening to the obscured man. It was almost like a language that she knew, but just not quite what she understood. It was his tone that made her uncomfortable. It was like the way that she would talk to her dog and that made her guts all unsettled as she tried futilely to look around. She then heard a high-pitched whistle. The man who had spoken to her whistled the same bars of a song that she thought was "What a Friend We Have in Jesus". It made everything that much worse.

She prayed for death.

It felt like forever before the vehicle that she decided was going to end up being a four-wheeler kept going. Of course, it had to be a four-wheeler with this sort of terrain. Her grandfather had one that he always took hunting. Missy realized that she was a part of a similar story. She was something they had caught in the woods. These pieces coming together were not making her feel any better about the situation. Slowly, there were steps that approached whatever was keeping her there. She heard someone spit.

"Good hunt, son?" asked the approaching feet. "What you got there?"

"Garoul," replied the other voice. "It got its tail snagged this mornin'. Ma saw it going down to the creek when we finally got it."

Missy jumped as she felt another body being pushed into the box -- which was resolving into a large cage -- with her. Whatever it was was far too big for it to be a human being as it pushed against her. Missy could smell sweat and heat. Warm fur pushed against her exposed skin. She knew that what was brushing against her was some kind of dog. That didn't make any sense to her. Dogs didn't sweat but she could smell human sweat on whatever was beside her. She jerked towards whatever it was; she felt her head lay against him.

Then, she heard the second man sigh. She knew that it was the sigh of someone who was disappointed. It was such a universal sound.

"Fool's errand," lamented the other voice. "Garoul, hunteth not high-lone. His kin shall cometh looking f'r that gent."

"So, let's findeth his kin bef're those gents findeth us?"

There was a long silence as the four-wheeler sputtered to life. There was a hard jerk before the vehicle lurched back onto the trail before them.

"One means more. We can't hunt for more if the gods aren't with us."

"I'm sick of shoat. Gods got to be one with us."

"We'll have to consult."

Missy wasn't sure which part bothered her more. The strange use of English that was just barely understandable to her or the fact they were talking about hunting. She didn't know exactly what shoat was, but she guessed that whatever the large fuzzy animal that was against her was "garoul". It was a new creature that she had never seen before. Missy had lived her whole life in the woods of these mountains, and this was new. That was less concerning than the other fragment she had gleaned.

She didn't know of anything that was shoat besides a pig, but there weren't any wild pigs in the woods near the trail. It was then that a weird fact floated into Missy's head. She had heard once that pig's flesh was a lot like a human being. The cannibals of distant islands had called human flesh "long pig," didn't they? She wondered if people were their pigs.

A sick feeling washed over Missy.

She tried to ignore the precise fear flitting through her head as they kept riding along. She felt herself drift off without really any sort of further thought about things. It could have been sleep.

Whatever it was, Missy found herself awaking from the state that she had hidden in. Her eyes tried to focus on what she was seeing. Based on the smell and the weird voices that she had been listening to, she was expecting to see something out of a horror film. She was convinced that it was going to be the set of a Texas Chainsaw Massacre before her. Her mind was preparing to cope with that sort of horror.

She couldn't have seen anything further from that expectation.

It was perfectly clean. If she hadn't been dragged through the woods, she would have assumed that it was another house that sat in the back of the woods like where her parents lived. It was clean. If it wasn't for the definite smell of death, Missy might have enjoyed it. She wasn't exactly sure how she knew the smell of death. Of course, she knew what it was, there was no shortage of times that an animal like a possum or rat would get stuck under the house and then die. But this was magnified like it hung in the air around the place that almost caused her to gag. Her eyes darted around, trying to find where the smell came from without fully taking in what was surely going to be a horrific scene. All Missy could see was plain grass that was turning a strange shade of brown but had been neatly trimmed like it was still growing. They passed a small garden that seemed to be growing only black plants that she wasn't sure would ever bear fruit. The four-wheeler stopped. Missy turned her head to one side as she looked up.

It was an old house with sharp angles that formed some sort of strange box. There were missing windows that had been boarded up with pieces of wood which gave it that abandoned look. It was temporary, something told Missy, they would be able to replace these things in time. It just hadn't been time. There was a falling porch that was well decorated between her and the barn that seemed to be sitting out behind the house. Missy knew where she was.

It was the Octagon House.

She'd never been out to the Octagon House. The road out to it was impossible, at best, to get to let alone why you would even go out there. There were plenty of abandoned houses throughout the region and she'd partied with her friends in a lot of them. No one ever went to the Octagon house for whatever reason. There was something about it that was perfectly evil and aversive that screamed the need to be left alone. As Missy was forced to be closer to the house, she understood why she'd never wanted to come here. She could see the decorative lights that were on the porch of the house. Instantly, she knew what they were.

They were human skulls.

Every part of Missy wanted to scream as she became fully aware of what exactly she was being forced to see. She twisted as she tried to let out a scream, but then stopped with only a gurgling pop that died at the gag. Her eyes closed as she tried to tell herself that this was not real. This was a bad dream. She was going to awake sooner rather than later.

"Didja find 'em? It smells bad out there like its lousy with garoul?" said a female voice. That made the wolf-dog-creature beside her shiver angrily. "Don't bring 'em inside the house. They'll stink up my kitchen. Put it inside the barn."

"Ma," a male voice interjected. "Garoul don't hunt alone. It might be one of them black Garoul. high-lone."

"I ain't stupid." Snapped back at the woman. "I need to see if the White Face God'll bless the Hunt. So go, find me a shoat. We need to prepare the ritual."

10.

In the world of many supernatural creatures there are some exclusions to what they eat. As you might already know from either these books, or some general knowledge of others, vampires drink living blood as opposed to eating a really good, rare cheeseburger. There are some witches who are primarily vegetarians or vegans. Werewolves are a different breed altogether when it comes to eating. While there are few foods that outright make them ill, mostly it's like dealing with a dog with a digestive tract made of steel. I do know that many of the werewolf packs that roam around do avoid chocolate because, well, let's just not risk it, shall we? I tell you all of this to point out that largely werewolves avoid food simply out of religious observations as opposed to some sort of illness or disease that it could cause. This leads me back to the Crowes. As far as Jodell could tell, the Crowes had only two taboos when it came to consuming food or drink. The first was more common than you think with modern packs, consuming the flesh of fellow canines. This is often done out of respect for fellow hounds except among the *conry* who had woven that into their ancient beliefs. They tell the less-known story of the Hound of Ulster who devoured the flesh of three wolf hounds and was cursed by the gods to spend the nights as one. If he or his descendants were ever seen they would be shunned and stalked by the mundane world.

The Crowes had extended that to an *amadan* or the mundane. This had been done out of survival when they came to the new world and went west with Daniel Boone. Boone had asked them to cross the trails of a place that he had named Wolf Hill because it was where his beloved hunting dogs were killed by a wolf. The Crowes went there hunting a wolf because that's what they assumed they'd find.

It was not.

To this day, Jodell didn't know how the family had been able to keep the first great pioneer, in the opinion of Lord Byron and many of his contemporaries that hung out at the Hardees with him, repeating the story of the wolves. She assumed that it was because it was only partly correct. Daniel Boone did come across a wolf there in his Hills, but it wasn't like any wolf that he'd ever seen before.

Jodell had every understanding from family legend that it had been the She-Wolf.

The She-Wolf wasn't a werewolf like her own family by any stretch of the imagination. This was an Old World vampire who had lost her way when she was exiled from Louisiana. If there was anything that she knew about the woman based on the Department of the Arcane records, Jodell knew that she was seductive and evil. It had led her to also believe that if Daniel Boone had stuck to his story about wolves then he must have been terrified of the things that she had made him do. She also wondered if it was why the *amadan* were considered kin animals to distinguish them from other things in the woods that would eat settlers. She knew there were other packs that would eat an amadan like her kin were preparing to eat chickens.

There were worse things that weren't them.

The second prohibition was that of alcohol. It was unusual that the Crowes didn't drink. Most mountain *conry* didn't only drink but they would make their own brew and looked upon those who didn't do either with great suspicion. The Crowes had been masterful brewers and runners of the shine using the skills they learned during the American Civil War to run and hide in the woods but that all changed with Cousin Harmon.

If you want an exact accounting of how Cousin Harmon was related to the Crowes, that is a problem because there is simply not enough space here to detail this complicated family tree. What I will say is that he was, indeed, related by blood or marriage (and it's possible both) and was *morrcan* which is a polite way of saying he couldn't shift into a wolf form. He did, however, have a head for numbers and was good at running a business which meant that he had the only bar in a dry county. For a while this was a good business for the family and Cousin Harmon. It had, however, become a problem for Cousin Harmon's business partner, Norman Church.

Church didn't know exactly how things worked in the county where the Crowes roamed. There was a time that a state line was as far as Beijing was from New York City. That man Church didn't know how things were run. You didn't buy from someone you didn't know or trust. Church wanted their product to come from over the mountain in North Carolina, but that wasn't the way that we did business. It had led to an impasse.

"I'm gonna kill that mangy son of a bitch," was something that had been overheard from that man Church.

That man Church learned a few facts that most average people never get to learn about werewolves. The first thing he learned was that even if a werewolf never shifts into any form, they are still stronger than the mundane who tries to pick a fight with them. The other thing to never threaten a werewolf, changing or not, with a gun unless you know what comes next. That man Church took the first swing before he pulled his gun. Cousin Harmon wasn't about to be a part of that. He grabbed that man Church by the throat and swung him down, breaking his neck quickly. This was a different time then it was now. Cousin Harmon knew that if he didn't tell the *athair* or pack leader, he would be in more trouble. Of course, at that time, the *aithar* was his cousin who was sheriff for the county.

If you thought that I was about to tell you a tangential story about how the town was corrupt and that justice was denied to the Church family over Cousin Harmon, that isn't the story that would be told. In fact, because of the conflict of interest, many of the things that happened were moved to another county. Let it never be said that the Crowes were dishonest people. They were many things, but honest was the most important. If they hadn't promised it would have been different, but there was a swearing to uphold the law and therefore Cousin Harmon would have his day in court. That time had come and gone, and it was decided that by twelve honest men, that it was self-defense. It should have ended here but like most complicated stories that involve families.

It did not.

That man Church had family who, despite the work of a court, still felt that they had been slighted by the system and were looking for a debt to be paid when it came to justice. When justice doesn't come to you then the next thing that you do is hunt for your own vengeance. They had first started by targeting Cousin Harmon head on. It was a failed bomb that caused Cousin Harmon to leave the house in an effort to protect his wife and children.

He was wrong.

Diversions are a wonderful tactic but generally only work when they are noticed. When Cousin Harmon fled to Johnson City ("no doubt to a flop house with some floozy," Jodell's Grandmother was often keen to say under her breath when the story was ever discussed) no one noticed. Instead, the family of that man Church bombed the house where Paulina, Cousin Harmon's wife, slept with their three daughters in the same bedroom. As it was understood that there were enough explosives bound to the foundation to level three city blocks.

No one survived.

Sometime in the aftermath, it was decided that they could no longer live in this sort of feud. It was decided by the Crowes that there was no reason to keep up a business that was going to lead to more death and fire. It was not worth that sort of temptation. In classic extremist form, they swore off drinking.

So, imagine Jodell's surprise when her mother poured her a strange smelling liquor into a red Solo Cup. She set it down on the table in front of her. She cast her eyes up at her mother.

"Don't give me that look, it ain't like I bought it," Rachel explained. "I made it myself."

"What are you going to do if Lord Byron catches you?" Jodell asked.

Rachel gave her daughter a prissy smirk that is often reserved for felines who have eaten small birds out of cages. If her mother hadn't been born amadan, Jodell was certain that she would have taken the head of the table after the death of Prince David. Even he had been cautious of his proud wife, there was a man who lived up to every inch of his name until his death at the Battle of Sugar Hollow. She lived in fear of no man.

Jodell wondered if Lord Byron feared his sister-in-law.

"I won't tell if you don't," Rachel said. "You look like you need it more than I do."

Jodell never liked when her mother had that sly smirk on her face when she knew more than anyone else. It was the only reason that Jodell could imagine that attracted her father to her. There was something "extra" about her mother. Some of the amadan had a little extra power to them. It seemed more common out in the hinterlands than in the city. She felt like it was spooky.

Jodell looked up at her mother.

"Is it that obvious?" Jodell asked before taking a hearty swig.

"Your daddy used to make the same face when something was troubling him. I'd have to be an idiot to not notice that in one of my kids. Is it because Bill is running the rocks today?"

Jodell was put in a position where she wasn't sure she could share her full thoughts. She hated the Running of the Rocks. It was a barbaric ritual of hazing that she never wanted to see her husband and the father of her children be a part of. She had visions of Vaughn having his full way with Bill and that would be it. They'd bury Bill in some grave out in the woods and pretend that he was never there. Vaughn had occupied her mind for most of the weeks leading up to this weekend.

That was all gone now because of Huston.

She wasn't afraid of Huston anymore. For him to have that kind of sway over her was quite far into the past. That changed very little for Jodell mentally. Part of her was still going to always be his favorite chew toy and he was out in the woods. She couldn't help but think that he was waiting out there right now. She couldn't tell her mother.

She'd lose her mind.

It's okay, she told herself, *the Department is handling it*. It wasn't her problem.

"I hate that he wants to do this," Jodell said finally. "He's going to get hurt."

"He wants to though," Rachel replied. "It's a big step."

"He shouldn't have to."

"Jo, honey. He wants to be a part of the pack. I think that's sweet."

"We don't need a pack."

"Yes, you do. Pack is a family. You'll always need family." Rachel sighed. "You're still hardheaded about this. I guess that ain't your fault. You don't think like a wolf.

Her mother had been saying that to Jodell for years. She didn't think like a wolf. She wasn't pack oriented. She had never been pack oriented. She narrowed her eyes at her mother.

"Still don't make sense," she snarled.

Rachel didn't answer her. Instead, she filled Jodell's Solo cup again

"You tend to be by yourself except for your family. That's not wolf mentality."

Jodell's mouth opened to protest.

"Oh, don't get me wrong," Rachel continued. "You love Bill and your pups but they come first and not the pack. It ain't wrong. It's just not wolf."

Jodell turned to stare out of a window. It didn't make sense to her. It wouldn't matter now. She would have to wait as time passed.

11.

It didn't take much for Ma to understand what had happened. She'd been in the woods as well. She'd seen the wolf pad towards her. She also knew that it would mean only one thing. She was going to have to speak to the black gods of the woods. If they had been given the right to be able to move along, then she knew that it would be time to keep going. It was something that they had been waiting for almost for generations. She knew what it would come down to with this: revenge.

She thought about using Missy as an offering to the black gods, but that wasn't correct. If she wasn't still a virgin, then the black gods wouldn't bother with her and she liked the idea of having a sow for breeding. Hunting was hard enough. They had been grateful for the attention that had been paid to the trail but with a breeding sow, they could lay low and eat for a while with a diversity in their food. So, she had Missy dragged to the cages back in the bright red barn along with the wolf that they found. He would probably turn back into his shoat form. He wasn't worthy of the black gods. Once they found the rest of his pack, she would be excited to kill him with the rest of the dogs. She walked with her boys as they took both towards the very clean barn. Missy seemed to have enough fight in her to let out a scream as she looked over at the faces of the people who watched in the cages. That's what occurred to Missy.

There were people in those cages.

In that moment, Missy mustered all her remaining energy to let out a hoarse scream of terror as she started to realize exactly what was going to happen. She felt her hands starting to shake the maintained cage door as she almost started to beg to be let out. Ma walked along the line of cages. One of the men from the four-wheeler looked at Missy. She looked away from him because her eyes couldn't settle on him.

"Don't you worry none, little Sow," he told her. "We ain't gonna hurt you. We got plans for you."

That did nothing to calm Missy. She had no desire to be hurt but she very ardently didn't want to be there.

Then, it got far more disturbing for Missy.

Ma walked towards a table that sat at the other end of the farm as she danced lightly. Her mouth opened and started to speak in a language that wasn't English. Missy had never heard it before, and she hoped that she would never hear it again. Ma danced on the balls of her feet as she picked up a knife that Missy knew was the length of a full-grown man's femur as she rocked back and forward. Ma's head dropped back as she hummed again while her hands waved the long knife towards the men in a cage. Her blade finally pointed at one of the men. He looked at the family as they started towards the cage. He fell to his knees as he shook his head begging almost without a sound.

"No, please, for the love of God, no," he said quickly as the men from the four-wheeler opened the door.

"You don't understand," said one of them. "God says it's your time."

The men pulled him out as he screamed and kicked. They were stronger than him and that was it. Missy watched as they led him out. Ma turned her head back as she held the blade up and followed the boys. She walked behind them in a muttering of soft prayer. Missy watched as she settled into her prison. She could imagine.

If she had the ability to follow them, she would have seen them walk over the hill. The man from the cage was dragged down the hill as he kicked and screamed. There was nothing that he could really do about it after all. They walked the man into the house from a back walkway that led directly into a center hallway. He looked around as he was finally hauled into a room with no windows. He felt his breath come up short.

Who builds a house with no windows?

The man was walked toward a raised chair on some sort of dais. He was forced down to his knees. There was a quiet few breath passing except for strange sounds of rat-like feet skittering quickly in the walls. Around them the burning heat of torches lightened the room. His nose curled up at the unpleasant smell of the fire. It was fueled by something repugnant like burning pork or bad lasagna. He looked up at the figure sitting in the chair. It was draped in a long black cloak that obscured the face from the man.

"You don't understand," he screamed. "I have a fiancé! She's going to miss me."

Silence emanated from the figure.

The man from the cage let out another sob before a heavy blow came down on the back of his head. Ma stood back watching as her oldest and biggest son proceeded to beat the man repeatedly until she could see the bone and brain flesh that peeked out from each scratch. She watched as the next one waited. There was still breath in their sacrifice. The second son looped a thick rope around the neck of their victim and then started to squeeze. The sacrifice didn't fight but the breath was still rattling out. He tilted the head back. That was for Ma.

If she didn't take his life, then the black gods wouldn't take the man. They wouldn't have favor. She quickly bladed the man's throat allowing the last bit of blood and life to drain. The sacrifice went limp. Ma reached down into the blood. She let the warm fluid coat her fingers. She turned to the biggest of the pair. She pressed her blood palm to his cheeks before leaning in and pressing her lips to his eagerly.

"Bring me their heads," she whispered. "May His bone white smile be on you."

12.

The one who sat at the head of the table for the Crowes was Lord Byron, which sounded like it might have been far too grand a name to be sitting anywhere but at the head of the table. Lord Byron would tell you that this was simply not the case. His father had been the man who became head of the table after a long battle and when he ascended, he knew that his mother, a highly traditional woman convinced that she would make their way, believed that her sons would have to have powerful names to maintain their authority over the family. It was why the oldest of them was named King Solomon. There had to be a belief that when King Solomon was born that there would not just be a family but an empire when it came to all the werewolves of the mountains of East Tennessee. King Solomon tried to live up to his name even as he marched off into war.

That is where he died as well.

After King Solomon was Prince David. Prince David had reigned longer than their brother and was a good man. He was almost concerned that he might slip into the pitfalls of his namesake, but he had been there for the fight until the last bitter battle. Prince David might have lived longer if not for the need to protect his son Vaughn. Lord Byron had no idea why his son was at the battle, but that had led to the end of Prince David's life at the Battle of Sugar

Hollow. His death resulted in everything being completely handed on to Lord Byron. He didn't want to be the king at peace time, but it was his life now. Lord Byron knew that it was going to be a terrible life because he distrusted an existence this peaceful and calm. It could mean only one thing. A time was coming when peace would no longer matter, and war would come. It would then be on him to protect the family. Lord Byron promised on the bones of his ancestors and with the blood of his body that they would stay alive like the mountains they inhabited.

No matter what would happen, they would survive.

While lightly jealous of his valiant but dead brothers, Lord Byron would never become a war time leader. His legacy would rest in a time of peace. He worried what that would mean for his spirit. They would remember the patriarchs who started their line and the generals that had led them to battle. Lord Byron could only hope that he would be able to be the father of a prosperous peace time. It wasn't time to worry about what he would be when he died. This wasn't a day for a funeral day and remembrances of legacy; however, it was a day of life and celebration. This day, he was high priest and that meant there were far more important things to be done than worry about the future.

Lord Byron could feel the weight of his heritage on his shoulders.

War or peace, Lord Byron knew that he had lived long enough to sit at the head of the table and that was the great honor of his life. He could have been killed for his seat by any member of his family as happened in some packs. That was the rumor, wasn't it? That there were a bunch of packs that would kill the head of the table for the seat. There were some packs that had more political intrigue than other sorts of stories that you hear about royalty. He thought that was disgusting. Above all else, you took care of your family and if there was someone who thought he couldn't take care of the family then he needed to be fought and then killed. Lord Byron hated those families because there was simply no honor in them. There were so many stories that he'd been told over the years of other packs. There was a legacy to be had when it came to peace time. If he was remembered as a great leader during a time of peace, then he could rest easy. Lord Byron would have the honor of being the first to die surrounded by his family and peacefully in the master bedroom before he was laid to rest with his ancestors.

If everything was done well, he would rest easy.

He was sitting in that very master bedroom at a vanity set that was older than him as he kept his head tilted back. The sound of a stiff brush pulling through his mid-back length snow white and black hair was punctuated by an intake of breath as his lip came up in a snarl when the woman who was brushing his hair got caught on a tangle. His clouding eyes cast up towards the woman who offered him an apologetic glance. She feared him. She had always feared him. Instead of hitting her as she expected, he reached up and patted her hand. She let out a soft sigh before she finished. Her small fingers started working on the tight braid. He watched her as her eyes focused on the weaving of his long hair.

He loved her too much to have taken her as a wife.

Sometimes, Lord Byron would watch her and wondered what her marriage had been like to King Solomon. She always seemed like she was scared about something. They had to be young when they got married. Sometimes you don't know how to treat someone when you are too young to understand. Barbra Anne was the queen for his oldest brother. When he died, Lord Byron thought that it was going to be the wife of his next older brother which would have been Prince David. Prince David had decided that he wasn't about to give up his *amanan* bride to make sure that Barbra Anne would be taken care of in the tradition of their people. Prince David wasn't good at tradition. It was Lord Byron who'd stepped up. It was probably better that Prince David had died and died a hero. Halfheartedly, Lord Byron had offered to marry Rachel in a way to protect his family. She had declined fiercely and married another member of the pack.

Lord Byron had been both upset and relieved at the same time.

It was that indignation that brought them all home today. That made Lord Byron secretly angry at himself for this. It was Jodell who had wanted to be free of the pack. That had hurt him deeply, but he understood. It was the old ways that had betrayed her when it came to Huston. He had been the one who arranged the marriage that he thought would bring peace. Huston was sort of an asshole and if he bothered to walk across a Crowe ever again, Huston would find himself being left in pieces. Vaughn had just made things completely harder. If he hadn't ended up in a fight with the outsider who had married Jodell they wouldn't be here. He had decided to approach it like they would normally. Anyone who wanted to marry into the pack would have to Run the Rocks. He wasn't sure if he liked Vaughn's methods of tricking her back into the fold, but at the very least Lord Byron was pleased to see her back.

He had missed Jodell.

He felt the line of blue being painted in a careful line along his face with an ancient paint that he'd never known how to mix. Lord Byron had never bothered to learn how the war paint was made but he knew that the ancestors would have had the woman folk work on this or at least the ones that would have not been in battle next to the men folk. Lord Byron pulled his head up higher as his spine lengthened. She was putting the crown that had been woven with teeth and the large black bone skull. He wasn't the first Crowe to wear the crown. It was an elongated skull of a deer with the sharpest teeth that had ever been jammed into a mouth. Its outstretched horns had been decorated with thick pieces of leather and bright blue and green beads. He looked like a warrior king.

"Well, mother," he said to Barbra Anne. "I suppose it's time."

She was glad that he said it and not her. He had to preside over the Running of the Rocks and there was something that she knew was his job and if she didn't want to be a part of that then it was time that he did. There was a terrible fear that if he wasn't there to watch over his younger kin, they could imagine what could happen. Vaughn was still an angry, angry young man and there was a boy that he was about to take that anger out on. While people had died during the Running of the Rocks, he was not prepared for that kind of casualty to be an outsider who happened to be a policeman. There were lots of issues that they would have to understand and that wasn't something they were ready to cover up. He stopped at the chest of drawers that was almost as tall as Lord Byron. He bowed his crowned head towards the pictures and reminders of his ancestors. Altars weren't as common as one would expect in the homes of packs. He liked to see the faces of those who were gone before he went to face those who were alive. He wanted to make sure that he carried them with him as always.

They would march with him in the procession.

The procession started at the porch of the farmhouse. The joyous noises of family playing stopped suddenly as if a loud gong had been sounded. Slowly, the family members that were present started to form lines on either side creating a pathway between the porch down towards the creek. Lord Byron stood still for a moment before he stepped off of the grass and walked, not paying any attention to the family members who watched him. He pretended not to at least, but he knew that he was being watched and he liked it to an extent, but it was selfish. This day was about the family and the things that family did for each other. He felt people follow him from behind. It was a part of the ritual. There might have been singing at one time in the past, but there was nothing but silence following them today. There was no need for anyone to speak when holy things were to occur. It would take a few moments before the women folk and anyone else who chose to not come to this ritual place would return to talking and playing games. For now, it was silence.

Lord Byron led them down a long path that veered off the main trail that led to the trellis. Under the ancient trellis were several smooth rocks lapped gently by the creek. Around the banks, jagged edges led over a small waterfall. Lord Byron stood on the high bank looking down. He waited until a camping chair was set down behind him. He sat, allowing his cloak to cascade over the back. He leaned forward, looking down as the young man Jodell felt the need to marry waded through the rocks and creek to stand in the middle of the running water on the largest and smooth rock. He looked up with his broad shoulders squared.

"What business do you have walking into our pack, amadan?" Lord Byron said as he overlooked Bill.

Bill felt like he might be freezing as the creek water soaked into his pants, making his skin pucker up pimpled flesh. He couldn't be cold. He couldn't be weak. Instead, he squared his shoulders as if he was not terrified, like he was a cop. He walked to the edge of the rock.

"I am William Alan Harris!" Bill thought that he might be yelling. It was the kind of forceful projection that you did when you were a cop. "I've come to seek the hand of one of your pack members to be bound to me in this life and the next."

"Who?"

"Jodell Ursula Crowe, daughter of Prince David and his Rachel."

"And you want to enter our pack for our daughter? For what reason?"

Bill wasn't sure exactly what he needed to say. It seemed foolish to ask to marry a woman that he'd been married to for almost four years and had a son with. He didn't care about splitting hairs today though. He had to just go through the motions.

"I have never cared for someone like I have cared for Jodell."

"She's got a husband." Bill knew the voice of Vaughn better than he wanted to. "Her laying with you has made her a slut."

If the creek could stop babbling at Vaughn's words, it would have. There was never an appropriate time for a word like that about the family. It grated on Bill and he almost wanted to spit at Vaughn where he was pacing at the top of the hill.

"You want to come down here and say that to my face?" Bill said, his big hands balling into fists.

Bill's first thought was to say that he loved her. That was very true. He had been in love with Jodell for a very long time. What he'd learned was that was not a good reason to fight.

Lord Byron put up a hand as he listened to the younger men exchange words. Vaughn took a step back as he spat in a place using all words in Gaelic.

"While Baron Vaughn mac Prince David, may speak his distress to this, Jodell is still in a bonded union to her first husband. Has Huston mac Whelan or any of his kin come to challenge for the honor of his bride?"

This silence was less painful. Someone should have mentioned this rhetorical, but required part of the process in advance, though it may not have changed anything. No one wanted to speak to the Whelans.

"Since there is no one who claims our sister as their kin, why do you, Baron Vaughn mac Prince David, challenge this union?"

"I am her closest male relative and his union with my sister has sullied her good name," Vaughn said. "I want my debt to be paid in blood."

"Is this something, that you, William mac Harris, shall consent to?" Lord Byron finally said.

"I'd go through hell and back for Jodell," Bill answered. "I think I'm willing to stand toe to toe with her family."

"So be it. Baron Vaughn mac Prince David shall then keep you in combat on the rocks until such a time that he feels that honor is no longer a question or his debt in blood has been paid."

Bill watched Vaughn climb down to the rocks. He waded through the waist deep water of the creek before climbing up on the smooth rock. He offered Bill a sharp-toothed grin as he stood with his shoulders squared to Vaughn.

"Glad you agreed to do this, gardie," Vaughn taunted. "I've been fixin' to fuck you up for making my sister a whore."

For the majority of his life and career, Bill had never been the man who would throw the first punch. You waited for someone else to go first. This was not one of those times. He had heard Jodell called a whore or a slut by this man more times that he was willing or able to let go. With a sudden loud scream, Bill lunged his shoulder right into Vaughn's chest. Vaughn was surprised. Bill was a big man for an amadan, sure, but he was an amadan. He was just a human being with no elements of the conry. Bill was the most in shape member of the Sheriff's Office, which honestly isn't saying much. It meant that he did quite a bit of deadlifting all sorts of people. He was also a man who had survived in Iraq. He was tougher and stronger than he looked.

He'd also never been this angry.

Vaughn fell backward and hit the smooth surface of the rock. Vaughn wasn't expecting Bill's first punch to land, let alone that Bill would skip right to a full-on tackle. He also didn't expect a fist to come crashing immediately towards Vaughn's face. Vaughn turned his head up. By the time Bill saw his brother-in-law's teeth, his jaw and lips had elongated into a snout that was only seen on a wolf. It would be a matter of time before the growling and the barking became a long bite to his throat. Bill put his hand up to block and his instincts were correct. Soon, predator sharp fangs tore into the broad side of his arm. Bill let out a scream. His head started to fuzz at the initial shock of the deep bite. Bill had to admit that this was all sort of surreal. He looked down at Vaughn. Those sharp blue eyes had become something more feral than was human. No, you don't break eye contact, he remembered. Normally in a bite you "feed" it. The more flesh that you feed into a person's mouth, the less pressure the hold can exert, so then the jaw would weaken, and you would be able to get out without leaving a chunk of yourself behind. This wasn't a drunk being escorted out of Cowboy's at four in the morning, however. This was something that he knew that wasn't going to have been covered in his basic training. What did you do when a wolf attacked you?

You fought back.

Bill struggled, kicking at Vaughn, pulling him towards the edge of the rock. He felt his body rock back as Vaughn shook his head, tearing his teeth deeper into Bill's forearm. Bill's free hand searched into the creek itself. Bill found his fingers gripping around a large rock. If he had thought about it for even a moment, Bill might not have done what came next, but Bill simply wasn't going to think about it. He swung his fist with the rock in hand right into Vaughn's elongated jaw. Bill heard Vaughn yelp once before he pushed his full weight onto Vaughn shoving him off. He swung again at the other man's head with his rock-spiked fist. Vaughn shifted harder into some strange space between wolf and man as he launched himself full force towards Bill. Bill cracked somewhere as he hit the smooth rock. He let out a hard groan as he pulled himself up. Bill had finally got to his feet before he was pushed again off of the rock into the deepest part of the water. Bill hit with a splash.

Vaughn let out a panicked gasp as he looked down. There was nothing that he could find that was a trace of lawman. He started to wade out into the water, hunting for Bill. He had to find him. There was a difference when it came killing a man outright and when an injured man was gone into the water. He kept hunting until something gripped the back of Vaughn's head and shoved it down into the water. He struggled for what felt like forever but couldn't break the grip or find the leverage to escape. Suddenly, his head was pulled up.

"We square now?" Bill panted out in a loud yell.

"Yea, we good," Vaughn gasped, a little surprised at his response and the turn of events.

Bill let go of Vaughn. He looked up at the crowd of faces. He wasn't sure if he was going to die had he killed Vaughn or not, but still it was a strange moment. Lord Byron nodded at him quietly.

"I don't think we have a problem with you joining the pack," Lord Byron said gravely. "All debts are paid."

Slowly, each member of the pack left the creek side. Vaughn looked back at Bill, offering him a toothy smile.

"No hard feelings, right?" he said uncertainly.

"Yea, only one," Bill replied. "Ever call Jodell a whore again, and I will skin you alive."

13.

Several hours later found Jodell leaning back on a blanket. Her nose twitched, smelling the crackling wood as it was consumed by the fire. Bonfires brought back a long flood of memories to Jodell. She loved the feeling. She could remember father standing beside her telling her that fire was something that he'd learned to make when he was a small pup. Every wolf needed to know how to make fire because they could get lost in the woods. The fire pit was important because fire meant that you could cook, and if you had small pups or people with you who can't shift, they would need to be warmed. This fire was not for heat or for food today. This was for the delight of their own life. Bonfires meant something that was deep and spiritual that she couldn't understand. You always ended a day with a ritual meeting around the fire.

She leaned back watching children stand hesitantly away from the fire. She crossed her legs just at her ankles watching Rowan with her cousins. She didn't look like Jodell's daughter at all. Rowan was a part of the pack. She was going to grow up and be like the other members of her family in a few years. Her lip twisted as she thought about it for a long time. Rowan was going to be a young woman soon. She'd be walked out on the trellis and then she was going to be turned or not. Considering that her father was a werewolf, she'd probably be turning. She belonged here. Rowan would be joining the Wild Hunt in time if the howl for war would ever come. It made Jodell's stomach turn. Some of it was simply that she belonged with the pack and Jodell had been selfish. She was terrified of losing her child. She didn't want to think about the amount of fighting that she had done to get her safe, only to let her go. It was a part of motherhood; she would have to let go eventually. She blinked, trying to hide tears running down her face.

Then she turned her attention to her son and husband.

Bill and Bill, Jr were standing a safe distance away from where Rowan was talking about how "lame" it was that they were cooking food over a fire or whatever. She knew that no one would admit they enjoyed it. Instead, Bill stood close enough to keep an eye on her in case she needed to be rescued by her father. Then there was Bill, Jr. He was gripping on the edge of a stick that had speared what looked like a large hot dog. His small child face intensely stared at the edge like this was the most important thing that he would ever have to do. Would he be able to join the Call when or if it ever came? She figured that he wouldn't have the ability to shift like other members of the family. She worried about what it could be to be a mutt that couldn't shift. She didn't change.

Stop, she told herself, *he's four*. There was plenty of time to worry about him, but this wasn't the time to do that.

Jodell wasn't aware that her mother had taken over with her son until she heard the low groan of a muscle sore body dropping next to her on the blanket. She offered him a smile as Bill looked over at her. She watched his face twist as he sat down on the blanket beside her as he let out a groan. She blinked as he leaned over and then offered her a kiss. She gave him one with a soft sigh.

"You've been drinking." he said to her in a low voice.

"Seemed like a better use of my time than watching you and Vaughn beating the tar out of each other."

She hesitated for a moment waiting for him to be angry at her. She was expecting him to say something about her dishonor or something worse. Instead, Bill shrugged as he looked back to the fire watching Rowan and then Bill Jr.

"Fair enough," he said. "Vaughn wasn't the best person then, either."

They were quiet for a long time. Bill watched his kids. His daughter playing with her cousins, delighting in a strange new life. His namesake with a grin on his face being taken care of by his mother-in-law. Bill furrowed his brow before he looked back at Jodell.

"Rowan acts like she ain't never done this before," Bill said, mystified.

Jodell was very quiet. Bill turned his head back to watch her as she took a swallow from a cup. It was pretty bold to be bringing that out there, but maybe things were easy to overlook when everyone was having a good time.

Jodell was suddenly not having a good time.

Bill sat up watching her. He had made an area of expertise of watching her and her moods as they changed. She looked back at him. She wasn't upset about the questions, Bill could tell from the crease on her forehead and the pursing of her lips.

She was embarrassed.

"Well, she hasn't," Jodell said finally.

She hated it when he stared at her with that neutral expression. He created some sort of vacuum that meant that he was waiting for an answer from her to see what information he could squeeze out of her. Jodell was convinced that given a few more years, he could be a detective. She'd still hate when he looked at her like that.

"Really?" Bill said, watching her as she started to fidget.

She didn't want to answer that. Jodell wondered if she needed to yell about seeing her lawyer before answering any more questions. It wouldn't help her case here.

"I couldn't do it," she explained, putting her hands in her lap. "Huston and I were married as a Beltaine marriage and I was pregnant with Rowan then. When we were together, Whelan rituals were more important than my family. I…."

It hurt to even discuss this out loud but she knew that she had to get it out of her system. Bill knew everything about her previous marriage and there was no reason to hide from him.

He placed his hand on her back.

"I couldn't bear the thought of coming back after my marriage fell apart."

"That wasn't your fault. Huston was no good to you," Bill said.

"It's not what we do."

"I know," said Bill. "It's family. We don't want to disappoint or shame family. It's a big deal to you. Shit, baby, it's a big deal to me, too. That's the thing about family. No matter how much of an embarrassment, they'll always love you. You've got to make things less awkward for our kids."

"Our kids," Jodell repeated. "It's always weird to me that you accept Rowan like she's your own."

"Yea, I adopted her now, didn't I?" He laughed softly. "Besides, do you think we'd just stop at Billy?"

Jodell offered him a sideways glance as she arched a brow at him.

"Excuse me?"

"Ain't that what we do?" said Bill with a half-joking laugh. "Barefoot and pregnant now that I'm a member of the pack."

She slapped his chest awkwardly. He grunted with a half grin. It might have hurt but only slightly. He then looked down at her with a smirk.

"You didn't marry me to be your woman," Jodell stated.

"No, but I wouldn't mind us expanding our pack."

Jodell put a hand on his face brushing softly over his bruised cheek. That was a conversation that she avoided for as long as she possibly could. She wasn't sure how the werewolf conversation had come up. It was easier with him being in law enforcement. After all, there was a chance that he had on more than one occasion where they had been able to fight through many things. But they had to deal with the idea of more children and that meant another conversation about the Blessing of Cuchulain. There was less of a chance of her children with Bill of ever turning: one in four if she understood genetics. That was a worse conversation than the one where they changed. Jodell had been the one they'd called at the high school when a girl turned when things got too stressful at the middle school. How do you explain it to kids when they didn't turn at the Trellis?

Jodell thought that might be worse.

She pushed her apprehensions to one side. She had no desire to allow her children to be strangers in her own family, let alone being a weirdo or outcast. It wasn't the time for that. She knew that it was worrying about something that might not happen for children who didn't even exist at that time. It was her great-grandmother who had told her to never borrow trouble before she needed it. Jodell didn't need it tonight.

And it was too nice of a night to go ruining it with trouble.

She leaned against Bill, letting her lips brush against his. Bill held her face against his and leaned forward into her kiss. It didn't answer any questions but that was fine. Tonight, wasn't the night to answer questions or make plans for the future. Right now, it was about the fire and the night and the family. Jodell felt a small tightness in her shoulders finally unwind. It was because she felt something that she hadn't felt in a long time.

She was finally home.

14.

When the embers of the fire started to die down with the sound of cracking of wood, there was a shift in the mood. Lord Byron had made his rounds to all the members of the family before he finally settled into a chair at the far end of the fire. The small children ran towards Lord Byron. It took both Rowan and Bill Jr a moment to understand what was going on before they joined their cousins. He leaned back watching them gather.

"Pawpaw," said one of the kids, "Will you tell us a story?"

"Don't I do that every year?" Lord Byron replied as he lit his pipe before he looked down at them. "Ain't you tired of hearing that story?"

There was a long silence. Lord Byron took a long puff on his pipe.

"What story do y'all want to hear?" he asked. He looked at the waiting faces of a younger generation. "Again?"

"We want to know how we got here," said another child.

Lord Byron took a dramatic draw from his pipe before he blew out a billow of smoke. He then told this story:

We've always been wanderers, timey. We used to roam woods that lined the outside of Arcadia when the land of dreams. They say we were the sons that were born after the first king of werewolves was shunned from humanity. I don't know if I believe it but I know that we once lived in woods that were burned down for a Hedge and our people spread and moved throughout the world. I like to believe that's how we came to Ireland. We were easy to move in the dark forests because we are black furred as we are now, but Ireland seemed to be where we belonged. We didn't have a city until it was founded but there was long ago, timey, a city called Ossory where we made our home. It's easy to think that it was a city like we know it. I don't think that's the case. I think that for a long time, we as conry had our own country and it was there in the city of Ossory.

After traveling for ages and being lost we had our first home where we lived in peace and would have been that way still if it hadn't been for one thing.

That damn Roman Pirate found us.

They say that he was kidnapped by Irish pirates and that made him a slave for a number of years. When he returned, he fell in love with the Irish people and knew what his mission was while he was in captivity. That might be true but I swear this, timey. If Patrick ain't never set foot on our homeland, we'd still be living as kings there. Once he came back, they didn't welcome these outsiders. You can't uproot a faith older than your man on the cross and then refuse our gifts. I don't know how he won over the amadan but it was because, timey, he came to Ossory.

Patrick came to kill our kind.

As the story goes, while Patrick was wandering around with the good word of his God and his good news, that's when he came upon Ossory. We were as kind as we've always been when strangers came along our people. We've never been okay with people coming to tell us that we're wrong. It's been the thing about being conry from day one. Not only were we out of strange, but we'd had our own faith. The faith that we took with us when we came to Ireland and that's the belief that our people had always survived with. What I will say about the Patrick is that he understood that faith was important to us and how to use that in its own way.

It was then he saw the faith of our ancestors.

Whether we were originally the wild sons of Lycaon or not, our people in Ossory lived like the wild men should have back then. We roamed the forests in a part of our mad hunts. We traveled in our clans and packs because that is what we are first and foremost, members of the packs. We also saw no reason to hide ourselves. This was our land and our faith. I don't know if I have the full understanding of what holiday that he found but I could only guess that there was a moon. We will always change during the moon. That Roman Pirate saw it and ran. We know what happened next.

By the next day, there were thousands of Irishmen who came to kill us all. We could have fought them off but our families were there, our old, our sick and our children. When the Howl of War comes, if you have been blessed like our ancestors, you will have to fight but never when you come to find our family. They ended our kingdom of Ossory and we scattered again. Timey, by then, we knew that we couldn't live in peace, so we integrated with the amadan. It's why some of you don't know how to change. Ain't nothing wrong with that, you are the ones who can keep us hidden. The Irish pretended that we weren't that bad, we were what was left of a long dead race of heroes. They weren't as bad as the English.

The English hunted us down for our blood and pelts.

I will always hate the Roman Pirate for bringing the Roman God to Ireland and making our lives harder, but I will never hate him as much as I hate the English. The English saw the island where we made our home as the next step of their own conquering. They took the language, they took the faith of the Roman god that had spread through the island. You can only imagine what they saw of us. We were backward pagans that had to be taught what happens to witches and there were plenty of people who believed that we were witches. I don't know how many of us were hanged or burned. I think we'd all been murdered if we didn't pass for the amadan, timey but this is where things are just going to get worse for us. No matter how bad the Roman Pirate was, that bastard Cromwell was terrible.

No, you don't ever say his name without calling him a bastard. It's the only good time to say this about people.

He thought of us as we were slaves and of course we were sold into it. I don't know how many conry died but I know that our family was forced off to Virginia. It was probably best for the English that we were taken to the new world. When we got sold to the English, we ended up at Jamestown in Virginia. Maybe it was the fates or the old gods saw it.

There was a hungry monster in Jamestown.

We're not like the other indentured servants that came from Europe. We could run and we could move faster from that. We could *also hide from those who brought us. The New World ain't much different from being back in Ireland. Once we had the moment, we ran. What we learned, timey, is that we found our own kind of people. Conry everywhere, timey and we found the First Wolves. They're like us, timey, we married into their packs. They were the ones that told us about the monsters.*

The First Wolves met the monster that they saw. They didn't seem like monsters, but we knew that the worst monsters are the ones that work in the amadan. This one was worse. The First Wolves told our people that the monster at Jamestown had been cursed. Curses ain't something we should ever deal with but there was something. We'd put our roots down in this place. We had timey born here with the First Wolves. We ain't about to go through Ossory ever again. We drove the cursed from this land.

We sent that curse out of the world.

I think that's why we came west when Daniel Boone told us about the wolves at Wolf Hills. He and his party were attacked by the wolves in the hills that ain't too far from where we sit now. There might have always been some guilt that came from being a part of the pack that came west. We knew that what had been cursed was there. We ain't never seen that curse here though we did see a wolf. We seen the She-Wolf. I don't know what Daniel Boone done with her but I know that he told people he'd been hunted by man-sized wolves when we imprisoned that bitch in the cave. We'd let him keep that story. After all, he was a great hero. Also that she-wolf was a dangerous vampire. It's why we stayed here.

We will always fight for this place. We fought for this place when the English went to war. We were at King's Mountain. It's how we got the land that you set on. We would burn the bridges when it came to the Civil War. It's why we live here and what we do.

That, timey, that's why we live here.

"How much of that do you think is true?" Bill whispered to Jodell at the end of the story.

Jodell shrugged as she looked back at Bill.

"Some of it but not all of it," Jodell whispered back. "You always want to look better for your family."

15.

Under a sick gray sky, there was a dead field that sat in the literal middle of nowhere. For as far as the eye could see, was nothing but dead white grass. That was impressive since there was no real sun to speak of hanging in the gray sky. The only other weather was a harsh wind that blew into the field. Of course, that didn't matter to the grass. One could gently blow on the grass and the fragile, dry stalks would snap. It would take a somewhat stern look to break the grass. The only thing that could be found inhabiting was this world was something else.

Death and decay were this world.

Death might not be the correct word to use. Death was the final and ending phase of the living world, but this was something else. This world was dying, but they would never just end. That made the smell of decay even worse. Decay came with death, but when it was dying and decay it was just the smell of sickness and that made it worse. The odor rolled through the field and coated the mouth and nose of anyone who presumed to breathe in the field. It didn't seem to bother the only person who sat in the field.

Yes, there was a person in the field.

In the dead grass, a path curved and twisted forming an elaborate maze that still smoked with the edges of white, blue magic and in the center of the maze sat the figure of a woman. She had been sitting in this maze for some time, though she couldn't tell you how long. Time and space had always been hard to follow, but it must have been a while due to the state of undress in the maze. She had taken off her the thin fabric of her blue blazer long before this moment and had folded it neatly beside her. After that, beaten up canvas high tops and socks had joined the jacket. Her socks didn't match each other but they had been shoved into the shoes. In a few moments, the purple tie would be joining that suit. She sat with her legs crossed in what someone would call Lotus position with her hands folded in her lap. If someone walked up on her, they would assume that she was perfectly normal except for one thing.

The woman was completely blue.

This is something that I should make absolutely clear. When I say that the woman was blue, I'm not referring to any sort of skin tone. Skin tone was not something that anyone could be able to really focus on, per say nor is this a reference to hair color or what remained of the suit. When I say that the woman was blue, I mean just that. There was a radiant blue light blasting out of her body. She was nothing but a being of bright blue light. Why would a woman made of bright blue light be sitting in the middle of a field? There was only one reason.

She needed to find a way out of this place sooner rather than later.

As much as she enjoyed meditating in this place -- everyone needs some time to collect themselves, but this was starting to become rather irritating. The problem with the field was that it was the only place that she was still a fully formed human being. If this place disappeared, she would be nothing but a sentient ball of light, which was what she actually was, but that led to a strange problem. She was comfortable with the idea of thinking of herself as a person. She wasn't sure if she was ready to return to her essence, a ball of power. The Blue Woman had been learning to accept pronouns which weren't something that she'd ever thought about before that moment. The Blue Woman had never referred to herself as "she". There were all of these things that she had taken up while she was living in a human vessel.

That was a strange thing for her. She'd slept for so long in the dirt and then one day had gotten bored. There was a witch and mage who were far beyond dumb and had engaged in some sort of coitus. At that moment, the Blue Woman was like, well, there we go. She had made her home inside this child and that was where she lived. He wasn't exactly a powerful magical being, but she had worked out a symbiosis with him and they grew up. She watched his life, and the Blue Woman was surprised by people. She loved him. Now, he was gone. They had been separated in the void of blackness.

The Blue Woman closed her eyes. She could see him as he fell through the blackness. His body was prone and floated lifeless in the infinite blackness of the Space between Worlds. Think of it as losing the remote control in an old couch with rogue springs that could reach up and scratch a deep scar in the back of your hand. There were thousands of dangerous things that would break magical beings, including her. She could see him as her body floated quietly down. The only thing that would stop her was the Grinning Shadow. The Blue Woman could move fast but the Grinning Shadow was the master of darkness and that included the blackness of the Between Worlds. At that moment, she had only one advantage.

The Grinning Shadow was trapped here with her in this place.

They were connected and the Blue Woman knew it. You couldn't have the light without the shadows that would be cast by it; inversely, the shadow couldn't exist unless there was light. It didn't surprise her that they were there together. It would be a race to find the vessel that she adored before the Grinning Shadow took him and used it for his curse. It wouldn't necessarily need her vessel, she rationalized. The thing about the Grinning Shadow was that it could find one easier among the races of men than she could. Human beings, in general, had a desire for power and easily gave in to fear. It would be home. She just had to wait for the Grinning Shadow to find her and attempt to devour her whole. Gladly the Blue Woman would allow this and once in the belly of the beast she'd explode, sending pieces of the Grinning Shadow flying everywhere. That would work fine except for one problem.

The third person in this place would simply not allow that.

The Blue Woman was an ancient figure. There were quite a few things that she had seen but she had never seen something like this. As the Blue Woman looked up at the sky, the Grinning Shadow loomed over her. She could see the bone white smile sneering down at her as it started towards the Blue Woman. Then there it would be. The third person would fly right into it and start ripping at the Shadow.

There was the Beast.

The Blue Woman didn't know where the Beast came from. It hadn't fallen into the Space Between with her and the Grinning Shadow when the world opened up and swallowed them both. In the thousands of years that the Blue Woman had lived, she had never seen something like this before. The Beast was shiny black. The Blue Woman could see the ambient light reflected in the wings of the creature that swam towards the shadow with large terrible claws bared where there should be hands and feet, glistening with the black blood of the Grinning Shadow. The Blue Woman couldn't tell if there was a beak or teeth. It didn't matter, the Blue Woman was always distracted by the noise.

The Beast was screaming.

The Blue Woman could hear the Beast from miles away. There was the sound of screeching that cut through the world. It was exactly like it was the sound of thousands of hawks all attacking at one time. The Beast would dive into the Grinning Shadow and then start to rip it apart. Once the Grinning Shadow was completely down, the Beast would stare at the Blue Woman. There was only a second before it would attack her. The Blue Woman would then explode. She'd find herself back where she was. It wouldn't stop.

But it had to end.

16.

Jodell wasn't sure if she was asleep when she heard the snapping of a twig. It might have been why she didn't react quickly. The fact that she could hear other heads snapping up at the sound convinced her that it was no dream. Quickly, she joined them in training her eyes on the black figures of the trees settled on the outside of the land surrounding the house. She could see nothing at the first glance. There were no sounds, which became more upsetting as the night pushed black clouds to cover the moon. She watched as those who could shift lengthened their bodies into large black lupine frames with their heads down towards the ground sniffing and staring into the blackness. Their eyes were better that way as well as their sense of smell. That was upsetting to Jodell.

If they couldn't smell it, then it could smell like the forest. There could be hundreds of them.

She would be angry if they told her that she had to go hide in the house. She was as much of a fighter as Vaughn or any of her cousins but that wasn't the point. She knew that she had to protect her children and Bill first. Before the pack came her family, and she'd take them over anyone any day of the week. This was only going to become more pressing as the seconds ticked away silently. They weren't talking. Once talking had stopped, everyone knew they were in tactical mode and that anyone who might be able to find anything in the darkness would be communicating the way that wolves had always communicated: through facial gestures. They were always her most confusing moments growing up. You'd see wolves howl in movies or TV. No one did that unless they were lost.

You never let the prey get the upper hand.

When all sound started to bleed out, Jodell knew that things were serious. It didn't matter how much fight she had in her, she had to get her family safe first. Instantly, she reached down to Bill who had been sleeping next to her and shook him gently. Bill had always been a hard sleeper and this was something that had been developed over time. There was no doubt that it had come from at least one of his tours of duty in the Middle East or the subsequent therapy afterwards.

"Bill," Jodell hissed as loudly as king cobra. "Wake up!"

Bill had more than enough experience with that specific tone to know that this is when he should be pulled out of a slumber and to action. Bug-eyed, he looked around almost demanding to know what was on fire and which child had set said fire.

"Something ain't right," she whispered. "We-"

Before Jodell could get another word out, the wind changed. She picked her head up, catching the smell of spoiled meat that wafted into the air. Jodell felt her upper lip curl as she let out a hard snarl like she was trying to make herself larger at a threat she couldn't see, but she could smell. Her eyes cut back to Bill.

"Get the kids inside," Jodell finally choked out. "Now."

In the time that Bill had been married to Jodell, he had been in many fights with his bride over what were perceived as "dangerous" situations. Much of this had been during the early part of their marriage and she was still working through her personal concerns of being hunted down by Huston or his kin. Bill wasn't completely blameless. No one ever came back from something without some sort of mental damage, and this had been the cornerstone of their marriage: PTSD. I only mention this to give you an idea that there was a potential for mild debate on whether or not this was overreaction, and it could have been, however, Bill heard the cousin closest to him pad towards the thicket with a snarl that he'd never heard come out of any dog that he was aware of existing in the wild kingdom. Without another thought about whether this was all far too much or not, Bill collected a still sleeping Bill Jr and Rowan with as much strength that a man of his size and weight could muster and ran towards the house. This was the best course of action: run and don't look back.

Jodell did not share his opinion on the matter.

Jodell was barely old enough to remember pack wars that had torn the mountains apart. Lots of people had died and much of that had become warfare inside of the pack dens. This was beyond savage and unnecessary. When the *conry* came around to realizing that they weren't each other's enemies, they agreed to drop all the old scores. In that moment, her mind instantly went back to figuring that whoever was planning to attack them didn't believe in the same rules as everyone else and that made her flat out angry. She knew that she had absolutely no choice but to be a part of this fight. With a light sprint, she headed towards the crop of trees ready to draw blood.

Then, she saw them.

Jodell stood on the edge of the bonfire pit when she saw the antlers moving out of the woods. She was not sure if she'd ever seen a buck with antlers as wide or big. She could have easily assumed that they weren't really antlers at all. They had to be some sort of stripped branches that rocked in the wind. That concept was dashed when the fleshless skulls rose out of the trees. The night air was quickly being filled with the sound of hard-beating hooves ripping the grass apart as they ran from the woods with its sharp snatching and cracking sounds. Jodell felt her eyes go wide trying to take in the scene. Suddenly, one by one, other heads and creatures emerged.

They were running so fast.

Jodell found herself frozen as she watched black shadows tearing up the ground with their thundering prance as they stampeded towards the waiting black masses that were her family. It was simply no match. She knew that the second that she saw one of the great beasts open its steaming jaws and crush a cousin's head between the teeth, not unlike a child with a grape. She couldn't find the will to move forward or even turn to chase after those who were running for safety.

That was, of course, until she heard a shrill scream.

For those of you who have never had a child, and don't worry I don't quite understand it myself, there is a strange thing that happens when you hear your own child's pain or fear. She turned quickly to see her youngest sitting in the middle of the campground, mouth opened in a high-pitched scream. Rowan was but a few feet away pulling on him to attempt to get Bill Jr out of the way. Jodell felt her breath come out in a fevered panic. There was someone missing.

"Bill!" she screamed.

There was no time for her to be looking for Bill. Just as the word left her mouth, she saw another one of the things. It loped at speed towards her children with its mouth open. There was no question about what she needed to do next.

It would be what happened next that made Jodell later question what exactly happened.

Jodell had started running with no real regard for the details. She was running. In a flash of brilliance, she had picked up a long abandoned croquet mallet as she started running towards the animal. That's what it was. She was going to believe that it was some kind of animal. With all the strength that Jodell could muster, she swung at the animal, cracking right at the jaw line and for a second, it stopped. Jodell stood panting, holding tightly onto the croquet mallet. She found herself standing between the children and whatever it was.

"Rowan, I need you to run," she hissed.

"Mommy...."

"Now, little girl! It'll be all right." She knew the second that she said it that it was a lie. "**Go**."

Just as she turned, it was there. Jodell stood staring at the dead eyes of a large bone white skull looking down at her. She was certain later that this was all much quicker than the timeframe Jodell was really experiencing. Everything seemed to move slowly to her. She saw the beast's mouth open. She could smell the acrid breath wafting out of the mouth from each of the teeth. She thought that she heard a low dead screech come through the teeth. She returned the screech with a sharp yell as she swiftly brought the mallet up. The teeth snapped the mallet like it was nothing. There was a second snatch of the rotted teeth. Jodell let out a scream as she felt her skin tear and sting under the bite. She brought up a hand with a sharp force to punch the monster as hard as she could.

Except, what came out of Jodell's mouth wasn't a scream.

She wasn't sure what it would be called. It was a howl, but it seemed to start from somewhere lower in her body. It was a rumbling sound before it came out of her mouth like a bellow that was louder than anything that Jodell had ever heard from any of the agile members of her family. In fact, it was so strange that she wasn't sure that it was coming out of her mouth. The creature sank teeth into Jodell's arm tighter -- almost straight to the bone. The enraged howl went deeper as a large black furred paw swiped down scratching at the sunken eye of the beast, ripping as black blood flooded out. The beast took a step back before it started towards Jodell again. She hadn't thought about what she was about to do but she knew that she let out a loud bellow again before she grabbed the beast by the neck and she hugged with a vice grip. Jodell found herself hugging the beast tighter until there was a terrible sick pop. Jodell found herself falling back.

Then, there was a thump.

Jodell wasn't sure how long she had been laying on her back. She was cold. Parts of clothes had been shredded and anything that had clung on was almost gone. She found herself shivering as sweat, blood and a black film covered her body. She sat up, her eyes looking madly around. There was soft horror that only came from an attack. That wasn't completely a night terror lie. She hadn't dreamed the horror that had been visited upon her family. She started to stumble through the wreckage of a good night. She'd hoped that Bill was there, but as each step progressed, she became less sure that she'd find them. She would have kept going except Jodell tripped over something. She turned her body to see what she had found. Before her was the body of the beast that she had killed except it wasn't really the beast. It was a person.

Jodell suddenly realized that she'd killed a fellow shifter.

17.

Oh, hello, I hope that you are enjoying the story so far. I don't mean to pause the book, but I do have a tendency to interject because I like checking in on the readers of this book series. I do value our relationship as reader/author, and I want you to know that this is important and that's what I'm doing here. Also, I feel the need to share some information that might be important for you to be aware of about the story. It's something that I've often done for the last three books. If you aren't familiar with this, allow me to explain myself.

When I was just a lowercase "S.C." I read two very different books that have influenced me. One of them was the Hitchhiker's Guide to the Galaxy. If you haven't been able to pick that up so far, then you should definitely go read these books. I do recommend them to most people. The second thing that I was quite in to was manga. My favorite growing up was called Fushigi Yuugi. I'm not name dropping a great manga/show/movie for a random reason. One of the reasons that I love this (and also the reason that I loved the Sailor Moon and Trigun comics) was because there was a side panel that was basically a discussion from the author to the reader about things that would be important. I learned a lot from reading Yuu Watase's notes about her work, and not just about Japanese culture, which when I was a lowercase "S.C." was somewhat of a mystery to me. (You see, kids, we didn't have the internet when I was your age) but also about the influences of her own work and found this as an important side note to have while reading this fantastical book. It's sort of like podcasts today where you feel like you know the hosts, like they were your closest friends. I hope we can be friends through this work, but I also want to tell you a little bit about the culture that you're reading about because I've spent a lot of time in Gaiman Heights, and this is perhaps new to some of you. So, let's get on with this, shall we?

Let's talk about werewolves.

It has been very easy for some people in the supernatural world to forget that magic is a part of every society that has sprung up. When the first human had their first thought, there was a sort of magic that was born. Because of this, several different schools of magic would change humans into some sort of different animal exist and it can be scary to some humans. I cannot tell you specifically as to why this is a fear of humans but, most definitely, people do fear the loss of their humanity. Out of that, comes the werewolf. To leave it at that, however, would be overly simplistic and rather terrible on my behalf. I would hate to think that I gave you bad information. Out of several different cultures, there are a number of species of shapeshifters.

In order for me to discuss werewolves directly, I would have to tell you that there are a number of species when it comes to werewolves. I'm not sure if the word species is exactly correct in order to discuss werewolves. Saying that there are different species of werewolves is like saying that there are different species of human beings and that would be based on where they are from in the world. There aren't different species of human beings and that is the same for werewolves. That is not to say that werewolves aren't their own species. If you want to ever end your life quickly, it would be to make this comment to someone who is a shapeshifter that isn't werewolves. You will not be kept together for much longer. If you need an illustration: imagine a giant bowl of M & Ms. There are all sorts in there, but they are out of the package. You could put your hand in that bowl and pull out an M & M. It is still an M & M but it's also a werewolf. More simply put by my father:

All werewolves are shifters but not all shapeshifters are werewolves.

For those people in the New World, werewolves are the most common shifter that people think about when it comes to the Modern Era. Much of this can be blamed on the popularity of werewolf movies in the West. I would love to tell you that there is a reason people liked them so much, that there was a deep psychological reason, but I'm not a fan of Freud and I don't have a good handle on Jungian archetypes to lecture here on it, so I will tell you that there are werewolves in almost every western culture. Like most supernatural species there is a definite division of how this race has been treated over the generations in relationship to where they were born. As much as I hate that my white privilege has been showing in this regard I do want to start with Europe. Some of this has to do with the better levels of documentation. By and large, werewolf populations in a Judeo-Christian setting have experienced a level of persecution that puts them on par with witches. While I would love to tell you that this started when a bunch of followers of a kindly Jewish carpenter decided to take things far too seriously, that would be ignoring a large book on my desk about Greek Mythology.

While there are scant references to werewolves found in classical literature, there have been a number of ancient Greek texts that refer to men who are able to shift into wolves. This doesn't count for the story of King Lycaon of Arcadia ("Not OUR Arcadia," says Amaya. "It's a different Arcadia. King Oberon has ruled since the Fourth Great Wave of the Sominal Epoch." "I don't know what that means," I said to Amaya. "Neither do I," she replies). King Lycaon was suspicious of the ability of the ancient Gods to literally know everything. Lycaon decided the only way to test this was to play a trick on the god Zeus. Lycaon thought it would be really funny to roast up his firstborn son and feed it to the god. Zeus wasn't that dumb and turned Lycaon into a wolf. There are some who will tell you that the fae were the ones who created werewolves from this incident. ("Yes, we did!" Amaya chirps. I asked Penny, who was also in my kitchen when I was doing this chapter, and Penny looked at me and simply said, "I don't know."). There are several packs who will tell you that they are descended from the houses of Lycaon. This seems to be a common theme among the wolf packs in their own stories of where they came from.

This might lead you to wonder how one becomes a werewolf. This is far more complicated than me simply explaining that there is only one way of becoming a werewolf. If you have ever seen the Wolf Man starring Lon Chaney, Jr. it very well could be believed that you become a werewolf by being bitten by the wolf itself. This is by and large, a load of rubbish and if you ever bring it up to someone who is, in fact, a werewolf, they will be greatly offended, and this isn't a safe place to be. Werewolves are very proud of being werewolves. Being told that they were a product of a random bite is one the most racist things that you can say to a werewolf.

In reality, there are two ways that one becomes a werewolf. The easiest way to do this is often to be born a werewolf. This is a trait that has been passed down from family member to family member through generations. It doesn't always lead, however, to a change. Sometimes a person who might be born from werewolves could never go through the change themselves. It is why there has often been an aspect of ritually forcing the first change to occur in teenaged children. There are also children born of werewolves that might not ever change.

The second way of becoming a werewolf is by being cursed with the change. This is not something that the werewolves want to speak about in a real detail. There is a ritual where the person who is going to be cursed is forced into a pelt of wolf fur. If I understand this correctly, there is a bit of a salve that binds the fur to the flesh of a person and there is something that is considered a drink of some sort of unknown potion. It is not something that they want to speak about because, well, people don't like to talk about their curses.

Therefore, curses are something that we will not be discussing at this time.

I'm about to wrap up this chapter because there is quite a bit of a story that I do need to get to for all of you, but I want you to be aware that I've only focused on werewolves here. Shapeshifters are something completely different than werewolves. Shapeshifters do exist in all sorts of societies. This is often due to a spiritual ritual and that is quite apart from this. Werewolf specific information is not necessarily applicable to other shifters. I did ask someone about this, and I was asked a question back.

"Are you a witch?"

"No." I said.

"Right," replied my supernatural contact. "That's what a witch would say."

I did get more details there, but that's not really important. Wolves typically band in packs of other werewolves. Often this is a family since the pack of werewolves bear other werewolves. It's a rare occasion that there is a "lone" wolf. That life choice often leaves people with someone who ends up being caught or dead. This leads to a phenomenon that can be seen in the cities. What we are bringing up in this instance is collective packs. These are packs that have been created, with an alpha male patriarch. If you want the best example that's the Sons of Sirius. While there are some of these types of packs in the cities, they are mostly loosely related urban packs built out of lost souls.

I would spend more time, but we do need to move on. I hope you find this information useful.

18.

Jodell wasn't sure if it was still night or sneaking towards morning until she saw the first rays of daylight start to peek through the cloud-shrouded mountains. It didn't matter, the only thing that she knew was that it was far too quiet. After all the screaming and terror from the night before, it was quiet. She couldn't stand it, but Jodell held her tongue as her legs pumped lightly rocking the porch swing back and forward. One hand brushed through Bill Jr.'s dark brown hair. He was soundly asleep using her lap as a pillow and a thumb wedged in his mouth. She was surprised that Rowan had left with her mother but didn't blame her. Rowan had been directly in the path of those things. She had to get out as quickly as she could, and it was safe now. She respected her seven-year-old's thoughts on survival. Bill Jr. was more fragile. She'd send him off in the morning when she thought that his head was fine. She was sure that he might have had a concussion but if he did, it wasn't a worry from the resident medic. Her cousin Charline assured her that it was fine for him to sleep.

"Your body goes into hyper-heal when you sleep. Best thing you can do for him is let that baby sleep." Charline said. "He's had a rough one, best for him anyway."

She wasn't going to argue with that. It was a bad day dawning and now, Jodell felt, it was only going to get worse from there. She wedged another cigarette into her mouth and lit it. She glanced down to make sure Bill Jr. hadn't woken up during that. He didn't, which gave her a passing moment of calm. She blew out a smoke cloud as her body settled. She could see the grass turning black on the campground like it had been struck with a sudden illness. It had been left over when they started removing the dead from the ground. It was the thing that she killed that left the blackest stain and was killing everything that it touched. Jodell hated it and whatever pack it was running with that brought this devastation to her sacred home.

They had tried to kill her and that's quite rude.

It was the violent fear of everyone in the family. It was something that they had a lasting memory of the War for Sugar Hollow. Even if they weren't alive then, they spoke as if there was some sort of shared memory of it all. She knew that her marriage to Huston was a part of the agreement that had ended the war between the packs out in the middle of the mountains. She wondered for a moment if that was why they were attacked. If she hadn't gone through the divorce and had even come back to him, then maybe there wouldn't have been a war. She thought about it again. The bone white face and the cold sharpness of the horns. That wasn't a wolf, and she knew that it couldn't be any kind of wolf. It was something different and far more dangerous and it told Jodell something that she wasn't quite prepared to reckon with just yet.

Strange days were here again.

Jodell had thought that the problems facing Gaiman Heights were going to be mostly a non-issue for those in the outside world. They had always been more obsessive about what should and shouldn't be known by the mundane world and that wasn't how business was meant to be done down here. That meant that they were entering a time when the rules of the world as they knew it no longer meant anything and that clearly meant one thing for her family. It would be war. Jodell knew that if she had to go to war with those things, she couldn't do it through the Department of the Arcane. They would simply not allow the pack to be as ruthless as they would possibly need to be. She had no choice; they had attacked her family and more than that.

Those things had carried off Bill.

All of Jodell's instincts told her that she needed to run. She needed to bound off into the woods trying to find some sort of trail that was dissipating the longer that she sat there. This was her first thing that she had to come to her thoughts. Then, logic seeped into the cracks of her plan. What was she going to do? There had to be more of them than there would be of her and she couldn't fight them all off. No, she had to wait and see if the pack had a plan and she'd run off with them on the Great Hunt.

If they'd let her run with them.

There was another thought drumming in the back of her head. Jodell was trying hard to ignore it, but every so often it would come back up as if it were on some sort of terrible loop. She had howled at the beast in front of her and swatted at it with great paws that she'd never seen before. When those thoughts came back, she could remember things that she saw and felt, and it was back on a sickening loop. Jodell knew what happened: she finally awoke. In the heat of great battle, the blessing of the ancestors came to her and she finally shifted, but that was disturbing to her. She wasn't one of them when she changed for the first time. Jodell had come out something else and it hurt to think about.

She wasn't *conry*.

I don't know if you've ever been faced with a moment of pure mental dissonance but when it comes to you, it's the most jarring thing that you can face. Jodell was in that moment. She knew that there was blood of wolves flowing through her veins. She knew that her father was Prince David and who her grandfather was before that. They knew their line of ancestors like cattlemen know breeding papers. She hadn't changed in her teens into a wolf and now, when she'd finally changed, she hadn't turned into a wolf at all. She'd shifted into something else and that meant that she wasn't really a part of her family in her mind. Tears forced out of her body and pooled in the corners of her eyes every time that she thought about it.

She needed a cigarette.

She threw out the mostly smoked cigarette and reached for another one. She repeated what she'd done before. She hadn't bought a pack of cigarettes since she had Bill Jr. This one was stolen off of Vaughn. Vaughn had shrugged it off. He'd always been the one who had given her cigarettes and sometimes a few beers. He wasn't putting up a fight. He never put up a fight. The more that she thought about it, she could remember the last cigarette.

Vaughn had driven her down to the police station feeding her cigarettes. He'd taken her through a Hardee's drive thru for breakfast that she couldn't eat. He took her to the station to finally file a complaint against Huston. It was amazing to her that he'd done it, but he was a fuming volcano of swearing that day. Christ, were her hands shaking then? Of course they were. She was going to lose her husband and it was all sorts of dishonor if she went to the cops. This time though, it was too much to tolerate. When she had been well enough, he drove her to the Sheriff's office.

"I ain't a fan of this either," Vaughn had said as he squirted grape jam on the sausage biscuit. "But fuck me, Jo. He's going to kill you and either we get the cops on him or I kill him. It's safer this way; the Elders think he done wrong, though his kin ain't too pleased, but fuck 'em. They think their shit don't smell."

She was able to get through that day. It was standing outside when she was at the point of tears again, that she almost prepared to run back in to demand that they overturn the charges. She could remember Vaughn telling her to calm down. She was crying again trying to light a cigarette. Then her hands were shaking too hard out of fear and pure nerves. That was when the deputy helped her with that. She'd nodded at him with a grateful smile.

"You are going to be okay," he'd assured her as she took a sobering drag. "You aren't a victim. You're a survivor."

Bill had gotten her to walk away. He was a good man. She had to find him.

Jodell went back to wondering if she could make the pack bend the rules to let her join the Great Hunt when she heard the screen door swing open carelessly. She sat up stiffly as she listened to the slow steps creaking across the wood of the porch and didn't relax until he was two feet away from her. She watched the gray light flickering over Lord Byron's face as he lit his pipe. Suddenly the morning air tainted by the smell of death and dew was suffused in the thick rich smell of tobacco smoke and it calmed Jodell because it was a comfort.

It told her that things could be normal again.

He let the flame dance before he shook the match out, before returning the spent wooden stick to the earth. He took a long puff as he leaned against a pillar on the porch.

"No one ever smoked in the house. My grandmother would chase any of the men out of the house when they lit a cigar or a pipe." He said quietly in some sort of explanation. "I own the house now, outright, could do whatever I wanted with it. But I swear to the Ancestors, if she caught me smoking in the house she'd rise out of the grave and rip out my lungs."

Jodell almost threw her cigarette away as she listened because, honestly, she didn't know where this was going. He lumbered towards her and then sat in a rocking chair looking down at Bill, Jr.

"How's he doin'?" he asked with a puff of smoke.

"He's a little banged up, but he's tough."

"Of course, he is," Lord Byron replied. "He's got Crowe blood in him. He'll be fine."

"I hope he's too young to remember any of this," Jodell said.

"Why?" replied Lord Byron. "He survived. That's something to be proud of."

That was it. She had loved Lord Byron, but then he lost it. She felt her eyes flash at him with a snarled grin as she pulled her arm around Bill, Jr. tightly.

"He ain't going to war for you or this family," Jodell growled at him.

"I don't want that for him neither, but that ain't my choice and it ain't yours either, Jo," he said with tired resignation. "If he's going to be a part of the fight, he'll know when he's ready."

Jodell rolled her eyes at him.

"Don't tell me that they filled you with all that nonsense of the English God so that you have given up the faith in the real one and the ancestors."

"Your ancestors didn't protect us," Jodell snapped at him. "The Old Gods let this land be defiled."

"Neither did Jesus," Lord Byron sighed. "Jo, we don't ever ask the Old Gods for protection. We ask for guidance, like we did when you were born."

Jodell turned her head to one side quizzically.

"I know it's a weird thing to bring up right now, but the Old Gods and the Ancestors always give us what we need," Lord Byron continued. "Like when you were born. Did you know you were born on this land?"

Jodell shook her head, listening to Lord Byron.

"That's true. We took your mama down to the creek and the knee women prepared your birth just like I was born and your daddy. You were the last to be born before my grandmama died. She did your blessing to Lord Eletha. She whispered what your true name was. The name no one should call you until you were called to change."

"What was it?" Jodell asked softly.

"Ursala."

Jodell almost asked a dumb question. Maybe it was just because she had experienced nothing but all of the children's movies including the one about the mermaid. The name Ursala didn't tell her about who she was apart from conjuring up the thoughts of a sea witch. She could see Lord Byron wanted to explain, but something interrupted. He sat back and then sniffed the air.

"Go prepare our sitting room," he said. "We gonna have some visitors."

19.

Long after the decaying smell came through, the sound of fresh tires struggling for traction as they almost missed a turn on the gravel road echoed off the distant shadowed hills and over the silent campground. There was a hard *thunk* as a pothole tried to humble the SUV as it turned off the path to the grooved land that had hosted more joyous arrivals less than twenty-four hours earlier. Lord Byron was not pleased with this intrusion. There was only one group of people that were careless enough to drive so casually up to a sacred space: The Department of the Arcane. Leave it up to a bunch of hunters and magi to just waltz into a place with no acknowledgement of privacy and always unannounced. Lord Byron couldn't think of a group that liked either the cops or the police. They had always been the hand of the highest bidder in the mountains. In their part of the world, they were the kind of people who would hunt those who ran shine or tried to unionize the mills and the paper plant down in Johnson City and Kingsport. They had always been able to fight the intimidation off and infiltrate them a little bit. It was the deeper mountains of Kentucky, West Virginia and Virginia where they were straight bastards to the working people. These anti-authoritarian feelings just spilled over onto the Department of the Arcane. Cops were considered bad news because they were usually in league with the highest bidder and those small-town officials who bought their positions, but the Department of the Arcane agents were either magi or worse -- people being paid by magi.

To the Lord Byron's mind, corrupt cops were no different from the Department of the Arcane. Definitely not his people.

Lord Byron knew that Jodell worked for the Department and that she'd remarried to a cop and it took more than a few leaps of mental gymnastics to get around those facts. He believed that it was something like an act of rebellion when it came to his niece. She had shunned the world that hadn't protected her, but once she realized that they still loved her and they could admit they made mistakes it would be like before. She'd come back and quit being their dog. That fantasy meant nothing just then.

He didn't invite the Department out here.

He wasn't sure how they got out here. It could have been a false flag attack. The magi were planning on going to war with the older tribes of the mountains maybe. It had always been a fear that they were planning on killing those groups they couldn't control. The younger pups had been talking about reading some of that nonsense on 4chantry, but Lord Byron didn't own a computer and had no time for conspiracy theories. The easiest answer was that one of the women or the *morrcans* called them when they got back to civilization. He wasn't sure he could blame them. It was like nothing they'd seen before. He had a plan. They could poke around all they want, but at the end of the day, he'd have his retribution for the trespasses on their land.

If there was anything left after that, the Department could try for their justice.

Lord Byron went to prepare the great room for them. Of course, that didn't mean that the Department wasn't going to be greeted by the rest of the pack.

They stood around the back of the house staring at the SUV with vicious anticipation. The Department shouldn't have gotten there that quickly. These were the same boys that had been padding circles around the house for several hours before and had failed to realize that anyone had left, so perceptions were clearly off. After that, the muttered spread of the same rumors read by the younger pups about the conspiracies on 4chantry had simmered into a high panic among the pack just as the SUV turned up.

At the end of the day, magi couldn't be trusted.

It was the passenger side that opened first to let the man out. A crisp pair of shoes dropped to the soil and walked along the ground. If the pack were hoping for a sign that everything was going to be all right, they were about to be disappointed.

They got Edmund Trumper.

If the cops weren't to be trusted and the Department was even worse, then Edmund Trumper was the worst of the worst. He was a clean man that found himself in the rural mountains for reasons no one ever spoke. People didn't like him for this reason and many others. Edumund Trumper was a meticulously clean man. It wasn't just the neat dressing, but an overly cleaned and pressed appearance of Edmund Trumper that set the rough-hewn, blue collar mountain folk on edge. He was a trained alchemist, along with being a mage which people found mysterious and distrustful. For his part, Edmund Trumper did nothing to dissuade anyone from hating him. He had a persona that was mostly a lie, because it meant that he didn't have to talk about his life. He didn't have to talk about his troubled marriage to his American wife or the baby that had died six months earlier that Edmund Trumper had always suspected she'd sacrificed. He never had to speak of Eddie from the North or his rough upbringing in estate housing. Edmund Trumper was generally cultured and well poised except...

"Bloody 'ell!" Edmund Trumper squeaked out in a thick Yorkshire accent. "Stepped in some shite!"

Edmund Trumper's wing tip sank deeper into what he dismally hoped was just mud. He pulled his shoe up and inspected it with a strange expression of utter disgust. He wasn't exactly sure what he was about to do until there was a light chuckle from the man who emerged from the driver's side.

"Shee-it, Ed," another voice drawled. "Even dirt hates you."

That West Texas twang was unmistakable. Really, there was only one person who talked like that and that was Arlis Thursday. Where people were put right off by Edmund Trumper, they liked Arliss Thursday. Some of this was his laid-back nature and the face that somewhat resembled Woody Harrelson, which made a certain generation think that he was cool. The other part of them thought that it was just a kindness to give the benefit of the doubt to him since many people just assumed that he was in some sort of strange marriage with Edmund Trumper. They were not more than work partners, but Arliss Thursday was gay, and most people knew that. Arliss Thursday wasn't one who hid much of anything about himself. He was gay, he grew up as a hunter in West Texas which is where his family was originally from. He was the first Thursday to come back east since the Mexican American War. He had helped to hunt the Lich.

He stayed because he liked East Coast rap.

None of this helped the rattled Crowes feel kinder towards the SUV's occupants as they paced and circled quietly, watching the agents approach the house. They moved slowly as they watched. There were few things more unsettling than a pack of werewolves on edge.

"Good morning, gentleman," chirped Mr. Trumper. "I'm Ed-"

"We know who you are." Vaughn had elected himself the spokesman of the pack. "What do y'all want?"

"May we speak to your alpha?"

That question was met with a serious snicker from the pack as they passed it along to one to another before they stopped.

"Alphas are a false construct that biologists created from observing captive packs." Vaughn explained. "Mostly, we create packs along familial lines and that means generally it's a parent or grandparent who takes care of the pack. Really you only see a struggle for an alpha position in non-genetically linked packs which is why there is pack fighting in zoos."

"Cut the bullshit," Arliss Thursday interjected. "Can we speak to your daddy?"

"No. My daddy has been dead for like twenty-three years," Vaughn smirked at the magi's ignorance. "Lord Byron done seen you comin'; he's waitin' for you in the great room."

Vaughn took a step back signaling his cousins to part ranks, making a path for Arlis Thursday and Edmund Trumper to walk into the house. They carefully entered the house, each member of the family following quietly behind them. Once everyone was inside the building, the farmhouse became silent.

That was when the person in the backseat of the SUV slid out.

Norvita wasn't quite sure if she was going to be able to handle all the negative energy and the dick measuring that went on in this place. She'd seen it before, but mostly when it was Carson and someone else. Carson always won or there was no contest. She never liked it, but now it was even worse. Still, there was a reason she was here, and it wasn't for whatever was going down with the politics of the region. She walked slowly across the front lawn of the farmhouse. She quietly stopped at the growing black spot. She knelt down beside the edge extending her hand over the desecrated area. She opened her hand, letting her mind wander over the death. She sighed.

"Oh," she said. "That's not good."

20.

The sound of defeated pacing attracted Ma's attention from the barn to the front of the mansion just as dawn appeared over the horizon. She knew that sound and it was never a pleasant one. It was the sound that came when a shoat slipped a trap out on the walking trials. She could remember it from when her brothers came back from over in Saltville after they were beaten back during the War. It was the kind of somber walk that was well beyond a funeral dirge, but full of tired sorrow edging towards misery. They had been defeated and beaten back and the morale was sinking low as the black blood seeped from open bites on their flesh. She watched them as they brought back what they could catch and that was a disappointment. One lousy shoat who looked like he'd die from the Curse before they ever got a chance to butcher him for the best parts. She put her hands on her hips and shook her head.

It was clear that Ma was disappointed.

Her disappointment was picked up on by Milo. He had been the oldest of the children and was now almost a man. He knew that when he could father a child that he'd become an adult and that was a problem. Pa would probably have him killed before that happened, but that wasn't his specific problem at that moment. What was his immediate problem was the disappointment of the woman. There was nothing more irritating than feeling like he was a small child compared to her.

Then, Milo really thought about what was making him mad.

He could accept that she had some sort of power in the household. She was, after all, the only female. She was the life giver and she bore the family for generations and she was his mother. Unless there was another woman who could withstand the Curse, she would bear his offspring in the next generations but that wasn't what made his insides boil. As she was the only female, Milo, as the oldest boy, knew that she was also the keeper of the arcane knowledge. She could read the augury and the signs and she had read them wrong. They were supposed to be victorious and they weren't. Milo marched away from his siblings and towards her. His big hand raised quickly and came down slapping out whatever taste was in Ma's mouth.

"You dumb bitch!" Milo yelled at her.

The shuffle of feet stopped as they heard the swear pass his lips. It was perfectly fine to hit a woman. If she was trying to be out of her place when they spoke, they would have to show a strong hand and that was all correct. What prompted the stunned silence was the swear word. Language wasn't something that you used coarsely around a woman, let alone the head female in the family. Breathing all but stopped as they watched Ma.

Ma let out a slow sigh unphased by the slap.

"It sounds like the Hunt didn't go well for us," Ma said gently.

"Of course, it didn't go well," Milo spat out black blood that burned in the dead ground. "This is your fault."

"How? I ain't the one who went hunting."

"You didn't read the portents right."

"I'm never wrong, boy."

"Then the spirits lie to you."

A gasp would have echoed through the boys if there was ever a chance to gasp. They never spoke ill of the spirits. If there was something that the Curse gave them, it was the understanding of the higher spirits. Ma reached over and grabbed the old shovel that had been conveniently resting on the side of the house. She swiftly swung it at Milo. The crack of iron and bone split through the night air and forced Milo down. She stood over him holding the shovel's head against his throat as she looked down.

"You hush up with that, now," Ma hissed at him as she looked down with icy calm. "If you cause us to fall out of favor with the black spirits that blessed our name, I will behead you here upon this ground."

"We were defeated."

"Because you mistook favor for a blessing. You're too young to ever hunt wolf. They ain't shoat, they fight back, and they will kill us. It's not the first time we fought them, but it'll be the last."

She looked up at her boys and she frowned looking at the faces.

"Who didn't come back?" she asked finally.

Ma took her shovel off of Milo. He sat up as he looked at Ma. He spat again before he cleaned up his face.

"Delmar," Milo finally said. "Them wolves got something I ain't never seen. She killt him."

"She?"

"She," Milo responded. "We had to run afore we could get the body."

Ma felt a little bit of sadness spreading in her. There was no mistake that Delmar was the youngest of the boys. Mothers always had a soft spot for their youngest, but that meant nothing when it came to the hunt. Delmar had been slow and more sensitive and that meant that they couldn't entirely rely on him in a fight. He made the family weaker by being alive. There was no doubt that at some point they would have to kill him. This way, it was better. He died in battle like a warrior, as he was born to be and she could mourn him as such.

"No body though?" she asked.

"No, ma'am. We had to leave him."

Delmar's spirit would never be able to rest, sadly. It meant that they would have to do only one thing and Ma was pleased with the development. In order to find peace and make things work the way that they were supposed to, they would have to kill each of the wolves.

They would have their revenge.

"I will see if Pa is willing to have a word for grace and we can have a funeral, but mark my words, my bear sons." Ma spoke quietly. "We will have their blood."

21.

If you were to fly a low air vehicle over the Cove you could see the Crowe home. It could easily be distinguished from the rest of the houses scattered throughout the Cove. Most of these houses were very modern and built by people who were looking for a quiet mountain retreat that was far enough from Asheville and Abingdon to not be too expensive, but close enough that it would be true to say that they had mountain homes. They all had names that were reserved for homes in a Bronte novel. Then, there was the Crowe homestead that had no name but had been rebuilt as needs served. There was a distinct L shape making it clear that this was exactly the case. The base of the L was the old part of the house that had been built on the foundation of the first home, which stood this way to keep a smooth breeze flowing through off the creek that was but a few steps from the back door of the dining room. It also made the coldest room where the kitchen stood. That had more to do with the foundation of limestone that had been built under the house, rooted in the creek-cooled mountain clay. It made the house cooler than most. That's what could have easily been the case anyway.

The glares that the Department agents got from the Crowes made the house absolutely frigid.

There were dozens of Crowes staring daggers at them. No matter where Edmund Trumper or Arliss Thursday looked, cold blue eyes were watching them as if they were trying to figure out exactly how to kill the men without anyone ever finding out. Of course, they'd get away with it. This was only made worse by the passing clouds that darkened the great room, causing their eyes to flash with a predator's glow. Tension hung in the air around this meeting and Edmund Trumper and Arliss Thursday knew that this was going to be a precarious position. This was a private place that outsiders were rarely allowed to walk into, let alone agents of the Department of the Arcane. It hadn't mattered to either of the men. They had a job to do and they would have to do it. Edmund Trumper cast a glance up at Jodell who was standing against a wall. He might have taken this as a sign of safety, that was the only thing that Jodell thought it could be when she caught his sheepish grin. She wasn't the only one who saw it.

That was how she knew it was a mistake.

If there is nothing else that you learn from this book series, please remember this: never show a sheepish anything in front of one werewolf let alone more than two. As someone who once fed on what they considered the weakest of the group, they'll see sheepish grins as something that could be construed as a weakness. Moreover, if you are present in a group of werewolves after they were attacked, they'll assume that you are covering something up and that is a welcome invitation to not remotely trust you…at all. That was what Jodell attempted to convey to Edmund Trumper through her raised eyebrows before it was too late. It was far too late. He knew that he'd made a mistake when he heard the sound of soft growling.

"Lord Byron has asked to speak with them," she said in a husky voice.

It was a harrowing sight to watch her kin slink back forming a path with family members on either side to the great room. She hung behind them as they walked in to stand at the end of the long table. The long table was far more frightening to her than she had ever seen it before. Lord Byron sat at the head with the oldest members of her family on either side looking up with no sound whatsoever. She wanted them to make some sound. If there was growling there would be something to respond to. This was just quiet waiting which meant one thing.

Planning.

Jodell handed off Bill Jr. to the closest cousin she trusted and stood at the edge of the room as Vaughn sat at the right hand of Lord Byron. She watched Lord Byron tilt his head back studying them. This was going to be a long morning. She knew that they wouldn't directly ask for help if they needed it though that and she knew that had to be the reason that they were out here. After all, something had to have come up and they needed some sort of guidance. She also knew that there would be no words mentioned about what had happened in the woods or last night. That was not for the Department of the Arcane. They would send a pack out for the Hunt and they would have revenge. Jodell knew that this meeting was not going to work out happily, but for now they were going to have to, somehow, break the silence.

That would fall to Edmund Trumper.

That wasn't exactly a surprise to Jodell. Edmund Trumper was a man who, in addition to being clean, was very good at being clear about what they would need him to do. Edmund Trumper took a step towards the table, placing his clean fingers on the surface.

"Good morning," he started. "I'm Ed-"

"Do you walk into everyone's house like that? That's got to get hard." Lord Byron barked him into silence. "We know who you are. Why are you here?"

"I don't know why you are askin'," Jodell's second cousin, Tyrone, muttered. "We get attacked then they show up. Be the magi sent them here to see if we'd all done got kilt."

Jodell wasn't proud of herself that she had thought about it too. She knew that it had been a distant possibility that this was some sort of attack created by the Department of the Arcane. She wanted to trust them and part of her did trust her employers, but things were getting strange and that made it stressful. She wouldn't put it past the magi to try planning on starting a war.

"We would never want to harm a peaceful pack," Edmund Trumper said sharply. He was quite offended by this assumption, but it seemed like there was some new piece of information as well that he couldn't help following up. "Your clan was attacked last night?"

"Maybe we were but that ain't really your business, *jake*." Lord Byron replied. "It's a family matter and we'll handle it that way unless y'all want to tell us something we don't know."

"What in the name of sanity do you think that we'd be hiding?" Edmund Trumper's crisp accent was starting to blunt. "There is nothing we'd hide if we had that information."

"They knew that Huston run off from his work release," Vaughn pointed out. Jodell felt herself die a little inside at that fact. "If the Whelans were planning an attack, they'd probably wait until he got out. You put us all at risk."

The room was quiet again and Jodell hated the anticipation crackling along the werewolves' tensed muscles. She could see tics moving along their faces -- a flared nostril here, and a glance with a twitch of the eye there. This was the silent conversation between the pack elders and Jodell was terrified. They were spoiling to attack for vengeance. All Lord Byron needed to do was say the word.

"I find it somewhat upsetting that this is the very first time that I'm hearing this piece of information." Lord Byron's tone was very calm as he uttered the understatement of the year, if one went by his body language.

"That sounds like a personal problem," interrupted Arliss Thursday. "If Jodell didn't want to tell you about her business, she doesn't have to."

Jodell had wondered if she could have leapt across the table and out the back door that was behind Lord Byron when she heard those words. If that was the case, then she could have ran and kept running for as long as she needed. This was not a smart plan and not even possible. Her kin were much quicker than her and they would have stopped her. Also, due to the many rebuilds of the house, there were no stairs under that screen door behind Lord Byron.

Without warning, Lord Byron slammed his hands on the table. His eyes flashed as he looked up at Arlis Thursday and Edmund Trumper. He stood up.

"That sort of problem isn't something you brush off to the timey." Jodell was a little bit hurt that she was being referred to as a child. "That is a threat to my family. That should have been brought directly to me!"

"Jodell is an adult. She is perfectly capable of handling herself," Arlis Thursday responded.

Jodell hated the fact that she was being talked about like she was a piece of furniture. She was about to say something before Lord Byron's hands came off the table as his claws were extended into the wood. Someone would have to fill that in and buff it out in the future, Jodell thought.

"That Whelan trash," Lord Byron spat. "Beat on my brother's only girl. Shamed his family, you don't think that he wouldn't attack us on a high holy day?"

"You got no evidence to back that up," Arliss Thursday pointed out.

"You do?" replied Lord Byron. "We have a family to protect and I'm sorry. I ain't about to trust the Department to hunt like we have. We'll find them and we'll be whole. If there is something left, y'all can have justice."

"Oi!" Edmund Trumper suddenly yelled like a northern English Soccer Hooligan. "You, mate, need to calm your knickers."

If they were planning to do something violent, the kin were derailed by Edmund Trumper and his strange outburst. Silence passed as everyone, including Arliss Thursday, attempted to figure out if there was some sort of demon that had taken over his partner.

Edmund Trumper cleared his throat.

"What you are talking about here is starting a war," Edmund Trumper's voice had returned to that sharp English accent that he'd carefully crafted. "It is the Department of the Arcane's policy to stop that by any means necessary."

"I will not permit the Department to handle family business."

"Maybe you should shut up and let the Department handle something," said a new voice in the room.

It would be a point of discussion at family gatherings as to how Norvita had snuck into the room and would add to her mystique of being a powerful psychic. It would only be Jodell, who later confirmed her suspicions with Norvita, who knew that she'd merely walked into the room during the most high-pressure part of the discussion. She was always naturally drawn to drama but found that there was no way she'd interrupt actual fighting. Edmund Trumper and Arliss Thursday moved away from the table, letting Norvita stand at the edge. She didn't smile but offered a strange scoff as she looked at the pack assembled before her as she tossed back her thick black hair.

"Trust me," she said finally, after skewering each of the elders with a soul-piercing look. "You are nowhere near capable of handling whatever attacked you."

"You don't know that" Vaughn retorted.

"Yea, I do," Norvita said quickly. "I'm a psychic."

"You boys brought a seer out here?" Lord Byron said, after deciding he wasn't that impressed with Norvita.

"Oh, they didn't have a choice. I made them do it." Norvita wasn't about to lose footing while men got into another dick measuring contest in her estimation. There was far more at stake than who was going to be in charge of what. "I've had dreams about it and trust me, my dreams are the last place you want to be. I am Swami Patel's Granddaughter."

"Your granddaddy don't mean anything to us, little girl."

"Yea, I figured as much but...."

Norvita suddenly waved her hand. What spilled out onto the table was a thick blackness that filled into a small circle. She waited for a moment before she flashed a terrible blast of purple that scalded the table as she looked down.

"Whatever attacked you guys was cursed AF." Norvita said. "And I know that a pack, no matter how powerful, can't go against it. You need at least a powerful magic user."

"So, that's going to be you?" asked Lord Byron.

"Probably not," Norvita answered. "I'd need someone to watch my back."

"Jodell can go with you," Lord Byron decided. "And you'd need to find em...or we will."

22.

Bill was in a dream before he woke up or he thought that it might have been a dream. He would never be sure. What he knew was that there was something that had kept him in a silent state longer than he would have ever been comfortable. It was a hard night for him overall, but at that moment he was trapped in a dream and that's what he was willing to call it.

In the dream, Bill was standing in a grey field that he had never seen before. It didn't look like any place that he'd ever stood in the middle of before. He thought about taking a step but the ground under him shook and died. He looked at the grass that rose up towards his dream self. He watched the grass break as he glanced at it. He almost frowned at it as he felt the ground below him shifting with each step. He looked around. The sky was dead gray but all he knew was that it was very gray and bright. He didn't know where he was but he hated it. It was like every fall when he would be asked to be with Rowan or Bill Jr.'s class as they went to the fort and the corn maze. He was always creeped out by corn. Some of that was because his cousin Buck had shown him Children of the Corn. It was a cheesy movie even then but he was a child when he saw it. It still scared him to this day. Bill kept walking until he found himself standing in the burned ruins of the grass. Bill walked along the path.

Then he saw her.

She stood up in the middle of the field, her large eyes staring at him like a rolling storm. Bill had to catch his breath. She was beautiful.

Not like Jodell.

Jodell was the prettiest girl he'd ever seen in his life, but she was mountain pretty. His shoulder ached at the time that he'd told her that, but it wasn't an insult. Jodell was the kind of pretty that people wrote sad mountain ballads about and that came with her willful spirit. This was a different kind of pretty. The only thing that he could think of was that she was heart-breaking sad pretty.

She was La Llorona.

Bill hated that these thoughts were coming back. There were these memories that he had kept filed away from himself because they had no bearing on his everyday life and now, they were rushing back to him like he had all the time in the world.

Like the Weeping Woman.

It recalled Gomez to his mind, his patrol partner back in the worst part of the world during his last tour. It had been just the two of them guarding a road in the middle of the night covered in desert cold. The pair would share their own ghost stories. He'd told Gomez about the phantom lights on the railroad or the Confederate ghosts that were supposed to haunt the hills. Gomez told him about La Llorona. She had been a pretty woman, the most beautiful woman in her village. That's why the rich man decided to marry her. They were happy for a time. She gave him two beautiful sons, but good things never lasted. He started traveling more and more. She thought that she had stopped loving him. She was right. He came home once with a girl who was young and pretty and the woman was getting old. Her husband told her to leave. She said she would but wanted to say goodbye to her sons. She did say goodbye by drowning both of them in the bath and then killing herself. Because she had committed murder and then suicide, she wasn't allowed to enter the gates of heaven until she can find the souls of her sons. They say she walks the streets sometimes kidnapping children and when they aren't hers, she drowns them.

"It's so fucking spooky out here, I half expect to see her here," Gomez had said.

"How many women do we see on a daily basis looking for their kids who are alive, Gomez? We'd never know if she's one of them."

"Yea, she'll be different. She'll be pretty, but sad."

Bill wasn't sure he'd understood until he saw the woman in the middle of the grass. She was different but she was perfectly sad.

The Blue Woman turned her head to one side as she watched Bill approach her. She walked a slow, slow circle around him as she carefully inspected Bill. Instantly he understood that she wasn't a ghost. Granted, he might not have ever seen a ghost, but this wasn't one. It was something that was very, very powerful. She would agree with him on that, but there was something that was far more important to her. She was disappointed.

"You aren't Asher," she said to him sadly.

"No," said Bill. "I'm not."

"I'm lost," she said quietly.

"That makes two of us."

"Yes, but you can't be here."

Bill didn't exactly have a desire to be there himself but if he could have left, then he would. He tried to open his mouth to say so, but then he heard it. It was the screeching of war birds. He looked up to the sky as he saw what he could only imagine was a war bird with its bright wings and talons outstretched. It was going to kill him, and he knew it. Suddenly, the Blue Woman shoved Bill out of the way.

Then, Bill saw a flash of bright blue light.

Bill's eyes finally flickered open as he looked around with a hard gasp. He wasn't sure where he was but this wasn't the field that he had been walking through. This was less of a delight than he thought it would be as he started to try to sit up. He was more and more confident that this was a dream. A dry cough came out of his mouth, surprisingly painfully for a dream. None of this was comforting to him.

This wasn't the Crowe Homestead.

Bill wasn't the most well-liked person in that household, but this was not what would happen there. They wouldn't have beaten him up and then discarded his body in the woods. Not after what he went through with the Running of the Rocks. Even if they had, he knew that Jodell would be right beside him if that were the case. She never left his side when he was sick or injured. Bill was as much under her protection as the kids were. He'd saved her once and loved her and now they were bound together. She wasn't there.

"Shit boy, I wasn't ever sure you'd ever wake up?"

Bill picked his head up and stared. At the other end of wherever they were was Huston. He was cross legged and naked. Bill tried to pick himself up, but he wasn't going to be able to do it. He wanted to spit at his wife's ex-husband but found his mouth to be too dry.

"Easy there, *jake*," Huston said. "I don't think that you are in any shape to fight. Just relax for a moment"

Bill slumped down with his head resting on the floor as he started to gasp again. There was a feeling of panic that came through him as he started to remember a few things that had happened, but he couldn't remember where his wife or children were. This was a fact that was becoming more upsetting when he realized that he was somehow with Huston. Whatever Huston had done to them, he was going to have to get some kind of vengeance for it. He would have to wait until the pain subsided.

The only thing was that the pain never came on how it should.

This was shock. There was no doubt that he'd been in a fight. He could at least remember trying to throw a punch or two. He could remember white teeth being borne and snapping down on his skin and there he was, he couldn't remember what kind of a fight it was or if it had been with a wolf or something else.

He knew that he'd lost consciousness between then and now.

After some painful breaths, Bill sat up and let his back settle against the back of what he quickly learned was a cage. He stared at the other man as he let out a slow aching grunt as he panted out another breath that made him see black spots. He could feel the sharp sting of pain. Gently, he looked down at his chest. At some point he'd lost his shirt which was unfortunate for him as he was greeted by the sight of deep bite marks all down his chest. They'd swollen up with red skin and yellow seeping in the open wounds.

There was no doubt that they were already infected. Bill shuddered to think about what else would be under the surface of these bites. Huston handed him a bottle of water, incongruous in its pristine plastic packaging among the backwoods hellscape.

"I know," he said, at Bill's disbelieving blink. "But they ain't broke the seal on 'em. I think they take 'em off those hikers they pick off the trail."

Huston wasn't wrong. The water had been from some sort of mass production. He drank it slowly. No sense in getting sick on drinking water too fast. He eyed Huston again carefully.

"I don't know what this shit is," Huston said. "They'd done killed my work detail and then I was brought here. You look like they got you good."

Bill shot Huston a scowl as he put the bottle down. He knew that he had to collect himself. He had to think quietly. He knew who he was. He was William Alan Harris. He was born in Franklin Memorial Hospital on January 27, 1982. He was Darlene and Jerry's second child. They'd lost a son three years earlier when the forceps had crushed his older brother's spine. He had a little sister and he was married to Jodell Ursula Crowe. He had two kids: Rowan Louise and William Alan Harris, Jr. Bill suddenly stopped.

Jodell.

Rowan.

Bill.

"Jodell?" he asked Huston quickly.

"She ain't here," Huston said. "She's gotten tougher than I remember if she ain't dead. It's just you and me, hoss -- at least right now."

"Right now?"

"Them folk who grabbed you bring some new livestock every couple of days, then they take them out and ain't never brung 'em back."

If Bill hadn't thought about it, he probably wouldn't have noticed the smell. Once he did smell it, he couldn't ignore it. There was a pervasive smell that Bill knew better than he wanted to. It was another one of those memories that turned over in his head. When he was starting out his career as a policeman, he was asked by CPS to help with the removal of a child from a dangerous situation. Everything about that job was imprinted on his memory and he wished he could forget. He couldn't. He'd never forgotten Madeline Grieves. She was a small child with dirty black hair and big eyes that looked up at him -- she was covered in filth. Bill was going to be grateful that he didn't know all of what had happened to her and hoped that she was living a great life now. He wasn't sure of that but he knew that smell because he was smelling that right now or not quite.

But it was very close.

It was the smell of human waste that was the strongest. Bill couldn't mistake the smell of human feces and urine for anything other than what it was. Over it was the smell of clean straw which was put down to be used and probably then raked over. Bill wanted to throw up, but he knew that he couldn't. He was going to resist both adding to the smell and then further dehydrating himself.

"Are we in a barn?" he asked confusedly.

"Yea, apparently, we're being added to the stock."

It didn't take too much imagination for Bill to realize what was meant by "stock". If there was something that he had learned today, it was the glaringly obvious use of humans as food for people who had decided that this was a good dietary choice.

The livestock was humans.

Bill wasn't going to try to fully understand exactly what that meant; he was going to spend far more time trying to figure out how they were going to get out. He hated Huston, but he wasn't about to let someone die in a cage even if they were a piece of trash. He tried to crawl towards the cage door.

Then, he heard sobbing.

Bill quickly looked over. He felt his body ease and twitch as he looked at her. She held her arms around her legs as she sobbed. Bill watched her and felt his heart twist.

"Yea, don't talk, hoss," Huston said.

"Hey," Bill coughed out.

The girl picked her head up, looking at them.

"He's not a dog anymore," Missy said awkwardly. "They'll kill him now."

"They?"

"The people. There were more in the cages, but not anymore."

"How long have you been here?"

"I don't know. It seems longer. They keep taking the others away. Makes everything worse."

"The others?"

"Yes, they bring men, two or three. They took them away."

Her lip curled up making a series of dents in her upper lip. She was going to start to cry again.

"I don't want to die here!" she wailed.

Bill's heart broke for her. He, as a lawman, never wanted to make a promise. Promises got you in trouble with families and victims. That was different from today though. When you're a cop, you always come in after the crime. He was on ground zero here, as much a victim as she was. In that case, he thought, it was okay to make promises. He sat up on his knees.

"My name is Bill Harris," he told her. I'm with the Carter County Sheriff's department."

"Does that mean someone is looking for us?" she asked.

"Yes," he said. "But we aren't going to wait around. I'm going to try my very best to get you out of here."

23.

Norvita couldn't get the A/C cold enough for her body to stop sweating. Her head felt fuzzy, and her stomach felt like it was spinning around in a circle. She tried to let her eyes drift out the window in a desperate effort to keep some kind of focus to keep from being ill, but this was to no avail. This wasn't something that she was willing to cop to: Norvita had always had a problem with car sickness. She had been able to keep much of this hidden from people as she would often refuse to take ride shares or taxis unless she was far too drunk to be driving. This was a secret that she had kept from everyone who knew her. Her grandparents knew about it, but that wasn't really her choice in the matter. She had been the one to puke all over the back of her grandmother's Range Rover on the way to the Berkshires when she was a small child. Her grandmother still screamed about it. Her grandfather was a man who just laughed quietly about all of these things.

God, that was a pretentious story, she thought to herself as she tried to fidget through whatever was going through her head now. Not that that was ever a problem for Norvita. She was wealthy and she had literally no problem with flaunting that wealth. She wanted to keep the part of herself that got carsick secret because it was a weakness that she couldn't control. She was hopeful that she'd even kept it from Karl. She didn't want him to know about it, but she thought he probably did anyway. Karl didn't need to be told. He knew everything. He'd been there for most of her life and she, honestly, needed his support to get through the idea of not having him in her life anymore.

To paraphrase Charles Dickens, Karl was dead as dead as dead can be.

Norvita was not really able to accept that concept in her life. This was another point of pride that she wasn't really sure that she was able to fully say out loud. Since the fall, Norvita had the hardest time connecting to the spirit world to see if Karl was on the other side. She would have been fine with someone or thing telling her that it wasn't exactly good for her to do that, but it would become like her dreams. She'd end up in that dead field watching some sort of battle continue and she wouldn't be able to move past it. She would just be in that field staring at the sky and the women and the rattling wind.

"Leeeet…. go…." it would hiss.

After that, Norvita stopped trying. It didn't stop the dreams, but she decided that she only needed that scenario in one place, and she was okay with her life. She had to rationalize her own grief. Karl was gone and he was in a place that she couldn't follow. She wondered if it was going to be worth it to follow Karl. She hadn't considered it, really, but Karl wasn't going to be her Karl anyway. He wasn't human when she saw him last, and it was why she had opened up the portal to send him to hell. That's what bothered her. She had sent him away. She had killed Karl and despite it being the right thing, she was still grieving and that was a new thing for her.

Norvita had never really experienced grief before.

She knew it was something that humans went through and she'd seen it plenty. As the granddaughter of the great medium Swami Patel, she had seen plenty of people who were grieving that came to try to speak to people on the other side of the veil. She had never understood it then. Her parents were dead. She had asked once if she could talk to her mother. Her grandfather told her no. That wasn't for her.

"Why, *nana-ji*?" she had asked.

"Because *poti*," her grandfather had replied. "Our people have moved on and they need to rest before their next life."

"But then, why are you able to talk to other people's loved ones but not ours?"

"*Poti*, some people don't move on," he'd said. "They will linger around. Not ours, but others."

"Why?"

"Sometimes because they can't let go."

"And other times?"

"Because their loved ones can't let go."

That was the theme of her life these days. It was time that she let go of Karl and everything else. She couldn't grieve someone who had moved on to his next stage of his own existence. It wasn't safe for her or for him. She was going to move on because he was in Hell.

That was something that she couldn't grieve at all... but she still did.

"You okay, darlin'?" Jodell interrupted whatever was going through Norvita's head.

Instantly, Norvita felt her face muscles tense as her jaw clenched at the word "darlin". She was moments away from laying into Jodell about the use of the word to describe her, a powerful psychic. If she had been feeling better, she might have started up like a New England machine gun, but being carsick made her sluggish, which was only working to the benefit of her rational brain. Rational brain told her that this was a term that was just used around here and to accept it. To be mad at Jodell for using a regional word would be like being mad at her grandfather for using "baby" to be casual with a customer service rep. The connotation was lost on both of them.

Norvita offered her a weak smile.

"Yea," she said finally.

Jodell wasn't exactly sure that she believed Norvita. If it wasn't the strange grayness to her skin and lips, it was the weakness in her conversation. Jodell leaned across her to open the glove box to pull out something quickly. She handed a plastic bag to Norvita.

Norvita stared at the object in her hands and blinked in confusion.

"Air sick bag?" she felt dumb saying it out loud. "Do I even?"

"I know that look," Jodell said with the wisdom of a woman who'd been there too many times. "Bill Jr. is the worst on car rides like this. It's his eyes. My momma thinks it's because he's probably more mixed than I'm aware of, being both *conry* and human. I think it's probably nearsightedness. Bill doesn't want to admit it, but he wears glasses when he rides. Either way, we'll probably have to see Doctor Cline sooner or later. You ain't used to our roads; Karl would always have the same problem for the first couple of days."

Jodell stopped abruptly leaving the silence echoing through the car. Norvita didn't want to interrupt out of decorum, but she was waiting for it.

"Sorry," Jodell said finally. "I didn't mean to bring him up. I know you two were close."

"Don't," Norvita cut her off. "Don't think I don't want to hear about him. I will always want to hear stories about Karl."

"I think the worse person I'd ever seen with car sickness was Karl. He always hated to admit he was wearing the wrong prescription of glasses. I think his eyes were better than he let on because of the demon, but he wanted to look like he was human. The first time he come down here, I took him over Hyter's Gap. That road turns on hair pins like it ain't nothing. I took that first turn on the gap and it was like he was that girl in the Exorcist."

Jodell stopped because that was the story. She expected to get a polite chuckle from Norvita and heard nothing. She frowned before she rolled down the window on Norvita's side. Norvita glanced over at Jodell, confused.

"Fresh air, honey," Jodell said. "Focus your eyes on one thing, not the speeding trees, it'll make you feel worse."

Norvita leaned her head against the cool glass of the window breathing in the air. Her body started to cool, letting the sickness dissipate. She still felt queasy, but it was better than before. She almost closed her eyes.

Jodell sighed disappointedly.

"I'm sorry about Karl." she said finally.

"Thanks," Norvita replied. "You're the only person that has said anything to me. No one ever talks about him anymore"

"Maybe people don't want to talk about Karl like that because he didn't die."

Norvita's eyes quickly opened as she sat up. Her head turned suddenly as she looked over at Jodell. Her mouth went dry as her heart leapt with a strange joy. She hadn't thought about Karl being alive, but maybe Jodell knew something that Norvita couldn't see. She could only assume that a second set of eyes might have been able to see something.

"W-w-what do you mean?" Norvita asked quickly.

"He didn't die like normal, right?" Jodell asked.

"No," Norvita said, crestfallen. "I guess not."

"Baby, if he'd died normally then there would have been a funeral and people could grieve normally but he didn't. He fell, right? Not even fell but done got swallowed up by the earth. No one knows how to react. If he'd just been an asshole before he was possessed, people could just say they weren't waiting for him. He was a good man and no one has the right words so they ain't gonna try."

"That's not fair!" The second Norvita said it, she became embarrassed. She knew how childish she sounded.

"It's not." Jodell was tempted to correct Norvita's tone, but she knew that she wasn't going to do that. It was better to let it go. "Magic doesn't make people less human. Sometimes when it comes to death, we're just as bad as the mundane."

"I still miss him." Norvita felt her skin heat up again because she sounded like a child to another person.

"Of course, you do," Jodell replied. "That was your daddy."

A sharp pain stabbed through Norvita's back and twisted around her heart, forcing tears down her face. It was the hard truth that Norvita wanted to ignore. She had pretended that Karl wasn't that important. She had a grandfather who loved her. She had a biological father that she didn't know, but whom she hated. That left Karl and Karl was the man who had cared for Norvita like a father. She covered her mouth looking down.

"You're the first person to understand." Norvita found her voice breaking.

"Course I do. Kin don't always mean blood," Jodell said. "You were as much his daughter as Annie or Nora, it's just not as obvious to most people."

Norvita couldn't bear to have this conversation keep going. She had to break away from it before it started to kill her. This wasn't a good time to grieve. She glanced out the window, trying to find something to distract herself from this conversation.

It didn't take long for her to find something.

If she was a super religious person, she would have assumed that it was God that had felt her unconscious prayer. That wasn't Norvita, but she did get distracted by a white cross placed on the side of the road. She sat up with a startled blink as she watched it pass. She didn't see the name because they were going too fast. She then saw another cross, but this one was decorated with flowers and ribbons. She saw another.

"What are those?" she blurted out.

"Hmm?"

"The crosses on the side of the road, what are they for?"

"You ain't never seen them before?"

"No."

"Sometimes people put them out on the side of the road where someone died or went missing from to honor the dead."

"Missing? People go missing from the road?"

"Closer to trail spots. You see it more around hunting season. Someone goes off into the brush, ain't never come back."

"How?"

"People get lost. The Department sends a couple of boys out in the woods to see if some of the packs or worse got em. We ain't never found anything. Most we ever find are sometimes bandanas tied to trees next to the Appalachian Trail. Just happens."

"Lots of things 'just happen'." Norvita muttered.

"Yea, I know. I ain't fond of it either. Grab tight to that bag. The road on the ridge has more curves than Elvira, Dolly, and Pamela Anderson Lee combined."

24.

The barn was quiet for a very long time after the last time they saw any of their captors. Ma had brought them what they assumed was food. No one was able to convince either themselves or each other that it was safe to eat. As far as they could tell, there was probably nothing distinctly poisonous about whatever the food that was being given to them. They were still alive for a reason. Ma had said as much to them. She stared at the three of them angrily.

"You ain't gonna let yourselves starve," she said angrily. "Sooner or later you'll either die or eat."

It was quiet after that. What that meant was each of the hostages were left alone with their thoughts and that was a dangerous thing for each of them. Huston was starting to brood and be angry. He had always hoped that he would die in the back of the mountains. It was where he was born and that was where he was going to die. What he didn't want was to die in the middle of a cage on a farm. This wasn't what he expected to see at the end of his life and he was angry about it. More than that, he was angry because he couldn't come up with a good plan to not end his life in a cage. He might have been able to come up with something, anything but he was distracted.

Missy was quite distracting.

In the short time that they had been together, Missy was starting to dance on Huston's last good nerve. She was far too fragile to be here. Despite Bill trying to calm her down, she was in constant hysterics. She would do nothing but cry or scream every time he thought that she had calmed down. It made it completely impossible for Huston to begin to speak. Huston just desperately wanted to punch her to shut her up. Huston realized that he wasn't much different than when he went to prison. Jodell would run her mouth the same way and she stopped when he hit her. He figured it would be the same for Missy, except Bill would probably stop him. Hell, in his estimation, Bill should be stopping Missy from going off the edge.

Bill wasn't helping.

Make no mistake, Bill was just as upset by Missy and her constant state of upset. He, however, was willing to accept that she was dealing with trauma. It wasn't every day that you were kidnapped by cannibals. She was welcome to be in a place where she couldn't understand it. Bill did find her voice trying at this point and it was making it hard for him to think. It wasn't the only thing that was making it hard for Bill to think.

Bill knew he was getting sicker.

He tried not to think about it, but the longer that was awake he could feel a fever burning his flesh and the infection from the bites was starting to be more painful. He didn't want to look at the skin around the wounds, but he could feel it. There was something moving through his body and it was slushy and black. He knew that he was going to have to get out of there sooner rather than later. If he didn't get out of there he was going to die.

It was around the last time that Ma came around he started to come up with a plan. It wasn't a plan that he was going to be executing by himself. No, if he was going to get out of there, then they were going to all be getting out of there. After he constructed what he thought was the best plan he presented it to Missy and Huston. Missy thought it was a great plan. Granted, she couldn't come up with a better idea, but she knew enough to acknowledge that she was out of ideas. Huston, on the other hand, had some questions. There was no mistake that they needed to get out of that place, but this wasn't the right plan. He did offer this as eloquently as he'd ever been known to be capable of.

"This is some bullshit," Huston said. "It's a bad idea and we're all going to die because of it."

The first thing that Huston's counter achieved was to cause Missy to cry harder. If there was some sort of glimmer of hope in her mind, it had been ruined and destroyed by Huston because, after all, if they were going to do this, they all had to be on the same page. Bill narrowed his eyes at Huston angrily.

"You got a better plan?" Bill asked dryly.

"No but yours is a fucking bad idea."

"Why? Is it because I'm the only one coming up with one?"

"You really think I'm going to be mad because you married my ex-wife and think that I'm going to shoot down your plan out of some kinda grudge? Get over yourself, *jake*. This is a plan that's going to get someone killed."

"Lot of words there for saying, yes."

If this were any other situation, Huston would have been angry at the idea of being accused of hating the man. He did hate Bill of course. Bill was the sort of guy in high school whose excessive honesty made the sort of benign actions that made life in high school unbearable for people like Huston. What did he do after

148

that? He was a cop which was exactly the same thing in the outside world. Then, he married Jodell and raised Huston's daughter. Huston knew that he wasn't a good father, and he could respect Bill for covering that for him.

"Bill, for this to work someone is going to have to stay behind and it sounds like you are planning on that."

"I'd be bad at my job if I didn't."

"Do you think Jodell is going to handle it if you die out here?"

"Whelan," Bill was talking slower with a light wheeze. "Look at me."

Huston looked at him with a quiet inspection. In the light of day, he finally realized that there was something else that was going to be worse than waiting. Bill leaned against the wall of the cage with a cold swallow. He had lost weight since they threw him in the cage earlier that morning. His cheeks had sunk deeper into the sides of his face as he tilted his head back. Huston, granted, was willing to accept that maybe that wasn't really the case, just a trick of the poor light, but he couldn't explain away the waxy gray skin that seemed to be covered in a layer of sweat forcing his hair back. The veins of black were pushing through his skin. Huston shook his head.

"Do you really think that I'm going to survive to go back to her?" Bill asked with a struggle.

"If you know what's good for you," Huston said.

"I have every plan of going home but... I can't wait."

"No ok, this is still stupid, but it's our only plan."

25.

By the time that they had gotten to the top of the Ridge, Norvita had become the worst kind of tourist. She had leaned against the window with her jaw agape looking out the window. If this had been in the setting that she'd been more comfortable with, say a city street, the sights might not have been jarring but this was not where they were. It was out in the middle of the wilds of a place that she had no basic understanding of personally, so she had been fascinated by the things that she saw. The first was the small family graveyards. This might not have been so confusing to her. Norvita, as the granddaughter of a powerful psychic, had been in many homes where the loved ones had been stored in urns and kept like some kind of weird family heirloom. Doyle had a personal family plot (though it was more confusing as to why a vampire would need a cemetery plot) in the Irish Catholic cemetery where he'd buried three of five of his children. He had an open place for his long dead wife and two he buried in Ireland, if he could ever remember where they were buried. All of those things made perfectly good sense to her. What she didn't understand was why would someone bury their family in the yard beside their house.

"Really?" Jodell asked when she brought it up to her. "That ain't hard. Some people have owned this land for generations. If your land has been zoned for farming, they let you have a graveyard for your family on it."

"But why? What happens when you move out or sell the land?"

"People don't expect that to be the case."

Despite this, that made some sense to Norvita. Humans, particularly the mundane, don't think of an advanced future. This is what they had, and they weren't going to leave. She wondered if that would be a problem during the zombie apocalypse. Why did Norvita think there was going to be a zombie apocalypse? This is a detail that is far more complicated than I have time to get into in this story. What really struck her were the statues.

Statues were something that she'd seen before and in lots of places. Norvita had gone to a very exclusive private school that had been run by the Roman Catholic Church. As such, there had been a number of statues of placid looking saints in places that people could congregate to keep them from doing sinful things like talk to boys or smoke. She had been convinced that her grandparents had a giant golden statue of Ganesh in their living room for the same reason. It was because god was always watching. She picked her head up when she saw the placid face of Christ on the side of the road pointing to his heart. Norvita wondered what that meant. She knew that she had seen statues in Gaiman Heights when she walked into different neighborhoods, especially when it came to the churches. St. Patrick stood waving with two fingers next to the Church of St. George and the Dragon. It was the guardian of South Gaiman (spiritually, Carson would tell you that he was the guard dog that hunted in South Gaiman). Most neighborhoods had that. Little Shi'an had dragons at the large gates that stared at you viciously. Norvita wondered sometimes if the Tak Lao ever modeled for them.

She wasn't brave enough to ask.

"There are statues," she said finally. "What's up with that?"

"What?" Jodell said, distracted.

"People like Jesus and statues." Jodell replied.

"That's it?"

"What?"

"Do they have deeper meanings or is it just that?"

"I think people have that St. Francis of Assisi because they like animals. I like that idea. There's a saint looking out for animals but other than that... I don't know, darlin'."

Norvita hated the phrase 'I don't know'. It was what everyone would tell her anymore and she thought it was a cop out. It hadn't occurred to Norvita that she was slightly spoiled by the fact that Karl had known everything. It was easy to ask him anything and he could just tell her. Of course, Karl was directly connected to the archives of Hell and he could easily access that if he had to for information. Of course, he always answered his questions and never made her feel like she was an idiot for not knowing something. Now all she got was a scoff.

"If you don't know, just look it up online," someone once told her.

She made a face thinking about it. She had been angry about that before she was distracted by a large satellite dish.

It was disconcerting for Norvita.

This wasn't really that new. Norvita had seen satellite dishes before. Her privileged experiences hadn't kept her away from the joys of that. The row houses of North Gaiman and East Side had small ones that grew outside of the buildings trying to gain some sort of secret knowledge. This one was bigger than that. She knew that the biggest ones were on the top of channel 5 that was in the heart of downtown that broadcasted for one of the major networks. In recent years, she found it creepy with a <u>They Live</u> vibe (prior to working with Asher, Norvita wouldn't have known what They Live was. It was something that Asher had forced on her. For this, and other reasons, she hated him because now she couldn't shake the paranoia).

"What is that *for*?" Norvita blurted out without thinking.

Jodell knew the answer to that question. It was a perfectly good question, and she was about to say it until the next thing fell out of her mouth.

"Many folks in the mountains are highly concerned about the search for alien life. We have our own version of SETI."

Jodell didn't realize what she said until the last words hung snarkily in the car. By then, it was far too late for her to take it back. She was absolutely terrified that she had said something very rude. She hoped that Norvita took it for what it was: a joke. It wasn't a very good joke. It was the kind of joke that you told to little kids to make them think about things in a weird way. She wasn't sure if she'd heard Bill tell their kids that line. She was almost sure that her father had said the same thing. That took Jodell back a little bit. She hadn't thought about her father in ages. You didn't want to think about the honored dead because they were just that: dead. They wanted to rest and only be called on when it was a moment of great need. It was in fact a great moment of need. She had things ripped away from her violently. She could use her dad now.

Not that she could remember him.

"Really?" Norvita asked, breaking into Jodell's maudlin thoughts.

Jodell almost laughed at the level of naivete that Norvita displayed. It was a dumb sort of thing that should haven't been a question. But she smiled at Norvita and then sighed.

"No, darlin'," she said to Norvita. "It's a joke. In the old days, that's how folks got TV this far down in the hollow. A family would share to save money back in the 80s or so."

"Oh, how do they watch TV now?"

"Probably the same way city folks do."

"Wait until it comes to Netflix then binge the fuck out of it over a weekend?"

"Or watch it the next day on Hulu."

Norvita wasn't expecting an answer like that or at all. She found this to be as perplexing as the statues or the satellite dishes. Maybe it was that she wasn't exactly sure where she was going with any of this in her head. Of course, she was also expecting things to be just a little different in her brain. She also had no idea what she was expecting. This was all cemented when they rose over the Ridge into the Camp.

Norvita wanted to tell you that she had no idea what she was expecting when she thought about the concept of a coal camp. These were words that were never really in her mind but that wouldn't be remotely true. She had decided that it had to be like the camps that she read about in a very popular young adult series. In this series, there was a post-apocalyptic society, and the heroine was from somewhere in the heart of the Appalachian Mountains. She was expecting to see poorly made, drafty cabins covered in filth. She also wasn't sure that was in the book or if she was combining that with the set design on Coalminer's Daughter.

It didn't matter. This wasn't what she was seeing.

There were evenly placed yards between each of the houses. If she didn't know better they would look like they were the same sort of house. They were small houses built of brick with some occasionally being covered in white paneling. She stared, watching as some chain link fences broke off little bits of grass for a shade tree and the odd picnic table. She liked the pretty yards. She wanted to ask Jodell as to what she was seeing.

Jodell stopped her before she could ask.

"They used to look worse." Jodell said. "Most of these houses were put up in the fifties. Lots of people bought them houses back in the eighties when some of the miners moved out of camp. They were making more money than the operators. They ain't bad houses."

"They are nice. I could see that."

"Darlin', you haven't seen anything. We're going to cross the tracks here in a minute."

Norvita didn't understand why this was very important until she felt the SUV bouncing. She looked up and her eyes started to focus on large houses rising out of the mountains and it was then that Jodell understood what it meant to be from the wrong side of the tracks. These houses were the nice part and the right side of the tracks. Each house was nicer than the last as she and Jodell went further down the path. She looked over at Jodell, about to ask about things and then she stopped. Jodell's mood was starting to become serious.

"Do I want to know?" Norvita asked.

"It's the management side of the tracks." Jodell said, her mouth set in a grim line. "Has been for years."

"Okay, why are we here?"

"Mullins owned the camp before he made enough to move down to Abingdon, but he left his attack dogs. If they are running a war, there is one bitch who would command it."

"Why?"

"She hates me."

"That's paranoid."

Jodell didn't say anything else as she turned down a main road.

26.

What has come up regularly in this story and has not yet been discussed at length is the nature of curses. I'm not quite sure how effective it is to explain what exactly a curse is and how it can do harm. I should tell you that magic has several different components. There is first, the material component. If you are a witch, then you know that it is highly important that you have to have materials to make spells work. Now, if you've worked with other types of spells, you know that words are perhaps more important than objects. If you don't have powerful components, then what you must have is the magical power to use those words and above all, the correct words. Words are very important, and this is where curses come from.

Curses are potent spells that are some of the most powerful magic that can be used by any person who has the intent. I've told you before that you will experience no fewer than six encounters with the supernatural and just forget that it ever happened. This is because the brain just simply cannot handle it. While that might be mostly ghosts or vampires or the occasional fairy, the other thing that happens is that we, as mundane humans, encounter curses on a regular basis. By and large, curses can be benign. Like if you have a co-worker that you hate and you mutter under your breath that you hope they choke, that's a curse. It is mostly harmless, although if you have some power, there might be a cough.

If they die of choking, then you are a natural spell caster and that's a lot to deal with.

I know what you are thinking, aren't spells something that you find in the Old World? It does feel Dark Ages to be saying something is a curse or the work of gypsies, but that would be a terribly racist thing to think. The Romani People have been through a lot and they shouldn't be dragged into your thoughts about curses. Curses are something that show up in many places and are a part of most cultures. There are remnants of the idea of curses that live on throughout the world and even in the United States. There are dozens of towns that have been cursed by the words or deeds or in blood. Some say that family lines have been cursed by people. I'm sure that you've heard of Montezuma's revenge. Make no mistake, curses come right along with any species that can communicate.

What is a curse, really? A curse is a wish of ill will that is called down upon another being out of spite. Like that whole example of you hoping your co-worker was to choke. Some of these are much easier to actually bring to pass because we're beings of energy. That's what human beings are: water and energy. This is an important thing to remember when you start using word working because you can, as a person, conjure a major amount of power. This is why the most important component in creating a curse can be: belief.

Belief is a dangerous weapon in the hands of someone who is not remotely aware of how they are going to use it. Belief in a religion can be used as a weapon that can cause things like repression, murder and etc etc etc. On a deeper personal level, belief can be used as a strong force that causes power to be focused. When you focus all that energy on one thing, then you can force a wave of magic that inflicts a curse. The second part of this equation is the belief of the person who is receiving the curse.

Have you ever seen the movie about the handsome squared-jawed lead who takes his doll shaped girlfriend to some sort of new and foreign town? There is always some kind of fear of a curse whether it's Old World Romani or some sort of dark magic that was bred in the Caribbean. It's always the doll shaped girl who believes in this sort of thing and causes all sorts of problems. If someone doesn't believe in the curse, then it becomes less effective. That, however, makes a boring story.

You don't want a boring story.

There are some rare moments that magical belief or disbelief is overrun by the curse itself and that's rare. Mostly this is coming from the power of the being giving the curse. A powerful magic user can cast a curse that is so terribly strong that it can be impossible to lift. Often this is an ancient magical being like a dragon. Dragons are able to give great blessings as well as some of the most upsetting curses that can be on generational levels. A curse from a dragon can last for generations. This isn't the worst kind of curse though; that would be a Gallows' Curse.

If this is the first time that you have ever heard of a Gallows' Curse, then you are probably not being currently afflicted by one and you are very lucky. Now that isn't to say that you aren't being cursed, but you didn't know that it was there which made it super easy to disbelieve, and now I've made things very, very difficult for you to go about your day. If this is still a foreign concept and you haven't experienced more strife after you became aware of this concept, then things should be going quite well and un-cursed for you and that's really good. For those of you who are now suffering the strife of a Gallows' Curse then, let me inform you. Human beings have lots of two things, energy and water. This book may be fiction, but I'm not even making anything up here. Your brain is nothing but a collection of microscopic batteries that are also sending information. Now, imagine the sort of the energy and stress that can cause an unstoppable curse that is born out of death. It can be devastating not just to the person that it was inflicted on, but also on the land.

Much like ignorance of the Gallows' Curse, I will forgive you if you haven't heard of Point Pleasant, West Virginia. It's a small town of about 4,000 people that sits at the spot where the

Kanawa and Ohio rivers meet. This might not mean much to you, but rivers are almost always a magical place as I'm told by a very excited little blue fairy. (She is still, by the way, screaming yes at me no matter how much I tell Amaya I have a migraine). That seems like a reasonable place to stop unless you are into cryptids and aliens. Since you bought this book, it's a good 50/50 chance that you are. Then you might know that Point Pleasant was host to something called the Mothman who showed up in November of 1966 and was seen regularly before the collapse of the Silver Bridge on December 15, 1966. This is me giving you some broad strokes and oversimplifying since you can go to Point Pleasant or read John Keel's book or see the movie based on that book. If you would like I can even tell you a number of documentaries, podcasts and the like through which you can consume every facet of the story. I don't need to do that for you here though -- message me later. What I can tell you here is that I've spoken to some of the residents of Point Pleasant about this and there is something else that had happened on the ground of this place that was there long before John Keel, Indrid Cold or the Mothman.

Point Pleasant has its own Gallows' Curse.

It might not surprise you to realize that white people were not the first to live in the Ohio River Valley. In fact, if you thought they were, then I need you to put down this book and find one written by a reputable historian and learn about American expansion. It will be better for you, me, and our nation. There were, in fact, lots of people who were here before the white settlers and they had lived a pretty normal life without the concept of white people. I won't say that it was without war, because that would be glossing over a number of indigenous conflicts that were among the tribes and it's a weird kind of tribalism that humans just can't seem to shake. However, I will say that it did seem like business as usual until the white people pushed forward.

For me to fully explain Westward Expansion, let me put it like this:

Imagine that you are sitting at home watching some singing reality show program on TV, minding your own business and then some random person pulls up to your house and kicks in the door. This would, more than likely, make you upset. After all, this is your house, and you belong there. This very well could cause you to start a war, which is what the native tribes did when settlers decided that they wanted to watch the Voice on their land. Out of this background of real history and sloppy metaphor was born a man by the name of Chief Cornstalk.

It would be completely stupid to say that Chief Cornstalk was his English name. This is mostly a translation of his name in Shawnee. I'd put that here, but this is not really important to the story. It was important to his story, but since this story is less about him and more about the idea of a Gallows' Curse on the city of Point Pleasant and they call him Cornstalk, I will too. Cornstalk was a Shawnee war chief. He grew up radicalized which definitely comes from being a native who has grown up with constant war on their front door. The funny thing about perpetual war, it causes people to learn that it becomes tiring. So, after several battles and a war that I would call the precursor to the American Revolutionary War, our hero became tired of fighting. He had become more inclined to share this land because there was no going forward so he, a fellow chief, and his son embarked on a mission of peace. Just you know, to try something different.

This was a terrible idea.

I'm being very brief on this because we have more story to get to but let me try to explain this the best I can. In an effort to make this peace work, the representatives of the Shawnee nations were taking hostages. I don't quite know what the point of this truly was. They were treated as guests and held hostage while a peace was to be hammered out and things were going quite well with this plan until they didn't.

This is by and large not something that is disputed. While on patrol, several of the white soldiers had been attacked by unnamed native forces and subsequently killed. This only brought on what I can describe as high tensions and a wave of panic. What you must understand is that in retaliation, the friends of the soldiers that had been murdered, executed the native hostages that they were holding.

What is disputed is that either it was Chief Cornstalk's dying breath that created the curse -- if he in fact did, but there are a few who will tell you that his death didn't curse the land and bring about the Mothman signs and destruction of the symbolic domination of nature by Western Civilization (the bridge).

I'm sure that you're asking yourself a few questions, mostly, when does the story start again? After this chapter.

Now the next question should be, what should you be thinking about the whole thing of dealing with curses? Well, there's not really a very good way to deal with a curse. You could ask the person who inflicted the curse to remove it. That could be easier said than done, especially if, as in the above example, they died while casting the curse. Honestly, I think the easiest way of combating negative energy is dealing with everything with good energy. If you approach the world with good intentions, it can take care of a lot of problems.

It's really the easiest thing to take care of a lot of black magic, really.

Easy.

27.

The second they were on the other side of the tracks, Norvita felt things change drastically. A feeling of animosity hung over the car. She looked out the window, eyes wide and staring to see what sort of world the houses was outside as they passed, began towering above them along with their rising price range. She bit her lip as she watched eyes stare at them from between the drawn shades and curtains. She knew those eyes. They were glowing eyes of some sort of judgement.

There were wolves in those houses, and they didn't like them.

Quickly, Norvita glanced at Jodell. Jodell had cranked up her personal scowl the vehicle bounced. She hadn't figured out where the animosity started, but it was a mutual feeling. Norvita was surprised. She had figured that most wolf packs had to hang together regardless. Of course, her only experience had been with the mixed pack of the Sons of Sirius. Cities had so few packs they couldn't afford to fight among themselves. She almost forgot that tribalism was all over the place and that included out here with the werewolves. Norvita was starting to become concerned as Jodell finally pulled up to a house. She was terrified when the car's engine shut off. Norvita was almost convinced by the aura of ever-heightening animosity that the second that she stepped out of the car, they would be ambushed.

That wasn't going to be the case.

Norvita had waited for Jodell to get out of the car first and she did. What she did next didn't exactly surprise Norvita. Jodell turned her eyes around and stared at the faces in the windows. Her bright blue eyes flashed as she bared her teeth. For a second, Norvita swore that she could see rows of sharp teeth that were too big for that mouth. Suddenly the eyes disappeared from the windows, leaving the curtains and blinds to swing in surprise. Norvita was about to say something, but she watched Jodell cover her mouth. The teeth's appearance had been a surprise to her and now an embarrassment. She glanced at Norvita.

"You didn't see nothing," Jodell said through a mouth that sounded like it was stuffed with marshmallows.

"See what?" Norvita replied.

Jodell nodded at Norvita's response as if this was the correct thing to say before she turned towards a path. Norvita followed and then realized something. No matter how uncomfortable the spying of neighbors was, it was nothing compared to the discomfort of walking on this land.

It felt like walking on a cursed ground.

She could feel the unease on ground where something terrible had happened. It was why she always hated going to places like Salem or Arkham. She could feel the madness of their past history in the ground that was below her feet. Even Boston was a problem. Sometimes history just soaked into the ground, but it wasn't like this. She had never been somewhere with a psychic stain so intense that she could see images in her head. Norvita felt her pace slowing as she could feel her head pounding as the images in her head were trying to warn her of something that she couldn't quite figure out. She wondered if Jodell could give her some clues.

Jodell wasn't in the mood to talk about rural Appalachian history.

Jodell was snarling harder as she almost hunched forward with each awkward foot fall, as she was trying to step forward down a path in a yard. If this was worth it, Norvita didn't see it. What she saw was an angry woman who didn't want to be out of her car trying to maintain control, so she followed behind. She then stopped and turned towards Norvita sharply. Norvita jumped as she looked at the woman.

"What?" Norvita asked.

"Don't embarrass me here," Jodell snapped.

"Oh, puh-lease." said Norvita, rolling her eyes. "I can be super appropriate."

Jodell narrowed her eyes at Norvita with a strange scowl. She leaned in, pointing a finger because she knew that there was something that felt oddly suspicious about her words. Norvita had yet to present information indicating that she was wrong so far, but Jodell's instincts were pointing towards Norvita making this harder than it already was. Still, she didn't have much of a choice. She turned and led Norvita to the house that they were heading for and it was quite a house.

The house that stood before them at the end of a cobblestone path might have been something created in a fairy tale. It was a Victorian style that had been popular half a generation before the house itself was built. There was a large porch that swung around the front of the house marked by hanging baskets and boxes full of bright flowers that stood out against the chocolate painted outside. The only thing bigger or more distracting than that was the large bay window that overlooked the front lawn.

It's cute, thought Norvita, why is it so brown?

It was the kind of brown that you expect to see as the outside icing on a cake. Coupled with the darker brown trim, it looked like something that would be served on the table of someone's fancy dinner and would taste like mousse as opposed to being a place where someone lived. Instantly, Norvita assumed that whoever was there wasn't living in a candy house, but if they were offering that as their vision, she couldn't exactly trust them. In Norvita's opinion, only evil women lived in houses that looked like candy.

This was a bad omen.

Jodell had finally stopped walking as she settled her path right in front of the porch. She turned her head to one side as she looked up. She was still hostile for a reason that Norvita didn't understand until.

"Verona."

Jodell's words were so frigid that Norvita couldn't help but shiver as she cast a glance over at Jodell, who stood with her arms folded staring up. On the porch stood a thin woman with a fiery red dye job. Had to be a dye job, surmised Norvita. She was at least twenty years older than Jodell and, judging by the folds of skin and the flaps that hung on her arms, was older than basically everyone else. She looked like Jodell could snap the woman in half. Fuck, thought Norvita, a stiff wind could snap this woman in half.

That was assuming she was that hard to kill.

Verona hadn't bothered to acknowledge either one of them. She seemed far more concerned with her hanging flower baskets and the bright red flowers that were burning in them. She slowly poured water from a fading plastic cup with the 1996 NASCAR schedule printed on it. The only other bit of action taking place was Verona taking long puffs off a cigarette that seemed both too skinny and too long. It was so quiet that Norvita wondered if Verona had even seen them.

"For a second, I thought something up and died under my porch," the woman said with a voice that had been scarred by years of cigarette smoke. "Then I seed you walking up to my house. All I can smell is that department smell and whatever shit smell that one has on her."

"I'm surprised that you can smell a damn thing," Jodell replied sharply. "I figured that you'd lost that sense from smoking them cheap-os."

It was true that racism and hate weren't new to Norvita. It was, after all, the price of being both brown in America and working for the Department of the Arcane. She had come to expect there to be some issues with all of these things. That being said, this was all very, very different. The fact that anything was said about her felt like an afterthought and it was. The hate was directed at Jodell and it was intensely personal.

Norvita found it distracting and that was saying a lot.

"Hi!" Norvita said loudly. "My name is Norvita Patel! Can we speak about the disappearances in the woods-"

"Some amadan go missing in the woods and they sent you out here." Verona scoffed as she went to another set of flowers. "That don't sound like our problem."

"It's going to be your problem," Jodell replied, all but spitting at the older woman. "The Department seems to think that Huston might be behind it. If this is the start of a war between our kin, I need to know now before they get involved."

"We ain't done nothing to your family," Verona said. "You already shamed us by putting him in jail. He'd done been decreed exiled by the other packs."

"He walked from his work release. If you are hiding him..."

"He got out and he ain't talking to me?" Verona sounded either hurt or pleased. Honestly, Norvita couldn't tell, and she was a psychic.

"If he ain't here, we don't know where he is," Jodell shook her head. "Can we come inside and talk?"

"I think that would be best."

28.

Norvita held her breath. There was one thing that she knew when it came to lifelong smokers, and that was the pervasive smell of stale smoke baked into every molecule of a surface of the building they lived in. She was waiting for it to slap her directly in the lungs and she was going to try to hold off on it for as long as she possibly could for the sake of her still shaky stomach. It would lead to another moment of her being on the edge of throwing up and that was probably not the best thing to do when you were in a new person's house, let alone trying to ask questions about some sort of violent event. Eventually, she couldn't handle it anymore and finally caught a shallow breath. For Norvita, this was a pleasant surprise. She had expected the smell of the bottom of an old woman's purse but failed to find any of that before her. Instead, there was chemical citrus pulsing heavier on a 30 second cycle. Norvita didn't know where the air freshener was, but she definitely wanted to tell the woman there were better alternatives to the one that she was using, although it was apparently doing a fine job repelling the secondhand smoke. She wanted to say something along these lines but kept her mouth shut.

See, Karl, I can learn tact, Norvita thought grimly to herself.

Despite there being an understanding of business, the hostile energy was still quite intense between Jodell and Verona. Norvita didn't know what the past history was, but she could allow her mind to wonder and create an entire narrative that made far more sense in her head than warring clans and an uneasy tension. Norvita hated the whole concept of palace intrigue when it was right in front of her because no one ever ended up happy when there was palace intrigue.

Dead wives and angry monarchs were nearly always the result. She wasn't okay with that.

It was counter to her natural existence. Norvita had always liked watching drama unfold and certainly wasn't above stirring some up herself. It was a poorly kept secret that she had resorted to cyber bullying herself so that she could get a little sympathy from someone when she wasn't feeling exactly the best. This was different. Werewolves were not going to say mean things online and then cry on their social media journals. They would claw and snarl at each other and then there would be a fight, like, a real fight with blood everywhere. Norvita was, under no circumstance, going to be getting between Verona and Jodell if that fight were to come.

She was a terrible referee.

Verona hummed as she walked the other two women down what felt like thin hallways with the world's oldest wood paneling. Norvita's eyes danced around looking at the walls on either side. There were some pictures. It was only then that she realized what exactly caused the animosity between Jodell and Verona. There was a picture on a wall of a man and woman in what she knew as the most western of wedding dresses (a part of Norvita was lightly jealous of white wedding dresses and another part was relieved that if she ever had a wedding, she'd never have to wear white) flanked by a group of either men or women on either side. She wasn't sure who the guy was, but Jodell was unmistakable. This was her wedding day.

Norvita was instantly certain that she wasn't currently married to the other person in that picture.

Verona let them into a room. This had to be a sitting room, thought Norvita. It wasn't that uncommon. Lots of people had sitting rooms and Norvita had been in plenty. This wasn't an unpleasant room, at best, it was cozy. Tables crouched beside what looked like overstuffed furniture. Norvita debated sitting on the couch covered in what looked like soft fur and the most obnoxious bright flower patterns.

But then she was far too busy being distracted by the fireplace mantel.

The Mantel was lower than she'd ever seen it on a fireplace. That had to be due to the lower fireplace which had what looked like poor proportions for actually holding a fire. Norvita had to take a moment to realize that it was a propane fireplace with fake logs. She was first taken by the clock that sat in the middle of the mantel. It was gold with cherry red finish. It would have fit with her grandparents' living room. It was nice to see some things that looked familiar. Around the clock, though, were small statues. Norvita half expected to see the small saints like people put in their yards, but they weren't. They were black coal statues with gentle faces of coal miners and some animals. That was where Norvita stopped looking at the animals. One of these figures was a wolf. It was a strange looking wolf. It was big with rows of fur on its back and bright red eyes flashing. Its mouth was open, displaying sharp teeth. She knew what it was.

This was a werewolf.

Nothing surprised Norvita when it came to werewolves. They were generally proud of their heritage as wolves. It was what was with it that got her attention. She saw the pictures lining the mantle. She felt that looking at these pictures was a personal intrusion, but she didn't stop.

Norvita wanted to make sure that she saw all of them.

She looked at each figure as she pursed her lips in thought. There was a picture of small children, mostly boys, thought Norvita, as they looked up. They were looking at someone with the hardened expressions of old men. Norvita could almost hear the voices of the children as they didn't die silently. She wanted to think that she imagined it, but there was the sound of high screaming and rocks falling. Norvita glanced away, but it wasn't going to be the last thing that she saw.

There were going to be more images and they were all going to be so much worse.

Her eyes drifted to another picture. It was in color -- three rail-thin men bound to what looked like a post. Their mouths were open in a silent scream as the muzzle of at least six large brown wolves ripped into their flesh. Let me rephrase that, to anyone else who would have seen the pictures, they looked like silent screams. Norvita heard them, along with the clacking of jaws and the delight of someone beyond her vision cackling excitedly. She turned away from the pictures of the black figures hanging from a tree surrounded by werewolves on their back legs and men in white hoods. She almost fell over and would have fainted had it not been for Jodell. She walked the psychic towards a couch.

"Oh, god," she whispered.

"I know, darlin'," Jodell whispered to Norvita. "I don't like their altar either. At least they only have pictures of their proudest moments."

Norvita didn't want to think about what that could have easily meant.

"Is she all right?" Verona asked as she settled into a recliner.

"Oh, yea," Jodell said quickly. "Just a little-lightheaded up this high on the Ridge."

"That's your own fault then," Verona said as she crossed one leg over the other, lighting another cigarette. "She ain't made for this place where she don't belong. Probably all them sand and sun that gets her into Allah Akbar or whatever."

If there was one thing that Norvita hated more than racism it was inaccurate racism. This was something that she had experienced a number of times. The fact that she was Indian was very confusing for people and did lead to many thoughtless statements. She would have corrected Verona, but then stopped herself. She felt sick with her head still swimming. She couldn't get her body ready to fight.

"When did Huston run off?" Verona asked with her eyes flashing.

"Sometime this morning," Jodell replied as she fought off the need to light a cigarette. "He was doing the death porter gig."

"I didn't know that" Verona said. "I guess he was learning to be on his own."

"The Department got called in because of the scene. They ain't able to find hide nor hair of him."

"Well, if he decided to walk off, ain't my problem. Once he walked out, he wasn't my son. You made sure of that."

"It's not that part that bothers me." Jodell said. "What bothers me is the fact that my family was attacked which is a part of the agreement that we all made. I understand that a contract was made that I broke, but that is no reason for you to attack my kind."

"What are you talking about?" Verona asked.

"Someone attacked my family."

"And you think that we'd do that? Over a shame?"

Jodell got quiet as she looked down at her own hands.

"Yes, obvi," Norvita said.

"That is stupid," Verona said snubbing out her cigarette. "We don't like you. We don't like your family, but I ain't about to start an all-out war because you chose to not keep your bloodline pure. Do you think we're the only ones who want to kill your family?"

"It was the first thought."

"No, Jodell, your family has been pissing people off for six hundred years. We're just the latest."

29.

The sound of pure anguish cutting through the farm's dead silence stopped Ma. She'd heard screams from the livestock before. It was what they did. If they were somewhat smart enough, they would start screaming or begging. Her favorite was when they would offer her things. There was nothing they could give her that she needed. She had everything she wanted except, well one thing, she'd love to have another girl folk to be with her. Because she'd been the only female to be born, she had borne the weight of everything. It wasn't important now, she would see another chance for that perhaps, but this was her more important issue. It was the screaming. She thought she could ignore it, but as Ma started cracking her green beans on the porch it just got louder. It was the female they had brought. Ma let out a sigh as she stood up. There wasn't a choice. She wanted to keep her sow prepared until it was time and that was going to be a problem if the dog had gotten loose or worse.

If the other one had turned.

She would be surprised by that honestly, but it could have happened. He'd been bitten pretty hard by one of the boys. Not many people survived the bite. There was every chance that he could succumb to the Curse and turn before dying of the bite. He wouldn't be family, but it would be interesting to see what could happen. She slowly walked towards the barn with an irritated sigh. That kind of noise would wake up Pa and she couldn't handle him being awake. There was nothing good that came from his interactions at this time. She'd have to take care of the animals before he took care of her. She pushed into the barn with her hands on her hips.

"What in tarnation are you going on about, shoat?" she said finally.

The cages were still intact which was a good thing. Ma was going to be supremely upset if they had broken the cages. The cages were fine and they all sat in their cages. Missy looked up, wide eyes glazed with thick wet tears. Ma made a mental note to give her more water later so she wouldn't dehydrate from her constant carrying on. Huston was sitting at the edge of the cage as he looked up. Out of all of them, Ma didn't trust Huston. He was one those dogs that ran in the woods and she knew he would be the one that would bite. He had to be one of the Crowes and she hated him.

"Well?" Ma said, almost barking.

"He ain't doin' so good," said Huston finally.

Ma let out a hard grunt as she looked down at Bill. It was confirmed that he was going to be dead then. She had half hoped that it wasn't the case, but then she saw his motionless body. This was really very, very impressive that he had lived as long as he had done, but still it was inevitable she supposed. She knew that she was going to have to handle this.

It didn't make her less angry at Bill.

He was too big to be easy to pull out and then composted. Most people who didn't survive the Curse were usually smaller. Their bodies were too tiny to handle the poison that came from the jaws. Still, not one shoat ever had survived the bite of the Curse. They hadn't been blessed with the strength to survive it. She'd thought this one might, maybe, with him being so large and fit. She knew that he was going to be a hell of a pain when he was pulled out. She was angry at him for dying so inconveniently and then she was mad at herself. She had cursed the fates and her womb for not allowing her to have a daughter. It would have made the work go easier.

Dead animals were woman's work.

Her anger wasn't going to make the work go any faster, but it would delay her and if she didn't handle this body sooner rather than later, it would start to smell. Shoat that died from the Curse would start to rot quicker than ones that just dropped dead on their own. If that foul odor hung in the barn, she'd face the beating of a lifetime from her brothers and then from Pa which would be impossible for her. Instead, she dug into her apron for the key which took no time at all to unlock the cage. She looked down at Bill with a mumble of irritation before she started to pull the body along in the silence as she swore in a series of archaic words.

At this time, I feel like I should tell you a little bit more about William Harris, Senior. Bill was a man who had lived a full life. We all have if we really look at it, but Bill's was still quite full. For example, he'd served in the Marines after high school for a lack of a better direction and decided that a boy from Carter County had no business being in either Afghanistan or Iraq. It was when he returned home that he'd gotten the job at the sheriff's department and had felt like he had a good path in life. Part of Bill's lack of direction was due to a love for acting and no good outlet for it. It wasn't something that was nurtured at home unless he was planning to enter a pulpit, so Bill had kept that desire to himself rather than auditioning for high school plays or trying out at his local community theatre. Why am I telling you all of this at this very moment in our story? Two reasons: I like adding some depth to characters which makes them more interesting, but it does seem a little late for Bill at this point. That brings me to my second reason. I want to tell you where Bill learned that he liked acting.

If you are from a rural area where there is very little do, you still have some options. One of these is to turn to stealing liquor and partying, but if you are not that kind of person then you end up becoming quite involved in afterschool activities. It shouldn't surprise you that Bill was one of those after school activities guys. He was involved in everything from Band to Bible Club (yes, this is a real thing), but his favorite thing was Key Club. For those of you who aren't aware, it is sort of like being a part of the Rotary Club for an adult. He did quite a bit of volunteering with the Key Club. Bill's single favorite thing to do with the Key Club was the Harvest Festival. The Key Club was very involved in that festival. Bill was always helping with the Haunted High School. This was a haunted house that they would put on and mostly it wasn't too frightening except for Brad Willis who would chase people down a semi-dark hallway with a chainsaw. Bill was also scary because he was very good at one thing, he was always the zombie. He was good at pretending to be very still and dead like a prop and then jumping out at the very last minute before people walked past him.

Bill was being very still as Ma pulled his full weight out of the cage. It was difficult for both of them and had Ma not been grunting with effort, she might have seen through it. She would have seen the toes on Bill's left foot twitch and then relax. Someone did.

That someone was Huston.

Like all werewolves, Huston was good at looking for subtle body changes. Let me remind you that wolves don't necessarily howl like in the movies. What they typically do, in order to hunt, is rely on facial tics and signals. Huston knew what exactly he was looking for and when he saw the toes, he knew that it was a signal.

It was time.

Huston had been working on summoning all his strength for this moment. It was a terrible plan but, again, it was the only plan that they had. He felt himself slap his chest as he pushed forward into the most painful transition into a full and large wolf that he could muster. He leapt forward with his fangs bared and landed on Ma pushing her down with a bone snapping charge. Ma let out a scream. Her eyes flashed into a black hollow as her jaw elongated. The pair snapped at each other as parts of Ma bulged out of her dress and smock showing coarse brown hide as she swiped at him. Bill quickly moved trying to get the cage lock off the door for Missy. Once the door was opened, Missy felt herself tumble out. She ran out of the cage and out of the barn. Huston reached down and bit at Ma's neck which only produced a terrible growl. Bill thought about running and then stopped. He glanced over at the farming implements on the wall. He grabbed what he only assumed was a pitchfork.

Bill would never understand what happened next.

Despite his warrior past, Bill was mostly a peaceable person. He wasn't a pacifist, but he was never exactly one who would have ever been a violent man. That meant nothing to him as the black blood was coursing through his veins. What Bill could feel now was dizzying rage. He was angry and he had to release this violence out somewhere. Where this went was Bill plunging the pitchfork down into Ma's face. A howl came out that was the worst thing that Bill would ever hear. That should have been enough. The woman wasn't moving anymore. Bill knew that he should have stopped.

He didn't.

Bill continued to stab down at the woman's face, allowing the same fowl black liquid to spread all over the floor of the barn. Bill could only describe this as a blind rage. He wasn't sure when he was going to stop. In fact, he wouldn't have stopped until he passed out from sheer weariness, until he heard the violent howl from Huston. Bill looked over at him with a dull blink.

"Go on to the Crowes," he struggled out. "I'll be behind you and Missy."

Huston snarled. It was the worst part of the plan, but it was the plan. He wasn't about to disregard it, just because Bill was an idiot. He didn't stop his quick run as he padded down the forest along a path. Missy had been running. Bill started to square his shoulders and started to run after them except…well…

He wasn't really running.

Bill felt his body slog towards the woods. He tried to run in place but couldn't get out of the path of his own feet. It felt like he was sinking into the dirt as he ran. His breath was labored with each step. Bill wasn't sure what happened first, he either fell or there was the heavy crack that went across his cheek.

Then, there was nothing…just blackness.

30.

Mid-afternoon was hanging on the red and orange foliage of the trees lining the roads as Norvita and Jodell hastily departed from the Ridge back towards town. There was no reason to hang around when they were out of any sort of help that they could get from the residents out there. Verona wouldn't allow them to ask anyone if they knew something and Jodell wasn't about to reach out without her authorization. Still, it was barking up the wrong tree, so to speak. Norvita knew that was correct. She would have been able to read something about it. Afterall, whatever had been running around in the woods was cursed and it was not something that you could hide or even if you believed that lycanthropy is a curse, it felt different. Norvita wasn't sure if lycanthropy itself could be called a curse.

Those people were a curse.

Norvita was having a hard time dealing with things that she had seen. Her brain was still swimming with all sorts of nightmares. She couldn't wrap her mind around it.

For a brief moment, she wondered if she should mention that to Jodell.

It probably wouldn't have surprised Jodell to find out that Norvita was having a difficult time trying to comprehend what was going on inside of her own mind. Jodell had always hated that the biggest ally to her family had been the Whelans. They were brutal people that had been on the payroll of the factory bosses to keep the Unions from forming. She was almost certain they were the running dogs down deeper south for the Confederate army. The Crowes were always pro-union in every sense of the word. They were proud of their service to the United States of America. Jodell was feeling very, very sick about realizing that she was the reason that they had backed her family during the last war of the packs. She had been traded as a bride and it was disgusting. She could only imagine what was happening with Norvita. She could probably feel the sins of the past. It wouldn't matter about being a psychic or not. She could feel it because bad always lingered.

Norvita had been quiet for far too long. Jodell had started to get very, very concerned. She looked over and quirked a brow at the other woman.

"Got something out there you want to share?" Jodell finally asked.

The short answer was yes. Norvita did have quite a bit going on in her mind. She didn't say this, however, because she was still working on processing what was on her mind and she wasn't exactly sure where to start. Mostly, it was that she was bothered by how she was feeling after she had left the Ridge. She wanted it to be just the visions. That would, of course, make more sense. Sometimes, a person can see something that was more upsetting that they would still be able to handle and that can cause terrible visions. She was more than willing to accept that. What she wasn't willing to accept was what she thought was the reason that she wasn't able to handle the visions. It was only one reason.

She was getting older.

It was the only logical reason that she had been getting tired and stressed out of all reasonable levels by the visions. She wasn't a teenager, and she was sitting on the start of her twenties. It would be a short decade before she was in her thirties and that, she thought, was just a point when she wouldn't be able to handle the visions. Her visions were growing in numbers and she was going to be getting sicker from them. If she didn't learn to cope with them soon, the visions would kill her.

No, she told herself, that couldn't possibly be the reason.

Norvita tried to push away the idea of being old as fast as she had the thought. There had to be another reason for this agitation and her inability to focus after the Ridge. It was something that Norvita had long been good at doing. She had learned that she was an Olympic-level mental gymnast when it came to thoughts. Mostly, it was how she told herself that it wasn't her fault, to reason away whatever terrible consequences that she had created with her actions.

After some time, she realized that it had to be the land that they were walking along when it came to the Ridge. She had memories of her grandfather taking her on a ghost hunt at Gettysburg for some deep cable special that he had been asked to be a part of. He hadn't been able to find a ghost or anything else for the mundane audience, but it had left a lasting impact on him. He had thrown up some sort of black ectoplasm for a week. She was terrified for him. Both her and her grandmother were convinced that he was going to die from this. Now, as they drove, Norvita could only assume, this awful psychic fallout was going to be her fate.

"Norvita?" Jodell said again.

She would have to find out what Swami Patel's coping mechanisms were. She knew that he'd done plenty of things in his life and he probably had something like a special meditative happy place he could go and dump his mental baggage. Of course, he was much older and he didn't see visions. That wasn't something that the men in her family ever did. That was something that her mother had suffered through. She wondered if her mother had done anything to stop them bothering her. Sometimes, she knew that wasn't the case. It was easier for her to think about that being the reason that her father had killed her and then himself. If it was something else, then —well—it would mean that it was something else. It was something far more horrible.

"Norvita?" Jodell tried again, snapping her fingers. "Hello?"

It would be easy just to dehumanize her father. He was a ghost, at best, to her and far off. Still, she thought that was probably not the best thing. After all, he had been in love with her mother. Norvita had been born out of that love. Her grandparents had started to love him enough to welcome him into the family. There had to be something there before she was born. Sometimes, it was easy to blame herself for what had happened. Maybe she was just a stressful presence. She'd never know. She would never have that partner to help her.

"Are you okay?"

Maybe that wasn't completely true. Norvita did have Carson, who had been beside her for a very long time or a long time in Norvita time even if it wasn't conventional. Nothing about Norvita was conventional, least of all her long term relationship with Carson O'Brian. Granted, there were thousands of paranormal romance novels about vampires and their psychic girlfriends but that didn't happen in the real world. Vampires made most magical beings very, very uncomfortable to be around and psychics were a pain for blood feeders. Still, Carson was great when it came to dealing with maudlin sorrow. He'd spent his afterlife listening to Doyle complain about his existence. Doyle was the saddest person Norvita had ever known. Carson would be great to talk with about what she'd seen. He'd always been good at explaining racists to her.

That wasn't an option just now.

At that point, sunset was hours away and Carson was very much asleep. It would be an hour after that before he'd be able to talk to her assuming that he wasn't serving at the pleasure of his king. That made Norvita roll her eyes silently to herself. Doyle had rejected the term king or prince when he rose to the throne of the vampires opting for the title of Taoiseach which as far as she could see was another word for moody manager. He was in a terrible place emotionally and that was coming down on her relationship with Carson. Maybe it wasn't completely his fault.

He'd lost someone too.

During the summer, Marcia has been murdered in a fairly violent manner by -- and this hurt for Norvita -- Karl when he finally changed. She was also dead but that wasn't the problem. For whatever reason the Department of the Arcane had yet to release Marcia's body. Norvita was sure that there was a reason that they had it but it was painful. It had been months at this point. The family hadn't buried her and Doyle hadn't been able to find peace. This was a bad thing for everyone. Doyle needed closure.

He missed his bride.

"Norvita?" Jodell growled at her.

Norvita missed her too. Norvita didn't have any siblings so it was like having an older sister when it came to Marcia. No matter how much Norvita had liked her, Marcia was far more important to Doyle than he would ever be to her. It was strange that she didn't see until now. There it was Doyle needed Marcia because she was the only thing that made him act like human. She probably could have kept him human. He had to provide some level of strength that he showed the world. He probably had no actual desire to relax. It wasn't just the calm. Norvita had the same problem. She was losing her mind because her tether to mundane humanity was gone.

Karl was gone.

Everything in her life was always about Karl. That was the grief, of course. When you lose someone, they always end up being the focus of your life. It was the complete end of normalcy for Norvita. She couldn't think of a time that Karl hadn't been there to be a part of her life. He had saved her from the murder at the hands of her father. He'd carried her around the crime scene until her grandparents arrived to take her away from him. If she had picked up the fit that she had with the woman from social services, he probably would have carried her to this day. He was gone now, and she was…lost.

"Norvita!" It sounded like a howl coming out of Jodell's mouth.

Norvita felt like she convulsed as she was startled back to the present moment by Jodell's loud voice. She cleared her throat as she looked down at her hands. Jodell offered her a soft smile.

"Honey, you okay? You sort of went off," Jodell said gently.

"There was a lot of bad out there," Norvita blurted out.

It was quiet for a moment as Norvita looked down, feeling completely stupid.

"You got that from out there?" Jodell asked.

Norvita nodded.

"Probably a lot of that," said Jodell. "They ain't all so civil. The Whelans are some of the worst people, but they at least act like people. If it wasn't them, I don't know who it would be."

"Curse," Norvita said. "It's cursed. Whatever is all over the ground out there is a curse of a nasty variety. Is that common around here?"

Jodell blinked at Norvita with a quiet sorrow. She turned her head to one side.

"You're kidding, right?" Jodell asked in disbelief.

"Yea, why not?" replied Norvita. "It's a terrible curse."

"Darlin', everything is cursed around here. You can't swing a dead cat without hitting a curse."

"Okay, so fine, there. It's the worst kind of curse," Norvita said. "Punishment. Does that help?"

"No."

"Ug. How about people who want your family dead and are cursed?"

"Well, that might be so," Jodell said. "The local offices have a record of inflicted curses. It'll take about an hour to get to Johnson City, but we'll be able to…"

"Or! Better yet! We could go to the library!" Norvita squealed in delight.

Jodell blinked softly in stunned silence.

"What?" asked Norvita.

"Nothing. I didn't expect you to be big on research or libraries."

"What? I read stuff," Norvita said quickly. "And libraries have all the weird shit."

Norvita was a fan of libraries largely for what exactly she had stated. She liked the weird things that she'd find in libraries. That was big city libraries (Norvita had only been to libraries in Gaiman Heights, which she was certain was the largest city that she'd ever been in and that was fine). She could only assume that rural libraries had even more secret treasures.

Jodell nodded quietly in a strange agreement.

"Okay," Jodell said as she started to drive in the direction of the library.

Just as they pulled up into the street closest to the library, a figure of a man walked up from the horizon. He was a strangely tall man who seemed to lumber quietly towards the car and then stopped. Norvita held her breath, unsure if he was real. The thought that there could be several residual visions that she could be seeing frightened her.

Jodell, on the other hand, saw him too. She stepped out of the car with her hands on her hips. They didn't have time for any sort of nonsense.

"Howdy, Jodell," said the man.

"What do you want, Cab?" Jodell asked.

"My missus needs to see the Patel girl," Cab said.

"What for?"

"Tilly ain't bothered to tell me. That's between her and the spirit world."

Jodell knocked on the passenger side window which Norvita rolled down quickly.

"We have a mission," Norvita reminded her.

"Yes, but the Witch has asked for you to come up and talk to her. You can't refuse a witch."

Ultimately, Jodell was correct. If you are ever going to be invited somewhere to speak with a witch, you should always go. After all, it's a terrible decision not to and Norvita, while famous for her bad life choices, wasn't going to add this to them.

31.

The next thing that Bill was aware of was a violent ringing in his ears that echoed out of his jaw and down to every living and dead cell in his body. The only thing that he could think that came close to what he was feeling was it was like being in a car crash. Bill let out a low groan as his eyes opened or attempted to with some difficulty. Bill was certain that one of her eyes was swollen from whatever had hit him in the face. Something hit him in the face. He could remember some vague and large hands on his skin. He shut his eyes again when they weren't able to focus on anything. He laid on the floor as he felt a groan trying to focus on anything solid. The world was spinning, and Bill knew it. From where he laid on the floor, he could feel every meter of the 460 meters per second that the earth spun. It made Bill feel even sicker as he felt the black push into his throat. For a moment, Bill wasn't sure that he had anything in his system.

He thought for a moment that he might have been drunk.

It wasn't a high likelihood, but the last time that Bill had been this bad off had been the last time that he'd gotten blind drunk. That seemed almost stupid since that was almost a decade ago and he was under the expressed opinion that there was no good reason for anyone to ever drink Everclear. Bill was confident that wasn't the case, but his theory was on shaky ground that wasn't helped by the music playing.

When the ringing in his ears subsided, Bill could hear something being played on a stereo. He wouldn't call it low-fi because it was beyond low-fi. Whatever sound system was being used, it was older than Bill and needed to be retired five years before that moment. Bill could hear that parts of a speaker was blown out by the overly high-pitched wail of Nashville string section which was made worse by the shaking bass of a song that sounded like it vibrated on the stereo. Because of this, it took a little bit of time for Bill to recognize the song but eventually he figured out that it was country music from a certain period of time. It was the kind of song you'd hear that people loved because it was that sort of party redneck music. Bill even recognized the song. Bill knew the song because he felt every part of his being wanting to yell back when the singer asked, "Why do you drink?"

To get drunk.

It might have seemed a strange subject of a song to someone who was unaware of whatever was being forced out of the rickety speakers, but Bill had worked plenty of bars in the county on Friday Night when someone thought karaoke was a good idea. There was a certain point of the night that one of three songs would be sung, it would either be "Friends in Low Places" by Garth Brooks or something by Merle Haggard. Once in a great while it would be this one. It was a song that he knew was going to lead to a terrible fight and that was going to be all sorts of issues if Hank Williams, Jr was playing a bar. Bill couldn't imagine that he was laying on the floor of a bar.

He could be laying on a porch.

It was a half hope from Bill's fever bitten brain that it was just that. He'd somehow, maybe he'd gotten wasted on whatever sort of mountain liquor that the Crowes had brewed, and he was still in some sort of state of inebriation. He was almost certain that if he rolled over that Jodell would be sitting beside him looking down a light smirk watching him sleep. She'd at least be there to keep him from doing something that was completely stupid. Bill opened his eyes again and had found that even without the spinning, she wasn't there. Bill wasn't sure he was quite ready to accept that he'd been through whatever you wanted to call this hellscape but there was a problem with his grasp at an escapist theory. Jodell wouldn't have allowed him to get black out drunk.

That just dawned on him.

She wasn't a drinker and neither was he. It was his clear belief that the only time that something like that would have happened was as a device in some sort of nefarious plan. Jodell was always willing to be the sober driver but she wouldn't have allowed him to get this sloppy. She would have to be gone or it was done by some sort of sneaky measure that would have kept her from stepping in. He could almost picture Vaughn and her cousins running a distraction, then he would be alone. What was the point of getting him drunk in the first place? Honestly, it didn't matter.

He was going to kill each one of them.

Despite the feeling of pure sickness that was in his body, Bill sat up finally as he looked around. He was looking for someone to tell him that he was wrong. He was dizzy to the point that he knew that his feet weren't going to work but he was determined to look whoever was going to speak to him in the eye. He felt his body retch before he settled to a sitting position. He wasn't alone. Before him was a man who seemed to be wearing a clean set of overalls. Bill watched the neat plait of silver hair hanging down to the back of the man's waist swing as he hummed deeply. Bill blinked again as forced himself to look at the man. In that state he could only think of one person who would bother to be this casual: Lord Byron.

Bill was furious.

"Lrrghath," he tried to muster.

Bill was almost grateful for the state of shock that his body was trapped in at that moment or otherwise, he might have felt the pain that was sitting in his jaw and face as his mouth filled with blood. Bill levered his body up and started to cough out blood as he felt both light and heavy at the same time.

"Larggath," Bill tried again, and it ended with the same result.

Bill's attempts to speak were met with a hollow laugh rattling from the man and then ending with a cough. Bill wondered if this was a real hollow laugh, or it was something else. He wanted it to be a hollow laugh because that would be a human response and he could handle the idea of being held by a human. Of course, that wasn't it. It sounded more like a sick hyena. Bill sat back as he stopped moving.

"I wasn't sure if you was trying to talk but I wouldn't if I was you," a deep voice said from the man before him. "Your jaw done got broke and that was a cheap shot. When my boys found Ma they got quite out of hand. Some of my boys ain't become men yet and they were her only option. You took that from them and I couldn't control him."

Bill neither liked nor was surprised by the words of the man who was sitting before him. He decided that it wasn't the incest that bothered him but the casual nature of the statements regarding it and violence in general. He hadn't stopped working on whatever. Bill jerked again. The man finally turned around.

He was big.

Bill had seen plenty of big men who had done their best to intimidate him, and they were usually very tall. This was different. He was tall, yes, but there was something that was well, larger than that; it was a presence that filled a room and that seemed to be a growing concern for Bill. He could feel there was a looming blackness swallowing the room. There was no safety net or backup here and he was on his own.

Bill was, for the first time, afraid.

Bill pulled back for a moment when he felt the chain around his neck tighten. He pulled himself down before he looked at the workbench. Bill wanted to pretend to see the piece of human that the man was working on. Instead, he looked back up at him.

"I don't think you are one of them dogs but you sure smell like them," said the man. "Don't surprise me if you like them. You are probably as strong as one of them. I know that because you ain't dead yet from the Curse. It's going to kill you, I know. You've got that glass look. You won't last long. I hope you make it to the night. We gonna kill them Crowe Dogs."

The man walked over and picked up Bill by the hair. He turned his head up as he licked his lips. Bill choked again.

"You have a woman there. I know that. I'm going make you watch as my boys take turns ruining her for this life and the next."

32.

I don't know how many of you have ever been in the lair of a witch, but I'm going to guess it is very few of you. Let me back that up, you have probably been in the lair of a witch and had no idea of it, if you are living in a more modern setting. When I say which, I'm not speaking of this sort of neo-pagan Wicca that might have a quaint altar somewhere facing the sun. They are, in fact, also witches, but what I'm speaking of is that of a weird sister. Younger witches are starting to become more comfortable with allowing people into their homes due to the rise of multi-level marketing parties and a lack of fear of an organized religion's crusades. This wasn't always the case for witches. At one time, witches were quite suspicious of people and would rarely let anyone into their secret homes, excluding Girl Scouts during cooking selling time, Mormons, door to door salesmen, and other witches. This is due to the pastime of witches, which is the gossip that witches will share with other witches and sometimes with cunning men (they don't like them as much as they like witches, but just about everyone likes cookies). Gossip is a strange thing that creates a cultural memory (this is not the same as race memory. In fact, race memory isn't real, and if you think it is, then please stop reading my book and walk away. I don't want you here.), that causes people to create a story that all witches go through. There is one name that creates this cultural memory for all witches.

Her name was Brunhild auf Housen.

I know that that name isn't familiar to you because you don't know her side of the story. That's sort of the problem as many historians will tell you about using only one side of the historic record, you don't get everything else that might have happened with the other players involved. It's also the fault of a historian to not get that and why for many years people really only focused on powerful white men as opposed to the other people who were also deeply involved with the stories themselves. In this case, you may just know the story of Brunhild auf Housen because it was recorded by a couple of German brothers named Jacob and Wilhelm Grimm. There is nothing wrong, per say, with what these two young men did. After all, they collected stories that they were told by various people that they came in contact with during their travels. For all intents and purposes, they were just stories, the kind of stories that you told children to either entertain them or teach a very important lesson. If you have learned nothing from these four books that you've read of mine (and if you didn't know that there were more than this, two things: 1: Thank you for buying and reading this book so far. 2: Please pick up the other three. I only ask because I think you'll like them), leave with this lesson: there is always more to fairy stories than just what you see.

Sometimes the stories we tell children are far more real than the history we learn.

There is a different story for Brunhild than the story that only mentions her as a violent demon.

When the world was young and green, there were natural witches that were embraced for their powers as such was the case of Brunhild and her sister. They were born in a small village in a long-forgotten place that probably is a pleasant visit if you choose to visit. For a time, they were all left alone living their quiet life. Brunhild was a kind woman who was able to conjure forth many things that had been known to please the townsfolk and was known chiefly for building large edible houses. What happens next is really a debate for scholars, but it's widely believed that a couple of factors occurred. One was a mini-Ice Age. At some point at the start of the Early Modern Era, Europe got quite cold, and this caused it to be hard to be a farmer which was the profession of most of the people in the lands that would, one day, be called Germany. This would generally not be a major problem, except that there was something else rising in Germany: Christianity.

By and large Christianity is not a terrible thing if one realizes that it is centered around a very kind Jewish Carpenter who lived some 2000 years ago teaching about how we should care one another, etc. This a good thing that had often been ignored by the followers of that Jewish Carpenter. In Germanic regions there was a rise of two very different types of this religion; one of which was centered around Rome which no one had ever been to, and the other was from a man who felt the need to post his disagreement with the other one on the door of a church. They were both offering some kind of help with this whole problem of a lack of food which made them important to their communities. While you and I might be fully aware that there are many factors as to why the famine might have occurred, this was, of course, long before the understanding of environments, weather patterns and the like, so there was a hole where an explanation should occur. What was used in that space was of course witchcraft. This is where some 60,000 people were executed in Germany as witches, but that isn't the story I want to tell (although, I should note that Brunhild's sister saw this all coming and chose to live the remainder of her days in a Bavarian convent which ended badly for her). I want to tell you about how Brunhild handled things. Brunhild was not going to allow herself to be murdered by the Catholics or the Protestants. Instead, she decided that she was going to be alive for as long as she possibly could, so she left the village and marched into the woods where she thought she was going to be safe. This next part is where things start going south.

Her story crosses with two children named Hansel and Gretel.

What comes next is, unfortunately, not an uncommon occurrence for the period of time in which this story takes place. When there is a shortage of food there are two groups who are always at risk: children and the elderly. Now, with the use of UN forces and various other things, this is less of a problem. I am, of course, oversimplifying all of this because there is far more that is going on about poverty and starvation that needs to be addressed and this is a novel about werewolves and magic. I simply do not have time to diverge into my political views on sustainability here. This all to say that there was quite a rash of child murders that went unreported from a time when people thought it was the best-case scenario for them and there was an easy excuse. For the stepmother of Hansel and Gretel, she had a perfect plan. She would ask her stepchildren to go off into the woods to look for food and then leave them there. They weren't very smart children because they were children. She had told them to leave a trail of breadcrumbs. This didn't work since breadcrumbs were then eaten by animals. So, the children became lost in the woods which was quite upsetting until they found themselves at the house of Brunhild who had magically had a homemade of food in the woods. Brunhild found them gnawing on the corner of the house.

"Stop that," she told them. "That's been out in the elements and it'll make you very sick."

"Please, Miss," said the girl. "We're really hungry."

"Oh, goodness, let's not eat my house." Brunhild said. "I'll give you plenty of food, but we'll need to get you home as well."

I know that this story doesn't sound like what you might have heard from the Brothers Grimm because they told a different story altogether at this point. Brunhild got these poor lost children fed and home and assumed that this would be the end of it.

She was very, very wrong.

In the time between the children getting lost in the woods and getting home the children had been found to be missing by their father who was a woodsman. He and his new wife were debating as to whether or not go off to hunt in the darkness for their children. This is what he would tell people. That the children were probably eaten by wolves. That being decided, there were his children standing at the door with several large bags of food.

"Boy! Not Boy!" he said, surprised. "How are you alive?"

"Oh, a witch helped us back," Hansel said.

This should have ended the story happily, but this wasn't what happened. The woodsman and his wife looked at each other and realized that if they allowed their children to speak with a witch they would have more problems down the line and so they decided that it was only fair that it was time to tell the church who also told the local witchfinder. The story ends exactly as you would remember, except substitute stake for oven.

Norvita thought about this story as she walked with Cab through the streets of Hamptons. There was never a time that a witch asked someone to come see them and this had to be an important message.

Where did she hear that version of the story?

She couldn't imagine that it was something that her grandparents would have told her. Her grandmother preferred to tell her stories from her childhood or stories about how to be a quiet and respectful wife which had the exact opposite effect. She assumed that it had probably been from Doyle and Carson who always talked about how much they hated European fairy stories. If there was only one very good indication of how much they hated stories, it was the story of Dracula. Doyle said a few things about him that were diplomatic and adult. It was what Doyle did. Carson would then spit and say the same thing:

"Fucking piece of shit."

It was Karl, she decided. If there was one thing that Karl always wanted, it was the truth. She knew that he would have told her the same thing about Brunhild and Dagmar and so on and so forth. She was surprised that she remembered any of it. She had never listened to him when he started talking or she'd thought she wasn't. Norvita would constantly have her nose buried in her phone. Maybe she knew more than she realized. Quietly, Norvita was angry with herself that she didn't spend more time with him. She hated that she wasn't more personal with him. It was too late now and she was trapped with a summons from Tilly the Witch.

It was never a good idea to ignore a summons from a powerful witch.

There are a few things that you should never do in life no matter how much of a rebel you are and one of those things is ignore the invitation of a witch to come around for anything. Witches are deceptively powerful and are known to be quite petty. If Tilly was anything like Mim, she would be the pettiest. The only thing that remained of the last person to say "no" to Mim was a single striped Christmas Sock.

Her mind raced with these random thoughts as she and Cab walked down the sun speckled street. A weird crop of buildings that had largely pastel colors painted around a storefront stood out from the old brick buildings lining the rest of the street between a weirdly homey looking jewelry store and an abandoned Italian restaurant. She wanted to think about Brunhild and witches but immediately, her mind went to playing marathon games of Candy Land with Scarlett which was far more terrifying than anything that could be channeled from the Abyss.

"Johnny Ace bought them buildings from our mayor when she had to pay for her husband's lawyers," Cab explained, sensing Norvita's thinly veiled apprehension. "He seen the row houses in Charleston, South Carolina. Rainbow Row?"

"I don't know it," Norvita replied.

"If youse a psychic, that don't surprise me. Charleston got to be hell for someone like you. We went once and Tilly hated it. She says the mundane ghosts there are the most pretentious in the South... well them and the ones in Atlanta. We've been banned from that. Johnny don't know that. He thought it would be classy. I think that it makes things look worse."

Norvita couldn't disagree with him. People try to change things by hiding the surface and ignoring what's under the surface. She did it all the time. She easily pretended to be the dumb entitled rich girl to hide the fact that she was more. She could see the pattern of the stone making her face cringe. If you looked close enough, the cracks could be seen. Everyone hid the truth, even herself and she was starting to think that was a bad idea.

Her thought pattern changed when she was confronted by the sight of Tilly's Boutique and its list of services. Tilly did hair, nails, tanning and fortune-telling.

"Really?" she said in disbelief.

"The tanning beds are really popular even with the increased chance of melanoma. Can't change some people."

"I meant the fortune-telling."

"Oh, that. Tilly ain't one to lie to people. She doesn't do much augury, mostly tea leaves and tarot."

"Doesn't she get into trouble for that?"

"With what? The Department?"

"It does fall into our purview when it comes to keeping magic from the mundane world?"

"Probably not enough people around here for people to care. I think they'd got more people other places who are doing worse things."

"How has it not been burned down by the...locals?"

"You think that there was a sort of Jesus people fighting us?"

She nodded.

"It's really classist for you to think that all rural people are either dumb or devoutly religious to the point where they would get their pitchforks and torches coming after us."

"Do they?"

"She does more hair and nails and that covers most of her serious witch business. People will overlook the thing they hate if you're one of their people. The people at the Tabernacle don't come to her but that's not hurting her. The Conference of Southern Baptist Churches sent a preacher here once that tried to get her to renounce the tarot. He fought for a little bit. He gave up, otherwise it's always the same. She's a good witch and people here know there are some things that are worser than her."

It wasn't something that Norvita had considered before. People kept everything separate when it came to Gaiman Heights. You knew that there were parts of town where you didn't go if you were a kind of magical being. She couldn't imagine what it must be like if you were a mundane person who had to live in the city. No one ever talked about weird things. It was different here. People accepted the weird shit and wrote it off as magic. It had to be why Karl liked it down here. He could be Karl and not hide his demonic heritage. He could be himself.

Norvita decided she'd hate living like that, though it would be nice to have fewer rules. Rules didn't save Karl.

No, they saved people from Karl.

"You better go on. She hates waiting."

Norvita glanced at Cab before she opened the store front door. She gave him one more glance behind her as she stepped in mentally preparing all sorts of things.

33.

Out of all the scenarios that Norvita had allowed to run through her head, she still wasn't sure what she was expecting when she walked into the hair salon. As far as she knew, she'd never been at a small-town barbershop, let alone one that was a front for a witch. She could remember going to strip malls with clean and fashionable store fronts for salon treatments. It always seemed like there was white everywhere like you were walking onto the set of some science fiction ship where people were working on hair and nails. It was all slick and very, very modern. This wasn't like that at all. This was once some kind of office or store from a time period that was more comfortable with warm wood paneling. That was another confusing thing. People around here liked wood paneling. It was like the height of home and office decorations peaked in 1982 and then just stopped. Norvita's eyes darted around the walls looking at the fashionable haircuts that were definitely sported by some models from the early 90s. Norvita apprehensively sat down on the couch. She looked down before picking up a three-year-old issue of U.S. Weekly. This only lasted for a moment until Tilly from the back of the shop. Norvita knew it because she could feel it at once. From the intensity of the aura, Norvita expected to see a tall and powerful figure of a woman when she looked up.

That wasn't the case.

Norvita had never heard the quote "higher the hair, the closer to God" before, but she would have thought that it applied to Tilly. Her hair was big. It wasn't just tall or piled up to a bouffant like it was still the sixties -- I mean it was, but it was more than that. It was puffed out like a blowfish, a halo of brightly red-dyed hair undulating around the woman's face and shoulders. Norvita hesitated. She was about as terrified as she had been of Verona almost to the point that she was looking for the long cigarette or the disturbing statues and pictures. She had to remind herself that this was a different person.

She was only a terrifyingly powerful witch.

"Can I guess what you're thinking?" Tilly said quizzically.

Norvita's eyes went wide as she looked up at the woman with her throat feeling thick and dry. She had nothing but questions buzzing through her head and she knew that there was no way that any of her questions could be voiced in a coherent or polite manner at this time. Instead, she nodded eagerly, hungry for any sort of information.

"You want to know why so many hillbillies have so many statues of Jesus."

Norvita felt her face fall flat at the notion of what Tilly had proclaimed to be the center of the information concerning her life. There were thousands of things that Norvita had started to think about, and she had started to find that her thoughts were all over the place and she had in fact, landed here. The conversation that they were going to be having would be about the stupid statues. She felt a weird laugh bubble out of her throat as she tried to say something to counter this proclamation. She didn't realize that she was being settled into the barber's chair. She blinked looking at the woman's reflection in the mirror.

"What?"

"I think there are personal reasons that people have statues like that. Each of them seemed really good for them. It must be strange for you. Your family has statues of what? Ganesh?"

"Yes," Norvita said stupidly. "Among others."

"I suspect that like the Roman Catholics, your people believe that the images of your gods are inviting the gods into your home. People don't think that way around here. A statue is a statue. It's like having a garden gnome. People love Jesus and that's why they have them. I have a statue like that and I'm not really all that about Jesus, but it's a nice statue."

Norvita didn't say anything as she heard the spritz of water dampening parts of her hair that was rapidly pulled back into toothed clips as she blinked softly. Norvita licked her lips as the clips released while hair was gently pulled in strands and clipped away, falling over her shoulders.

"I…don't…"

"My granny had a statue in her house, it was Mary. You know, the mother of Jesus," Tilly said. "She made it when she won a series of pottery classes. She wasn't a Catholic, but she loved it. When she passed, I asked for it because I loved her. It makes me think about her when I look at it."

Tilly paused and looked at Norvita's expression of pure confusion.

"What? You ain't the only one with psychic powers."

"I don't care about the statues anymore," Norvita said finally. "I have other questions. Why am I here? Like, here right now?"

Tilly laughed quietly before she went back on the delicate work of cutting Norvita's hair.

"I get the feeling that this is the first time you've asked that question. Have you tried asking yourself?"

"What?"

"Sweetie, I can see the future or I used to could see it. Things ain't as easy as they used to be for me. Ain't you havin' the same problems?"

Norvita choked for just a moment as she tried to inhale and exhale at the same time, before she looked back at Tilly. She hadn't realized how old she had gotten in that short of a time. It was like the stories that she'd heard of the changelings who had come back from Arcadia. You change when you are in the dream to the point where you might not be able to recognize yourself. She looked like she'd been worn down and she was starting to pale like the world outside them.

"I can't focus on anything apart from the same vision. I've seen it over and over," Norvita finally said. "I can't..."

"Find the balance?" continued Tilly. "I was afraid of that too. I can't find a good point either. It's like something has been taken from this world."

"Or someone," Norvita countered. "Someone like Doug?"

"Doug?"

"The Nexus. You can't pretend that you don't know what it is."

"I ain't going to try. But if there ain't no light then there is no shadow and we're all stuck."

"Then what am I supposed to do?"

"Get your hair and nails did."

So far, nothing that had happened to Norvita today made any sense to her in any meaningful way. And while her hair looked amazing, it didn't do anything to resolve her concerns. The world had fallen into, well, she couldn't call it chaos. It was more like some sort of sick rest of a coma and she knew that she had to fix it. There was nothing about this that was going to make anything better and least of all, doing all the things that she would do normally. If the world had made any sense then sure, Norvita would be happy to do her normal enthusiastic investigation and resolution of the problem.

The world did not make sense.

Tilly squeezed Norvita's shoulder reassuringly.

"It's all right darlin'," she said. "You need to do this."

"Why?" Norvita whispered.

"You need a little TLC. I think the kids call it 'self-care'."

"Self-care?"

"Self-care."

Norvita didn't remember how she got into the back room or what she thought was the back room of the salon. It didn't match the rest of the store front. It was a clean and strangely white space. She could see a weird bright light. She could see a strange airbrush painting that looked like it was taken from the cover of Duran Duran's Rio album. There was light samba being piped in from somewhere. Norvita found herself sitting at a table as she looked around confused while her fingers soaked in warm water.

"The hell?" she muttered.

She stopped when she felt a small hand pull hers out of the water and start working on the cuticles and cleaning her nails quietly. Norvita went awkward again.

"Amaya?" she croaked out.

On any day of the week in Gaiman Heights, you could come across a small blue and white fairy named Amaya. Much of this is because Amaya does several jobs in the city from announcements for the metro station to making your coffee. So, it wouldn't be surprising for Norvita to see her. That being said, this wasn't Gaiman Heights. This was East Tennessee, and this was very very jarring for Norvita who was already plenty jarred enough to be stashed in the cold cellar she felt certain would be underneath this building.

"Oh, hiya, Miss Norvita!" Amaya chirped excitedly.

"Hiya, Amaya…." replied Norvita involuntarily. She liked that her name rhymed with her standard greeting and therefore it was always good to start that way. "Why, why are you here?"

"Doing your nails?" Amaya asked quietly. "I have this sort of elderberry jelly purple that I thought we could…"

"No!" Norvita squeaked irritatedly. "Why are you doing my nails!"

"For funsies…duh."

"Amaya, it's been a long day. I'm really tired so can we just figure out what you're doing and what sort of squirrelly fairy trick this is?"

Amaya pulled her lower lip out, pouting at Norvita.

"Because you aren't taking good care of yourself. You need help with that."

"I take great care of myself."

"Not for a while."

"Since when?"

"Since Mr. Karl died."

"He isn't dead!" Norvita protested with another squeak. "He's just lost somewhere, and I haven't figured out what to do to find him."

"Well, have you considered not doing that?"

"What?"

"You've decided to focus on the serious task of finding Mr. Karl so that you're letting other things fall to the side. You, hair, your nails, saving the universe from implosion."

"That's not my job," Norvita said.

"It is, but you don't know it is all. You have decided that you are now key focused."

"What? Key focused?"

"Yes, you know, you have a set of keys and you have one place where you keep it at all times. You come home from work and you put them on the counter."

"How do you know that?" Norvita asked.

"I've been in your apartment. Anyway, you come home one day, and you were really tired or because it's you, really drunk, and you put your keys somewhere else."

"When did you go to my apartment?"

"I've been to your apartment lots of times. You have a really bad problem with pixies."

Norvita was at a loss for words. There were many times that she had found Pixies in her apartment. There was a natural spring that had grown up under the building that they were very fond of and it was terror for her kitten. Amaya was also the best of getting rid of pixies and that meant that she'd probably been in her apartment more than Norvita wanted to think about it.

"Anyway, you wake up the next morning to go do whatever you do, and you can't find your keys. You look everywhere and they aren't in the place you left them. So, you look all over the place for them tearing the apartment up because you need those keys."

"I feel like the reason I can't find my keys is because you took my keys."

"It's quite possible; I do like shiny things and your keys are always very shiny. You should really look into getting less glittery keychains for them, but this isn't about me. It's about your keys that you've lost."

"That you stole."

"Not aaaaaallll the time but this is about you focusing on keys. So, when you can't find them, you get the spare and then you go to work and then you find them later in like a shoe or something."

"You mean, you returned them in a shoe later after you stole them."

"Hey! Listen! It's a key obsession as a whatsit, metaphor, and what I mean is when you stop thinking about things, you end up finding a solution, so go do other things."

"Like getting my nails done."

"Yea!" Amaya said.

Norvita sighed.

"I'm being told how to relax by you and…wait. Did you come alone? Aren't you usually shadowed by Penny?"

"Yea, I brought Penny too. She's over there."

Suddenly, Norvita looked over in a previously unnoticed corner. She watched as the head of coppery red hair bounced over the edge of what she thought was maybe a guitar. She wasn't sure how she didn't notice the changeling before or the strange picking sound that came with tuning an instrument.

"What is that?" Norvita asked no one in particular. "A guitar?"

"No." Amaya said. "Mandolin."

Before Norvita could ask another question there was a thunk, and the feeling of blackness around her.

34.

It wasn't too long after they had started their run away from the farm house when Huston made a decision about Missy. Missy was about a foot shorter than him and her legs weren't going to be as fast as his. Because of this, she was going to start falling behind. It wasn't really Missy's fault. Huston had run around the forest since before he could talk. If it wasn't on all fours as he bounded around like a wild hound, it was in the course of his outdoorsy life. Missy wasn't exactly familiar with that sort of lifestyle. Because of this, it was making his life a little harder to get away from wherever they were and whoever had them.

Whoever?

Whatever.

He was all but convinced that their captors were not even anywhere near human. It was still not anything that he was going to think about directly. At that juncture, they couldn't bother with any sort of mental processing. They had to go. He knew that he was going to have to run faster and there was one thing that he could do to make progress more quickly. He was going to have to pick up

Missy and run. It was an adult choice that a Huston of three to five years ago and four years suspended wouldn't have made. If this was the Huston before he went to prison, he would have ditched her and kept going. That wasn't the Huston that was running down the wooded side of a hill almost dragging a girl with him. He was doing this. It was the plan that Bill had sketched out. Huston was angry at the institutionalized person he'd become. He never questioned the orders from a jake.

He wasn't ditching Missy because Bill had asked him to take care of her.

Huston was trying to find a reason to be angry at Bill. He knew that he had every reason in his mind to hate him. He didn't like Bill when they were in high school. Huston was probably about three to five years older than Bill which meant that he was still hanging out with friends from high school. Bill was the kind of kid who came to school with clean pressed shirts. He had cousins that had gotten into trouble for smoking because of Bill. If he wasn't bad enough then, he was now a cop. The kind of cop that couldn't be bought and those were the worst kind of cops. There was an understanding that you look the other way sometimes just for things to function. That was what the Department of the Arcane was for. The Department was good to look the other way for people like the alchemists who made the best moonshine you'd ever drink. The packs that roamed the woods knew that and had for generations. Bill wasn't the kind of guy who would do that.

Bill had also gotten Jodell to leave him while he was in jail.

That was the reason he had to hate Bill. Bill had told Jodell to leave and then they were together. He was raising Huston's daughter and then had another kid with her. Bill was the enemy. Of course, at this point there was a bigger enemy. That meant Bill, for a time, was his ally. He could hate Bill when they were all out of danger.

Bill should have been the hero.

Bill was supposed to be leading them out of the woods and back to safety. He could easily talk to the Department stooges or his own amadan jakes that would have been able to save a ton of people from what was going to be coming. No, Bill was still at the farm and dying. He was dying anyway. There was a curse and a disease coursing through Bill's body. He was going to die one way or another. If he was going to be able to allow people to get out before he did, he would though. He was the hero. He was Captain America. Captain America was going to be claimed by a curse and die.

Fuck, thought Huston, *Jodell is going to kill me.*

If she didn't blame him for killing Bill, then she would blame him for not bringing him back. However, this went, he knew that there would be a lot of screaming. She would be able to understand eventually. Suddenly, Huston decided that this was probably the fates intervening. With Bill gone, he could simply slide back into place and be by Jodell's side once more.

If, of course, they made it back alive.

Any sort of fantasy of his life after all of this would have to wait until he knew that they were going to be okay and survive the woods. He wasn't sure that was the case just yet. He could only assume that the things in the woods would be waiting for them if he looked back. If they slowed down for a second, they would end up exactly like Bill or even worse. That left the problem of Missy who was indeed starting to lag behind. Huston knew what they needed to do. He was going to have to put the extra kick into the tank, if you will. He was fast on two feet, but he was much faster on four. He knew that this could be a problem. He'd already shifted once today, and it was daytime. It was easier to shift at night and less of a strain. He thought he might be less fatigued if they were still close to a full moon.

He'd be still weak.

His strength wouldn't be up to par and if he took one good blow, he'd be just as hurt. The longer he waited, however, he was just going to be even more tired. With one loud growl, he bent forward. He howled as his body lengthened and grew the coarse grey fur. He let out another howl before he looked at Missy. She blinked twice at him and swayed slightly before accepting this new craziness as she climbed onto his back. He shook his head for a moment before he began sprinting on all fours through the woods. Missy should have been to the point of being traumatized, possibly incapacitated. He expected more obnoxious wailing any moment.

Missy was well beyond comprehending any new information.

If she had a chance to understand what she saw, she would have been elated to have a question answered. After a lifetime of reading supernatural fantasy novels that were not exactly made for YA, she had always wondered about whether or not werewolves got to keep their pants when they changed into animal forms. Of course, there was the Hulk who got to keep his pants but that was a different case. That wasn't real. She was, however, riding on the back of a werewolf so she wanted to know. As far as she could tell, there were no pants. In fact, before she had gotten on his back, Missy had been distracted by the furry sheath that dangled behind powerful hindlegs. If any of this would register later, she'd have to tell someone. That would be later. After she realized that she was sitting on the back of a werewolf bounding down the wooded slope, she really wanted to scream but couldn't find the words or the strength but, honestly, she was just too tired. That was what she was going to tell herself. It was a lie.

Missy had reached critical mass and had started to shut down.

I don't know how much you are aware of your brain's processes when it comes to the strange things that exist in this world. By and large, you will see something that you do not understand at least four different times in one day. Sometimes it isn't anything super important like a pixie buzzing by your face or the anger of a ghost with a sad story. Sometimes this might come through and make an impression, but mostly your brain forgets because this is what your brain does to protect you. You have no idea of the mental gymnastics your brain does to keep you from seeing all the sort of strange things in the world that you would then have to come to terms with. This only works if you aren't constantly bombarded by all sorts of weird things that you cannot even begin to comprehend or glide over. As is the case with Missy, she had long passed the moment where things didn't make sense to her and now, she had given up understanding everything. Missy believed that this was just the world that she was going to live in now.

She would have to explain it all to Paul.

She hadn't thought about Paul in ages at that point, or that's what it felt like. She had long forgotten that she had a loving fiancé let alone that she was ever going to see him again. Now, as she held onto the tufts of fur keeping her cemented on the back of the large wolf, it was going to be a piece of reality that she was going to face. She was going to see Paul at the end of this. He was waiting for her and would be thrilled to see her. She would have to be able to move beyond what had happened to her and live a normal human life with Paul. She was going to be married. None of this seemed real to her until now. The reality she recently faced was to be eaten or worse. Instead, she was going to be living a normal life far away from this experience. There was only one little problem with this.

She didn't know what normal was anymore.

She couldn't bear the idea of living as Mrs. Paul anymore. The idea of sliding back into the normal life that was on the other side of this horrific experience was impossible for her to think about. She wondered if it would be better if she had died out on the farm. That seemed to make more sense. She thought about letting go of the fur and sliding off the running wolf. She thought that she had to get out of this life and live in a new one. It would be better for everyone if she died.

It would make things easier. She had a classmate who'd talk about thoughts like that when they were talking about their suicide attempt. This meant only one thing to her.

She was going mad.

It was the most appropriate phrase to describe what was going on in Missy's brain. She couldn't use the term 'crazy'. Crazy was too mild and fun a word to describe what was going on in her head. It was fast and felt like it was tinted with pop music and candy. You told people that something was crazy when you had a strange but positive experience with the unusual. Oh, hey, did you know this was just insane. This was beyond that sort of thing. This was madness. This was a wife locked in an attic. Missy knew that this was something that felt old and Gothic like it was out of a Bronte novel. This was something that was madness or not far from it and she was going mad.

Suddenly, Missy secretly prayed for death.

There was no other way that she was going to cope with this experience. She didn't think that this was something that you went to therapy for. She wasn't going to blog about this experience, and it couldn't be the case where you give inspiring speeches to college students a year later. Missy knew that it would be on her before it was the end. She would live her life and then one day, she'd completely snap. She would never have any way that she could ever explain it to anyone exactly. She couldn't wrap her own mind around what had happened; there was no way that she was going to be able to explain anything. She expected that death was on its way. She was going to wait for her death.

Huston wasn't going to wait.

He wasn't traumatized by the experience in the woods, or he was going to tell himself that he wasn't. After all, he was much more aware of the scary things that were in the woods. The real truth was that he was just as disturbed by the incidents in the woods, but he was going to ignore that for now. Panic and trauma were human thoughts, and he knew that human thoughts would slow down his dog brain. He liked to keep his dog brain to the front. He was terrified about slowing down, but that wasn't a problem just yet. He liked being in a wolf form. Of course, this had its own problem.

He needed to know where to go for help.

His first thought was going to the Ridge. He knew that his kin would have enough firepower to fight off whatever sort of animal, beings, whatever were trying to kill them. He also knew that he had no desire to fight with them. There was no guarantee that they wouldn't kill him on the spot between the girl on his back and the dishonor that he had visited upon his family. He knew there was only one place that he could go.

The Crowe Homestead.

If there was anyone who could be able to point him in a direction where he might be able to keep them safe from the things in the woods, it would be the Crowes. They would be able to direct them towards Jodell and the Department of the Arcane. This was something that definitely fell into their purview. He knew that he could be killed by them. After all, he did nearly beat Jodell to death, but that was an exceptionally long time ago and a very different time. She was well over him and he was a different person. He also was sure that he was still exceptionally good, good friends with Vaughn. He half expected to be welcomed with open arms or the barrel of a shotgun. You know, it was probably fifty-fifty.

You can guess which one he was greeted with at the edge of the property.

It stuck out of the early night shadows brighter than anything else with a glint of metal and polished wood. Huston almost laughed in a strange relief. There was a chance that he was going to be gunned down by a silver and mercury bullet on the porch of his ex-wife's house. For him to come all this way through the monstrous horrors and then to be struck down in this almost normal way, would be hilarious if it wasn't actually about to happen. Huston slowed his padding steps as he lost his grip on his wolf form. He wearily put his hands up as he walked towards the house.

"Wait," yelled Huston. "Don't shoot."

"Huston?" Vaughn yelled back. Huston was thrilled to be yelled at by his old best friend. "You better give me a good goddamn reason to not blow your head off."

"Oh, I want to," Huston said quickly. "Where's Jodell?"

35.

It felt like the day was slipping from afternoon toward evening in the Hamptons as Jodell drove down the west part of Main Street heading towards the library. She pulled her vehicle into a lined parking space across the street from the library. She paused briefly to look around to see if there was anyone else out on this Sunday afternoon.

There wasn't a soul.

It was always a weird thing to go out on a Sunday in the South. Stoney Creek wasn't much better. People took that whole "day of rest" seriously unless they were in line at the deli counter at Sam-Mart. Once church was over for the most part, it was like walking into that episode of the <u>Twilight Zone</u> where there are no people. Hamptons was asleep.

Jodell didn't want to be here.

Some of it was the discomfort of walking around a town that was sleeping like the dead. It was completely unnerving walking through a silent town, like walking on the spine of a sleeping giant. If she stepped in a wrong direction, it would wake up what rested under her feet and roll over only to make the world shake and fall asleep. She wanted to say it was that. That would be all that it was on a normal Sunday. This wasn't a normal Sunday. A normal Sunday was a day spent at church with Bill's mother and maybe even Bill if he had that Sunday off. All that would pass with an anxiety-ridden lunch which would end with a lazy Sunday afternoon. Jodell had given that up for her family gathering which she'd figured would end up exactly how it would have gone. The men would do whatever dumb hillbilly thing that they would have been doing on Sunday, while the women and children hung around the house. Her aunts and her mother and female cousins would be chatting about whatever nonsense that she didn't understand while the children would be playing some sort of game. If she was lucky it wouldn't be Uno. Jodell had a scar above her eye from when she played Uno with her cousins. Short of the ritual combat that came when they first turned, it was the only other blood sport that the children would be permitted to engage in. Bill might be with Vaughn and the men but most probably he'd have started digging into a few things around the house, including the papers from the Knights of the Ku Klux Klan that her great-Uncle Tyrell had collected while living at the house. Not everyone was a saint in the family, but the irony wasn't lost on them. If the boys in white sheets knew there were werewolves they'd be in as much trouble as everyone else.

None of this slightly boring day was going to happen for Jodell.

No, Jodell was not in for a quiet lazy afternoon of cuddling with a child or her husband. She was hard at work and her displeasure with this was indicated by how heavily she was letting her feet hit as she marched up the stairs of the old Victorian house that was the public library. She wanted to be angry about all of this, but ultimately, she knew that this was in fact a comfort. If anything had been stable in her life, it had been the job. This was her doing the job that had protected her from dealing with the horror of her marriage to Huston. It had given her the strength and the money to move on with her life. If there was a place that was going to keep her safe it was her job. She knew that she needed to be at home with the kids. Protect your cubs. She was protecting her cubs.

Her steps stiffened as she could almost hear Bill's tongue do that strange click noise, he only made when he was mocking her with disappointment. He always told her that she spent too much time working for the Department of the Arcane while not going anywhere with the agency. They liked her, sure, but she was doing the same job that she came in doing almost eight years ago. He knew that she would work as much as she could if he didn't. In that way, they were very, very similar. He would have told her to go home. Hug the kids and stay with them and let someone else do the job. She was sure that he'd thrown that impression around the mountains and into her head like a dying wish. Jodell was going to ignore that thought. There was no way that she was going to accept the idea that Bill was, in fact, dead. She had a job to do. Someone decided to hurt family and she was capable of finding out who did it. Jodell knew what she wanted.

She wanted revenge.

Jodell stood on the step watching the paint flake under her boots. I want to take a moment to tell you about the library building. The library did not start its life as one. It was the first building that had been put up in the Hamptons when the railroad started to spread through the mountains. It had been the offices of Emperor's Coal and Iron Company. They didn't last long there. Eventually, the house was sold to Doctor Webster and his wife who made it their home as well as the practice for Dr. Webster. Dr. Webster was beloved by most of the people in the families in the Hamptons as he had been the only Doctor that settled into the mountains for a very, very long time. It would be fair to say that they wouldn't have survived without the Websters. The Websters were long dead, but the family had flourished. When Mrs. Marjorie Webster, Webster R. Webster's beloved wife, had died in 1952, the family donated the house to the public library system of Carter County.

This building is quite haunted. Jodell was prepared for this.

She wasn't prepared for what happened next.

Jodell reached for the door of the library. As she pulled the door open, she saw neon red letters on the black background that apologized for the fact that the library was closed. If Jodell had been driving a vehicle, it would have instantly slammed directly into the front of a very heavy wall. All of her seemed to crumple forward and then deflate like a fiberglass bumper. Instantly, her head was starting to work through who she needed to blame for this. This wasn't logical. If Jodell was being logical, she would have remembered that it was a Sunday. There might have been a library open in a larger city or even up north on a Sunday, maybe, but this wasn't a big town or up north. If she had forgotten that, then the memory of billboard about "Blue Laws are the path of Satan" that was over the liquor store for a number of years should have reminded her. The idea of doing anything on Sunday was a nightmare. She would have to accept that she and Norvita would have to drive to Patrick Henry Wesleyan College. It was a forty-five-minute drive, but it was the oldest college in the area and if anyone had the resources that they were going to need, it would be there. This sort of logical problem-solving would mean something if Jodell was being rational.

Jodell was far from rational.

Jodell was starting to find herself facing another dead end which only added another wave to the stress of dealing with an already stressful weekend. She knew that she needed information that was in the library and this was just another roadblock dropped in front of her, making it impossible for her to achieve her goal. She had to save Bill. He was in a world of danger and only she could stop it. Anything she could do to move forward was beyond the door that she couldn't open. Jodell let out a yell as she pounded her fist against the door with a loud scream. A chill went through Jodell as she saw a figure move towards the door. Jodell felt her eyes go wide as she watched a ghostly face appear in the door. She swallowed, staring into the face of a dead woman.

I feel like I've mentioned this before. The Library is quite haunted. If you spend any time in the magazine room, you might be able to detect the faint smell of tobacco smoke and hear the rustling of newspapers. This is generally assumed to be Dr. Webster who spends his time in what used to be his study. Since no one ever asked him questions about medical information, he was content to stay in what was once his study. That wasn't the same for Mrs. Webster.

By all accounts, Marjorie Webster was a tough woman who had been the driving force of Dr. Webster's practice when she was alive. She had the benefit of the early education of the Episcopal Deaconess education that taught her that rules, above all, had to be followed. It was forced into her along with the education that she received at Southwest Virginia Institute. None of these things had changed when she died. If anything, she'd become more serious after death.

Jodell was learning that by staring at the cold dead eyes from beyond the thick glass.

"We're closed," Mrs. Webster said matter of factly.

"I need in," Jodell replied. "I'm on Department business."

"We're closed," repeated Mrs. Webster.

"The Department of the Arcane," Jodell said with a growl. "Let me in!"

I hope that this series is informative for you. There are several lessons to take away from these books. One of these lessons is that you should never argue with a ghost. I'm sure that we all have that one family member that you know is going to be set in their ways come hell or high water. It can ruin many a holiday. Ghosts are dead. That is obvious and part of this is that ghosts don't change or grow or learn and they do adhere to their rules. If you don't also adhere to those rules then, well, they do have a tendency to get violent like Mrs. Webster is about to do. Her pale gray face went gauntly skeletal as her hair flew up. A greenish fire burned in her eyes as she let out a howl on an otherworldly frequency. Jodell was blown back on her heels and then quickly tumbled over her feet and then half stumbled, half slid down the steps, landing on her back in the grass before the library. She picked herself up from the ground, brushing herself off. Her foot idly kicked a rock, scaring one of the many small cats that lived around the library.

"God damn it," Jodell muttered. "It ain't fair."

It was then that her cooler head prevailed. It was going to mean waiting on Norvita to be done with Tilly the Witch and then driving down to the Wesleyan college. She was starting to collect herself as she walked out of the yard and past the wrought iron gate. For a moment she paused and stared up at the sky. The pinks of sunset were starting to bleed across the blue. The pale yellow-white disk of a full moon shone above her. Jodell let out a defeated sigh. The library at the college would be closed before she got there, even if she left right now. She was tired and now, all she had was the last thing that she could do appeal to the Old Gods.

"You owe me," she said coldly to the moon peering over the darkening mountains.

Here is the second lesson from this chapter. If you worship the older gods, the sort of gods that reward blood and violence, it's probably wise to be assertive rather than passive and pleading. They have a tendency to listen to that sort of aggression, or that was Jodell's thinking when she heard rumbling. She quickly snapped her head forward as she looked around. A vehicle was moving quickly down Main Street and she knew that truck. She regretted not having another rock to throw at Vaughn's truck. She most definitely wanted to when the window was rolled down to reveal Huston in the passenger seat.

"What do you y'all want?" she snarled.

"Get in," Vaughn said.

"Not with him."

"You ain't got a choice. He knows where Bill is."

36.

Norvita had started working actual cases after getting through orientation at the Department of the Arcane. This was, by and large, the same standard orientation stuff that most people are forced to go through when beginning a new job. This included many power points on policy, paperwork and, of course, videos about what to do during an active shooter event and what was not acceptable interactions with co-workers. What wasn't uncommon, by typical orientation standards, was that every new agent of the Department of the Arcane was asked to take a vision quest with Exposition Jones. Exposition Jones was the official bard for the Department and before you start getting angry at me for using a D&D term let me just stop you there. Bards have been a particularly important part of many societies for a number of years. We are, after all, what our stories tell us. Bards have the ability to see stories through their own magical means. It is important for all agents to be able to confront not only their past but anything that might be brought up in the line of duty. Norvita had gone through this as well. It had been instigated with a considerable bang on the back of her head with a heavier guitar. She suspected that something similar had happened when she woke up outside of Tilly's shop, though she was expecting to be somewhere else. She was expecting to have woken up somewhere with insane tea parties or something else vision questy. Norvita didn't quite know what Arcadia looked like but it wasn't this so she hadn't been kidnapped.

That was positive.

It didn't help Norvita in pinpointing exactly where she was, but knowing it wasn't Arcadia made her feel marginally better. She quietly took a step forward as her eyes searched around the gray skyline. She wouldn't put it past Penny and Amaya to have dropped her in the Hedge. In order to survive, the Hedge had taken on different aspects to match where it started to bleed into their world to protect itself. She knew from reports that it looked like an urban wasteland in the thickest part around Gaiman Heights. She assumed that it had to be the same when it came to places further out. Norvita could be forgiven if she thought that where she stood looked like the place where she had just stepped off until she started really looking at it. There was a space in the back of her mind that told her that this wasn't the case. She started to cringe. She'd been here before.

She'd been dreaming of this place.

It had started to occur to her when she saw the grey dead sky above her. It was the same terrible gray. She thought about what she had experienced before as she walked. They had done this before. She walked down the black path that led to her way through this. If she kept walking, then she would find the stairway and she'd end up in that horrible museum. Of course, that did nothing for her. After what felt like hours of walking but was probably only a few minutes, Norvita came to a conclusion.

"Well," she said to herself, "this sucks."

There was nothing helpful about saying that. The fact that something sucked, while quite true, didn't help her understand where she was or even to function in the world around her. Still, she was here. She took another step, hearing the shattering of grass and dry dirt under her feet. Her head swam as she started to focus her energy. She needed a clear direction to focus herself. It was no use.

All she could feel was anger.

It wasn't the normal type of anger that Norvita was familiar with and she was quite familiar with anger. Norvita had been angry plenty of times and it was one of her favorite moods, but this was a different kind of anger. This was the kind of anger that came from somewhere that was far beyond a mortal state of being. She paused. Someone was far angrier than she had ever known. She ignored that it could have been something outside of herself and reflected that it was everything. The visions that had brought her here were dumb. This whole case was dumb. She was in a static space that couldn't be fixed, and she hated it.

Well, the first step is admitting that you have a problem.

Norvita caught herself with that thought. Who would have told her that? It wasn't a Karlism. Karl would have never said that sort of glib statement. His advice would have been matter of fact coming from practical observation, which is what Karl did. No, that was a coffee-stained stupid observation that came from someone who had read it on a white poster hanging over people in a circle of self-improvement. That was part of a twelve-step program. Out of all the people that Norvita could think of who might have been in a twelve-step program, only one name came to her: Asher Stone. It would have been something he'd said after getting flattened by something. It was probably said as some sort of joke like he was the cocky never-say-die hero of the piece. It was supposed to endear him to Norvita.

At that point in time, it did nothing for her but make her angry.

Norvita could almost see him standing beside her with that stupid sword that no white man should ever be swinging slung over his shoulder like he was waiting for some high energy J-pop to start so he could go bouncing off to a fight. He'd have that stupid smirk on his face like he knew what was going on which was, at best, a lie. Asher barely knew where he was and what was going on, let alone being the hero of anything. He was supposed to save everyone from this sort of confounded, facing unsolvable horrors life.

He had done none of those things.

Asher had fallen into some sort of crack at the same time that Karl was pulled into hell. It was a strange night all around and now he was gone. For a few weeks, everyone was okay with this. When Asher had been awoken as a powerful being, the sort of crazy things that people had seen in Gaiman Heights had only escalated, including the thing that had ripped up the world opening up the rift for Karl to fall. And for those of you who haven't read the first three books that's a general explanation of what you've missed except for the vampires. I didn't mention the vampires but there are vampires, and battles for dominance and thrones and all that. You know, because they're vampires. And dragons. I'm sorry, I'm getting off topic here.

Everything that she had felt about Asher's whole existence came back to her in glaring detail and only made her realize exactly how angry she was at him. Norvita stopped quickly again.

"Fuck you, Asher Stone," she screamed at the sky.

Norvita felt her words echo through the dead sky. The ground vibrated in tune with her rage, pushing her through the dead world until she spilled forward. She threw her hands out to catch herself before she fell completely face first. Norvita lay on her stomach before she looked up to the grass before her. Her eyes went wide as she looked at the charred grass above her. She knew the bright blue flame that it burned with. She quickly got to her feet and started to run through the burned-out labyrinth of vegetation. She then stopped mid run when she saw the figure at the center of the maze.

"Doug?" Norvita whispered in disbelief.

The Blue Woman stood up and stared at Norvita. She wasn't wrong. She could see the long and different tattoos that had the power to protect and to do any sort of damage. They were at least on Asher's body to protect and bind the pair of them. In theory, Doug should have no form. It was, after all, nothing but it and a being of pure energy. Yet, Doug decided that it was she with all the sorts of energy and looks of Asher. The hair swept up in a pompadour and the calm looking smile. Norvita smiled back, relieved at seeing a person, or a person shape, that she knew.

"Doug." Novita said a little louder as she took another step forward.

Doug stood slowly as her head turned quizzically to one side. It took her a full minute to recognize Norvita. This sort of thing was easier when she was inside Asher. Asher's recall for people was much quicker than Doug's. Doug didn't particularly care for names. Names would change but energy had never changed. She had seen the rise and fall of thousands of people who had the same energy. Sometimes it came back in different forms. Sometimes it would become part of her. It was hard to remember names. Asher knew names. Asher cared for people and not energy. It was strange, but Doug half understood it seeing Norvita in this place. There was something comforting about seeing a familiar face.

"Norvita, you came," Doug said. "It is pleasing to see you."

Norvita felt light blue hands gently laid on her shoulders. Norvita breathed out a soft shudder as she looked into the pale face. Her anger was gone for a moment as she exhaled, shaking her head. This all seemed far too stupid. Norvita wanted to cry.

"I didn't understand what you wanted," she said, unable to hold back tears any longer. "I would have come sooner if I knew…"

"Strange days are with us once more," Doug said. "It isn't your place to understand them."

"What the hell is going on?"

"We fell from the paper world into blackness. I lost him there. I was looking when this came and swallowed us whole."

"Wait, us? Is Asher here?"

"No, he is lost. I cannot find him…too much light."

"I could take you back with me. I lost someone too…Karl."

"The Marked One?"

"Yea, he fell and died too."

"Do you think the Marked Man is dead?"

"Isn't he?"

"Those who are lost are not dead...just missing. We are all lost now."

"There's that 'we' again," Norvita said angrily. "You need to be more specific."

Doug extended a long finger up towards the sky. Norvita turned her head to look in the direction, her eyes went wide as she stared up at the sky. She watched the sky fill with large black wings dancing like smooth, molten stones in bright sunlight, sharp-edged and terrible. No matter how sharp the wings might have looked, it was nothing compared to the violent talons jutting out from under a cloud of shiny black. Norvita wasn't that interested in the body of what she was seeing.

She was focused on her face.

In the swirl of blackness and anger, and there was so much anger, she saw a round face peering down at her. There was something almost unrecognizable under the skeletal length of the beak as she looked down. Norvita locked on for only a second with the burning eyes as the realization came to her that made her chest lighter with terrified delight.

Marcia was still alive.

Norvita quickly turned to look at Doug with her jaw agape as she marched towards The Blue Woman. She pointed a finger up as she looked squarely at the Nexus.

"How? I saw her..."

"Are you sure?" Doug asked. "I would say that it's wrong though she'll die and die and die."

"Why are you being cruel."

"I wish I were."

It was almost a lighting and effects cue as a wind blew in. The ground cracked as the dead grass snapped under the chill sinking over it. Norvita felt a gasp work through her as she looked up. The sun was gone, only to be replaced by a bone white face with long forgotten eyes over a high row of pointing teeth arranged in a smile that was far too large. Blackness spread out that was darker than the feathers of Marcia's form. If she were hard pressed to describe it was the color of nothing, just darkness and it spread above them smiling all the time.

That horrible smile.

"No," Norvita whispered.

"She will fight it and tear at it with her claws and it will eventually kill her. It is far too large and too powerful to not survive. It has always survived."

"Then why fight it?"

"You were born with your visions. I am always what I am. We know what we are and have always known. She is new to all of this and is zealous in her compulsions. She has no other understanding as to why she should not be."

"She can't let go." Norvita whispered.

"It will consume her, and this place will fall apart and the cycle will begin again and we will be trapped."

"You could kill it," she said softly. "You are a being of pure magic."

"I could no more kill it than it could kill me. If we could break the cycle we could move on. I could find my vessel and she could find the thing she is fighting for."

"What is she fighting for?"

"What would you fight for if you were her?"

Norvita thought for a long time as she stared at the fight. She knew the answer to Doug's question. Despite everything, Norvita knew that Marcia loved Doyle and their strange child. It was family that called people back. She'd kill people for Karl and that's what this was about. She opened her mouth and then stopped.

"I can't…. stop her," Norvita said.

"You'll have to," Doug said. "She won't listen to me. My voice isn't this strong."

Norvita narrowed her dark eyes before they started to dance with bright purple sparks. She reached up, her hands bright purple with energy before she let loose an echoing clap. She felt the ground shake under her feet and then stop. In that moment, everything froze as Norvita stared up at the beast.

"Marcia!" she yelled at the top of her lungs, her shout vibrating through the sky. "Stop it."

Norvita wasn't sure if it was going to work until she saw Marcia's head turn towards her. She almost took a step back in terror when she saw the powerful eyes and talons, before her face softened. Norvita let out a soft sigh of relief when she saw the human face of her best friend and odd sister in all of these things.

"I can't," she called back with the strain in her voice clear. "I have to protect Scarlett."

"You have no idea what Scarlett is. She can protect herself." Norvita screamed back. "You can't protect her from in here."

"Then do what?" Marcia screamed again. "Let it win?"

"Yes. I think Doug can handle it."

Marcia's shoulders relaxed as her body started to sink from the sky. The blackness started to close in around her. Norvita watched as the jaw dropped, the beak folding into a more human aspect. Norvita turned back to look at Doug with a terrified questioning expression.

"Oh, it'll be fine," Doug said. "I've got this, as you say."

"Doug," Norvita asked. "Will I see you again?"

"Of course," Doug replied. "We have much to do together."

37.

No one touched the radio in the truck cabin as it barely held on to the hairpin turns of the mountain road. This was something that made both Huston and Vaughn uncomfortable. There was always the sound of music when you were preparing to hunt or go to war. Vaughn could remember the sound of the drums and the old words when his father and uncles went out for the war that ended wars. Huston's memory was the same. The chants were what connected you to the path of the old ones. If you closed your eyes long enough you could feel the feet of your ancestors marching beside you as they went off to war. They would snarl and fight with you as you went into battle. There had to be music. Instead, there was no sound but the racket of the engine. Jodell was sitting in the middle and neither one of them was quite prepared to reach over Jodell to turn on the radio. She was an angry that no one had ever seen before.

It was scary.

Eventually the quiet was broken by the sudden stop of the truck's engine just on the outside of the trail head. Jodell didn't wait for Huston to get out of her way. She crawled over his lap and out of the car and marched off into the brush without a second thought. She quickly disappeared into the dark foliage. This left Vaughn and Huston staring blankly at each other. Huston shrugged. He was aware of what was in the woods waiting for him. It was why Huston was hesitant to follow after Jodell. He looked at Vaughn. Vaughn scowled at Huston.

"Go on, go get her," commanded Vaughn.

"You ain't my daddy," Huston spat back.

"She's going to get hurt and you want me to be your friend. Go get her."

"She's your sister."

"We're going to need more than you and me," said Vaughn. "Go get her."

"Where are you goin' then?'

"Raise the pack."

Huston wasn't going to win a fight with Vaughn. After all, the Crowes were their best bet to fight off whatever was in the woods. More importantly, Vaughn had a better chance of being able to call on his shifting skills quicker and with less pain that Huston would have. He'd already shifted at least twice in the last twenty-four hours and that was starting to wear on him. He was already feeling tired. He would have easily been subdued by the larger man. He wasn't about to fight with Vaughn.

He was also not thrilled with the idea of chasing down his angry ex-wife.

That was it wasn't it. Jodell wasn't his problem anymore. She'd been passed off to someone else and that meant that he wasn't supposed to have to discipline the woman or keep her in line, yet there it was. He was being told by his former best friend that he needed to go save her. Part of Huston was resentful. Then it started to make sense to him. With Bill dying in the woods and probably dead, Vaughn was giving his consent for Huston to go get what was once his. He said nothing else and started off the trail to find Jodell.

This gave Huston a bit of time to think on his own.

He wasn't much of a thinker and decided once that he breathed the air of freedom for good, he was never going to be introspective ever again. He was planning on spending his days being impulsive and keeping his head down from this point forward. Still, as he quietly walked through the woods, he found himself thinking about her. How could he avoid it? He was hunting for her scent in the woods and all that brought back was memories. She might have belonged to him after all. That was something he'd have to bring up to her, but that meant that he was going to find her first. He continued his path down through the thicket. He let out a snarl of irritation. He had lost the scent. He growled again before he saw her.

"Jo, girl," Huston yelled. "Wait up!"

What Huston heard was the snapping of a branch with the echoes of a terrible nightmare. Then, as if there was some sort of preternatural force driving her, Jodell was behind him. He could see the light of the late afternoon reflecting off of her eyes. This wasn't Jodell, per say, it wasn't the woman that he had beat down. She turned her head to one side staring at him. She let out a soft growl. Huston thought about the woman that he had left behind when he was being escorted out of their house and dragged off to prison. She was so soft and frail. This wasn't that woman. There was something absolutely terrifying to him about this woman.

It took Huston back.

"Slow down, girl," he said, finally fighting through the fear of speaking to her. "You don't know where you're going off into the woods. Ain't sure you want to get lost out here."

He watched her stop again as she turned her head to one side as she let out another growl, her nostrils flaring and eyes narrowing. Something was keeping Jodell barely together and he wasn't sure what it was, but it wasn't going to hold on for much longer, not if Huston wasn't extremely careful and he was starting to be aware of that. He cleared his throat.

"I know where Bill is," Huston said quickly. "If you runned off from me, I can't take you there."

Jodell said nothing.

"I know you don't trust me, girl," he said. "We were not good to each other, but I owe your man. I will take you to find him."

Jodell took a step to one side as she let out a snarling exhalation. Huston smiled at her before he walked past. It wasn't what Vaughn asked him to do but it was going to have to be one step at a time.

They walked off into the thicker part of the woods.

38.

Norvita wouldn't call the state she was currently in the middle of falling. Having been jettisoned out of many a realm and done some falling, she knew what it felt like. This wasn't falling. It was sort of a strange flight, but it wasn't weighted by the feeling of gravity reaching up to pull her down towards reality and the hard earth waiting for her below. It was almost floating, and she was content to think of it as floating for a period of time until she felt the stinging that shot up from her feet, past her knees and into her hips. That was the kind of feeling one had when they landed hard on their feet and wasn't yet sure if they were going to fall over. Norvita wobbled for a moment on her unsteady legs with her mind still reeling from anything and everything that she might have seen. After a few seconds of collecting herself, she found herself walking. It was well beyond foolish to stay in one place. Norivta had to be going somewhere. Not that she knew where that was, she knew that she had to be back in a physical place so she did what seemed right at the time.

Norvita had to keep walking.

When she took that first step, a swear boiled past her lips. She might have stayed standing but that didn't mean that everything below her hips didn't hurt from the impact. This was a new feeling for her. Visions didn't really physically hurt, nor should exiting out of one. So, she was experiencing a new thing as she limped forward. After the pain started to subside, her eyes finally focused around her.

Instantly, Norita was freshly pissed off.

"Am I back in the fucking forest?!?" she screamed. It echoed off the trees of yes, a forest.

It wasn't the forests that surrounded the northern part of the park in Gaiman Heights or any of the number of national forests that Norvita had had the misfortune of hiking in as a girl scout. Norvita, for the record, hated being in the Girl Scouts, largely due to the weird outdoor component. She'd made an agreement then that if nature would leave her alone, then she'd try her hardest never to be in it again. This was the second time that agreement had been violated by the forces well beyond her control. This was the last place she'd ever want to be. She hated being lost in the woods and yet here she was, in real fucking life and not even a vision. She hadn't stopped walking, but it started to put her ill at ease. Had she really left the vision that had been forced upon her in the beauty salon? She was terrified that this was still the vision or worse. With the involvement of Amaya and Penny, she could easily be in the Hedge. It was hard to get a psychic like Norvita to cross into Arcadia (the land of the fae) but the Hedge was an easy place to lead anyone into. It was the twisting space between worlds and if someone spent enough time in the Hedge they could change. This was going to be harder for Norvita with each passing moment.

She couldn't trust her own perceptions.

Norvita suddenly realized that this had to be insanity. If you couldn't trust the reality around you, then whether or not this was her reality, then she was insane. She wasn't planning on letting that win for more than the two seconds it took her to think about it. Norvita's entire being focused on what was the real world that was around her. If Doug or Amaya wasn't making any comments, then she had to believe that this was reality. Because of this, she picked a direction and started to walk.

She needs to let go.

That thought flittered through her head yet again. The words *let go* stuck in her mind and she could have learned how to focus on that from what she had seen, but the problem was that the visions were starting to fade away from her. The longer that she thought about her vision the less she could remember. She could only hold on to the last two words and what they meant.

She knew that she had to let go of Karl.

It was the only thing that she could pull out from the vision. She knew that it was all about letting go. If there was only one thing that she had left to let go of it was Karl. She knew that she couldn't just let go of Karl though. If she started to forget about Karl, then there would be no one left to think about him and then he would really be gone. She couldn't hope that Monica would hold on to his memory. She'd forgotten about him the second he became possessed by the demon that had ruined his life. She had moved on to Richard Duchesnzy and had been married to him for the last two years. Norvita hated the man who called himself the Red Right Hand for lots of reasons, but she didn't hate him as much as she hated Monica. Norvita was the one who had to remember Karl and tell Annie and Lenore about him. If anyone was going to hold on to Karl, it had to be Norvita.

Let go.

That was the theme of the day, wasn't it? Everyone was letting go and it wasn't exactly working out for anyone. Doug had let go of Asher and where was Asher now? He was floating in the darkness and Doug was trapped in some sort of tiny pocket dimension unable to move past where she was stuck. Doug had to hold on to something to keep from being swept away, and obviously her identity with Asher was giving her that anchor. That was working out for her, right?

Let go.

Letting go seemed to be making the world a bad place now though. She looked up as she let her head take a spin at the idea. It was in that moment, she realized what Tilly had been trying to tell her. The world was cold and there was something gone from it. It wasn't that Asher was gone; it was Doug. Doug was a font of magic and was still absorbing energy and nothing was right. Everything was out of balance. Doug and Asher fell with the Shadow and there wasn't any way they were going do something right first time. He had to do it, if for no other reason, than to save everyone.

The Shadow was evil.

Even if this was for everyone to be safer, was that the best? It started to seem to Norvita that the world needed the shadow of evil to feed into the world for good. Balance was a way to keep the world going. Nothing was keeping the world moving forward. There had to be away to go forward.

Let go.

This was not the easiest train of thought for her to focus on. If she could just hold on to one thought then she could be all right but trying to actually think about letting go of Karl failed her, like trying to catch a slippery minnow with your hands. This couldn't be the point. She couldn't think right now about what she needed to let go of. She needed to get out of the forest. Nothing good ever came from her being in the middle of nature. She had to get out as soon as possible. Norvita stood tossing her hair back as she let out a lofty sigh. She stretched her fingers and then clapped. A quick pulse wave shook the land. Norvita sighed as she finally saw the path that had been laid out for her. She was hopeful that it led out of the forest.

What she wasn't expecting was a gentleman standing right in the middle of her predestined path.

Norvita let out a scream when she saw Vaughn. Vaughn blinked at her in confusion. Women generally didn't appear in the woods and usually not right before him. There was a moment in which Norvita was going to be an adult, full of smug psychic mystery. Instead;

"Fuck!" Norvita yelled in his face. "Watch where you're going!"

Then, Norvita looked at Vaughn. He hadn't said anything to her, but stood where he was, gazing slack jawed at her. He wasn't too unpretty in her opinion. He was a tall dark-haired man with piercing blue eyes. Norvita instantly knew what he was standing in front of him. Whether he could completely shift or not wasn't all that important and she knew that there was a Carson waiting at home. She knew how to handle this.

"Heya," Norvita said, unable to stop her flirtatious tone.

"Hey yourself," Vaughn replied automatically, mostly thrilled that Norvita wasn't yelling. She was kind of cute when she wasn't, and oddly scary when she was. "Can I help you, darlin'?"

Norvita couldn't stop giggling at that. Accents. Then, the thought of what they needed to do was deal with reality snapped her back to reality. She cleared her throat.

"Yes," she threw her hand up with her badge. "My name is Norvita Patel. I'm with the Department of the Arcane."

"Department of the Arcane?" Vaughn wasn't really that disappointed. "You work with Jodell?"

"Yes."

"Oh good, she done runned off in the woods."

"What?"

It was at this time that Vaughn explained to her what Huston had told him and how his sister sprinted off. I'd go through it again but you've read this far, if you've been halfway paying attention, there is no reason to go over it again. Norvita's face fell as she listened and then paused.

"Okay, we're going to need back up. How far is your family?"

"Not far, why, we gonna need all of them? Your bosses at the Department said to stay out of it."

"Yea, they aren't here, and this is shaping up to be a real shit show."

39.

If Jodell had been in a place to appreciate anything about Huston, she would have done it begrudgingly. What that would have been today was his ability to keep pace with her as she started running through the forest. He'd stayed right behind her with each passing step and hadn't lost his pace. That was dependent on a few things. One of these would have been Jodell being aware that Huston was behind her. She was far more preoccupied with tracking down Bill's scent in the woods. This was already hard for her. Jodell had been told that since she hadn't the traits to shift into a wolf, that her sense of smell was probably worse than her siblings and cousins. Slowly, as she was trudging through the woods as quickly as she dared, she started to realize that this was wrong. She could smell something in the distance. It was sweet and pungent like rotting flesh and fresh blood.

She could smell the fresh blood.

This situation was frustrating to Huston. He had been in charge for the length of their marriage and the longer they were walking in the woods, the less he believed that he'd actually been in charge then or now. That would mean, as much as he hated it, that they would have to go back to the homestead. Jodell had no business hunting down whoever had Bill and she needed to be safely out of the way. Huston did not want to be the person to tell her this, however. None of this was right in his opinion, but he was still keeping pace with her as she was sniffing out a direction better than he'd ever seen anyone else do it.

That was when the pain started.

It had been something that he'd ignored while he was in his wolf form and had been able to pretend wasn't there while he and Bill were formulating their plan to escape. Now, he was starting to slow down. The thing about your body, even a werewolf's body, when you start to slow down from survival mode then everything starts to hurt that you were ignoring before. Huston was starting to feel the painful spread of something foreign in his blood. He had suddenly realized that the same blackness that had likely already killed Bill was spreading through his body. Of course, he'd be infected. He spent too much damn time with Bill to not be sick. He knew that he would only have a few minutes to an hour before he became too sick to function. He knew that he might be worse than dead.

This was going to be a problem.

Huston didn't know what he was going to do, but he needed to get Jodell back to the pack before he betrayed her and himself.

That was the problem. He was slowly fighting back his thoughts. It was going to be easy enough to just tell Jodell to go back.

That's when the thoughts started to seep into his brain.

It started with a soft whisper. He was watching a woman that he had owned for several years. She was marching through the woods not listening to any sort of logic and he watched her. She had left him, of course she had left him. She ran away after he had beaten her repeatedly. That was a violation of the rules. She might have been married to Bill legally in the laws of the court, but that wasn't the rule out here. He'd never challenged for her. Bill didn't have her. Huston was still her man.

She had to be reminded.

He thought about this and for a moment, he knew what this would be. This would be a fight. Huston knew that she hated the fights, but those were her fault or that was how Huston saw it. He knew that she would become obstinate and that would make Huston angry. Once he was angry, he'd have to get violent with her. He knew that he was wrong to feel justified in that, but it was no longer correct. You didn't hit your woman because she didn't listen.

You didn't in amadan world.

This wasn't the world that the prison therapist had been preparing him for. After all the promises that he'd made, he was back in the world that he was supposed to be leaving behind. He had every desire in the world to leave this world in his past, but he knew that this wasn't going to be the case. Not today. This was the ancestors providing a path back to the life that was his before he went to prison. This was the way things were supposed to be.

How would he tell Jodell that?

It was the pause of a thought that he wouldn't have had before he went to prison. Before prison, he would have just told her that she needed to come with him. She was a different person than when he left her. Jodell had matured since then. Huston wanted to take responsibility for it, but that wasn't his hand. It had been the hand of Bill that had crafted Jodell into a better wife and mother through his love. If it wasn't for him, they wouldn't be here now. Bill died for him to be back with her.

Bill was no doubt dead by this point.

If they hadn't killed Bill during the escape, then there was no chance that he wasn't going to be dead by now. The blackness coursing through his veins would have killed any average human being. It was a miracle that Huston wasn't dead yet also, but he was starting to feel the effects now. He couldn't let it go on before telling her everything. He was going to tell her one thing. He was going to have to tell her that Bill was too sick to worry much about saving him. This wasn't a thought that he'd have had five years ago.

Prison had made him soft.

It would be enough to just let it happen and let her collapse into his arms. He would have been in a perfect position to allow himself to be the hero. Bill, however, had sacrificed his life to save Huston. After everything that had happened, Bill was still a bigger man than Huston could have ever been, and he hated him for that. At the very least, he owed him the courtesy of letting Jodell be ready for what was coming.

"Jo!" he called to her. "Wait up."

Jodell's pace stopped so quickly that it wasn't human. It didn't much seem like a conry movement either. Not that Huston hadn't seen the conry pause like that. There was something else that Jodell was channeling though, something more... massive? Maybe. She turned back, looking at Huston. Huston hadn't seen anything like this: not in her or anyone else. Maybe it was the shadow and sunlight playing tricks, but her eyes were different. It took a moment for Huston to remember. Jodell had one eye that was blue like the rest of her pack. It was how you could tell one of Them Crowe Boys, they all were dark haired with bright blue eyes. At that moment, both her eyes were a dark brown like a wide-eyed predator. He paused.

"Don't," her voice rumbled with a low roar. "Don't you dare think about talking to me about us."

If nothing else, Huston was angry at her. He wasn't about to be intimidated by his woman. It wasn't even that. He had something he had to do.

"Jo," he said with an answering growling sneer that showed her all his teeth.

"We ain't got time for any bullshit right now."

"Before we get there, you need to be ready for this," Huston said. "Bill ain't doin' too good. I don't know if he's going to be ... all right when we get there."

Jodell blinked long enough to pull her out of whatever rage she was feeling. She looked at Huston as she thought about snapping his head to one side so she could continue. He was concerned for Bill, at least there was that going for Huston.

"What?" Jodell asked. "What do you mean?"

"Whatever got me and him, they beat the tar out of him. He got sick from it. He might not be alive when we get there."

"We need to go," she said quickly. "I need to find him."

"Don't be a fucking retard, Jo." Huston said far more forcefully. "There was all sorts of different monsters out there we can't fight on our own. We need more people. We'll need your family."

"He's going to die if we wait."

"Christ, Jo! Your head done gone soft. He's probably already dead's what I'm sayin'. Let's get out of the woods before we get the same."

"He's my husband!"

"No. I am."

If you could have a moment that was totally quiet in the woods, it was then. Jodell's eyes darkened back to the heavy brown that swallowed up the blue as she cocked her head to one side, listening to him. She slowly walked towards him, every fiber of her being silently radiating *WHAT did you just say, now?* This wasn't the teenager he'd married long ago, it felt like, as she stood in front of him. She was so, so much angrier than that girl. He wasn't about to give up any space to her.

"What did you say?" her voice was back at that dark heavy growl that rattled one's bones subsonically.

"I'm the one you were ordained to marry," Huston growled. "It's time to go."

Jodell pushed him away from her as hard as she could. Huston stumbled back, almost tripping over a downed tree. Huston was horrified by Jodell. This was the moment that he should have walked away but something snapped inside his head. Maybe it was his irritation with her demands to find Bill. No, this was something worse. It was the fact that he was starting to feel the defiance that came from her. She was always headstrong, and Huston knew that there was only one thing that he do to could easily take care of it. He brought his hand up and moved to slap her as hard as he could. It was his best tactic to get her to calm down and it had worked every other time.

It did not work today.

Just before his hand connected with her cheek, Jodell grabbed Huston by the wrist. She turned her head towards him as she let out a loud roar that he'd never heard come from her before. Huston snarled while howling in pain as a sharp twist shattered every bone in his hand under the force of her grip. Huston looked at her, his eyes starting to water as he pursed his lip.

"What has gotten into you girl?" Huston whispered.

"You smell of death!" Jodell yelled.

Huston suddenly realized that if he didn't put forth an effort, there was not a good way that this ended for him. He tried to summon all the strength to pull up his padded feet. He swung at her. Before claws could meet flesh, Jodell swung him away as hard as she could. She felt his arm pop out of place as she let go. She started to take a step forward as she looked at him. Jodell covered her mouth in a gesture of shock. Huston spat.

"I didn't…" she whispered.

Before Jodell could get another word out of her mouth, there was a rush of wind. She watched as a black blur rushed across her vision and swallowed up Huston. When she looked again, he was gone in a flurry of black. Jodell tried to move forward before she felt something hit the back of her head with a hard sound. Jodell fell forward trying to pull herself up. Only then, she felt a boot slam into her face before it pressed down on the back of her neck.

"I'd kill you now," said a voice. "But I got plans for you. We ain't done yet."

40.

When the blackness lifted and she felt the world slip back, the first thing Jodell had was her hearing. All at once, the sound of the world came rushing back to her like someone had dunked her head under the sounds of the forest. It was all too much. Then, she picked out a single sound. At varying degrees of respiration, Jodell heard what sounded like rasping breathing. Her head was too heavy, to move to see where it came from specifically, but it was around her. Her eyes opened to see only blackness around her. All that did was make her angry. Unless she could be convinced otherwise, a feat that would be difficult at best, she had to believe that Huston had managed to hit her hard enough to bring her down to her knees and lose consciousness. She had promised herself that this was something that would never happen again. The only thing that kept her from being completely enraged at all of this was the sound of raspy breathing. She had no doubt broken a rib or two during their fight and she could be proud of it. She had hurt Huston, at least, breaking his ribs leaving a wet gasping to press out of his body. It was then that she opened her eyes to realize something.

It wasn't Huston.

Huston was lying prone not that far away from her. They were eye level to each other. The only difference was that Huston's eyes had a light going on slowly. There were masses of black figures around him. She watched as their bodies hunched over Huston. Jodell felt her body heave violently as she tried to fight against something, some pressure she became aware of. The boot on the back of her neck pushed down.

"No, darlin'" the raspy voice above her spoke. "You don't want to move. Just close your eyes. You don't need to see what's comin' next. My boys are hungry."

Jodell was never one to turn away from terror but loosely, she couldn't hold on to her consciousness either. Slowly, she closed her eyes again.

Sometime later, Jodell returned to her thoughts. She let out a groan as she felt her body drag heavily against gravity. She tugged as she tried to listen to the dying raspy voice she remembered. There was nothing like that now. It was gone. She kept her eyes closed as she listened. Before she could hear anything, she could smell him. There was the smell of death and human waste but under that was the smell of something that was familiar. It was the smell of aftershave that hadn't changed in years. Probably something he picked out in high school and never updated. She could smell his sweat. Her heart bounced against her chest.

She found Bill.

Quickly, her eyes flew open. All that she was greeted with was the roof of some sort kind of barn. She felt coarse ropes tug around her wrists, neck and feet. She took a breath in against the gag as she turned her head to one side. Instantly, she regretted it. Beside her was a crumpled body. His head was bowed over his chest as black lines crossed over his body in thick lines along the veins that popped out from his skin. Jodell knew that was a curse choking the life out of him. She bit down in what she could only assume was a gag in her mouth. That was better because the sob in her throat choked back her sorrow. She was terrified to see him like this. She didn't want to see him like this, but she had to look at him.

She needed to see him.

She tried to call for him. Bill turned his head up as his mouth opened pushing a labored breath out and into his body with desperation. Every moment of watching him was twisting like a nightmare in her belly. He was pale, very pale. She couldn't call what he looked like pale, more like a terrible grayness that came with a waxy expression. She didn't want to say anything as she looked at him. Bill licked his lips as he stared at her. He barely pulled on the choke chain firmly placed around his neck and then he stopped. He was too weak to fight the chain. He was dying.

Jodell wanted to cry.

Bill rallied long enough to realize that Jodell was there and watching him. He licked his lips as he pulled himself out his haze. He blinked slowly, making Jodell whimper harder as she tried to not cry for him.

"J…" he stammered pathetically. "Don't."

She stopped looking at him almost angrily. He didn't have the right for her to be upset about his suffering. Then, she looked at him. Bill had a moment of clarity that she knew only came from one very serious point: law enforcement. He was making sure that she wasn't about to give up some sort of information to their captors. She swallowed pushing the gag further into her throat. He was trying to instruct her for her next steps.

This was self-preservation that could only come from a life in law enforcement.

She probably should have picked up on it sooner, but she wasn't thinking, not really. She was far more concerned about exactly what had happened, since she'd spent most of her day looking for Bill. She had found him. This had put them both in a compromising situation though. With that, she realized what Bill was doing. They had been taken hostage. She assumed that Bill had done something to insult their captors. If they figured out anything about the pair of them then, well, they would be doomed.

As much as she wanted to weep for him, Jodell would hold it off for another time.

It felt like this went on forever. After all, she wanted to tell him everything, but stopped short, not least because her ability to talk was all but disabled by the gag. It was very quiet for a very, very long time until the door to the barn opened, forcing Jodell to shut her eyes. There was that same raspy breathing again. She wondered what Bill had been doing until she heard a wheeze of a laugh. It was then she realized that there was a hand on the outside of her right hip accompanied by the jangle of a choke chain.

"I think we found your old lady," Pa said as he looked back at Bill.

There was a quiet moment as if either Bill or Jodell was supposed to respond. Pa wasn't exactly waiting for a response. Pa dragged a chair up beside Jodell as he looked over her quietly before he shook his head.

"They tell me you kilt the youngest of my kin," he continued. "My boys were wanting to get their piece of your flesh when we found you, but that ain't right. I made a promise to your fella that I'd let him watch. See, he kilt my beloved daughter which is a problem for me. The ancestors didn't see fit to give my branch of the family another girl and I ain't about to let our blood pass out to some sort of shoat or even a dog like you. I figure this is the end of my line and that's fine by me. We ain't goin' down without takin' your family with us, Crowe."

Jodell opened her eyes and looked up at the older man. He didn't smile but there was a pleased smugness in his face.

"I know who you are and we've been waiting to find your family for a long time, Crowe dog. We have a grudge to settle. You see, we cursed. We cursed because of you."

41.

Pa told her this story:

I didn't know if we'd ever live this long to see your kind again, but here we are. It's nice to see one of you, little dog. My oldest tells me that you killed his baby boy. I ain't surprised. That boy wasn't right and probably wasn't that hard to kill. I'm glad we found y'all. I wondered if you were the kind of dog we've been looking for, but the fact that you look all sorts of scared at me right now, I'm going to guess you are. Oh, little dog, this is a long time coming.

We've been waiting for your kind to come across our paths again.

My family ain't from around here. Neither is yours. I know where your kind come from but we came over too. My family starts back in Scotland. Do you know where Scotland is, little dog? Probably. I ain't sure what people know anymore. The world is all sorts of weird. My great-great-granddaddy was born in the large family that lived in the highlands when the world made sense and the youngest of thirty. I think his daddy wanted him to be just like him digging ditches and trimming the hedges but that wasn't the life that my great-great-granddaddy was destined for. He was a better man than that. He threw off his Christian name and became someone new.

He started to call himself Sawney Bean.

My great-great-granddaddy knew that he was different from the rest of his neighbors. Sometimes you just know that you ain't normal. Like once in a great while someone is born to a higher purpose and that makes him the sort of king of all things. That was him. It's why his first thought was to take what he could get from passing travelers. It wasn't regular work as highwayman but when he was good at it, it was very good. He enjoyed his wine, women and songs, but his family was big. If there was something that my great-great-granddaddy needed in his life it was a partner. He wanted the family that he knew for his support. So he prayed. I think he started with the English god but that never did nobody no good. When it didn't give him what he wanted, he met the Smiling Black God with a White Face. My great-great-granddaddy pledged himself to the Smiling God and he would be given a bride.

He was given Agnes.

I think the shoat would call her a witch. There is no mistake that my great-great-granny was already attuned to the world that she drew her power from and could fight as good as any man. It is no surprise that the Smiling God had found favor with her. She was loyal to the Smiling God. From what we know, she hunted like my great-great-granddaddy, but gave her victims in honor of the Smiling God. If she hadn't been hunting then she would have never met my great-great-granddaddy. She had tried to hold him up and he'd nearly killed her after that. I don't know how long it took them to realize that this was their future. I can only assume it was the Smiling God. They consummated their union on the road and built their home in a cave protected by the harsh sea.

Agnes started to see visions next.

Agnes had seen visions since she was a little girl. It was exactly why her family had shunned her. I don't know if my great-great-granddaddy felt anything towards her witchy ways. Once you start to fall in the line of the Smiling God, then you can stop questioning things of a supernatural manner. The women folk in my line have always learned to perform the rituals that had been handed down from my great-great-granny. But she'd seen our future. She saw us standing on a hill looking down. Below us were the races of men. Our Smiling God told us that we were not like them. The morality bound to the English wasn't the morality that we'd need to ever worry about. We weren't men, we were something more. We were the stewards of the Smiling God and the Smiling God would provide. We'd live our lives and keep to his ways and he would bless us. She told my great-great-granddaddy this vision. I don't know if he believed her until she told him to bring the first victim back to her while he was still alive. He did and much to his surprise, Agnes said a prayer to the Smiling God and killed the shoat like he was another animal.

Sawney Bean understood after that first taste of shoat. The Smiling God would always provide.

In that environment, my family thrived. Great-great-granny was able to bear forth fourteen children, mostly boys but there were girls too. From there we spread to a small army of grandchildren that knew how to hunt for the betterment of the family. Ain't that what y'all do, little dog? You have to keep the blood pure and that means not fucking an animal. We were the only ones like us, so we married in our family and the Smiling God blessed us. None of us have ever been sick and he provided for us. We were the best hunters in the region. We could easily track at night and take what was ours and then disappear. Every time we hunted back then we gave our part to the Smiling God.

English made good hunting. Their Scottish subjects didn't mind how many of them went missing.

If this was the end of the story, then it would be the best life that anyone could have ever had. We ran the countryside killing and feasting on the blood. We ruled the land in our homeland. It was something else that happened.

Agnes had another vision.

She stood on the hill above our cave. The sky started to blacken as the moon turned towards her. She could see the face of her Smiling God look down at her. Agnes looked up at him and then stared at the tree. Beside her, she saw three bodies that she knew to be her, her beloved husband and their oldest daughter hanging from the tree swinging. She watched as their bodies turned and then fell to bone. She cast her eyes up to the Smiling God begging for understanding before she turned. Below her, she saw our family spreading out from the cave to all the corners of the earth. Agnes spent a great deal of time contemplating her vision. She knew that it would mean her death was coming but that was nothing compared to the survival of our family. That's what she told Sawney and he never believed her. He should have.

Agnes was never wrong.

I don't know if you could really blame my great-great-granddaddy. The world had left them alone for so long that it was hard to think that anything was going to change. There were lean times, sure, but people went missing all the time back then. Sometimes, you dropped a kid off in the woods because you couldn't feed them no more. Other times you just got lost going someplace and would never, ever be heard of again. We were doing everything we could to survive and the idea of throwing it off was scary to him. He was the king of his own domain. We are everywhere anymore, I bet and keeping his faith. Oh, am I boring you, little dog? You seem to be whining a bit.

Hold still, this part ain't gonna hurt.

Where was I? Oh, right. Lost my place.

I suppose we couldn't keep going without getting to be caught, but of course the Smiling God had told us that this was coming and this was the event that would spark our flight from our homeland. We were hunting on the old roads one day when we came across a newly made couple as they were leaving from their wedding off to living a wonderful life together. We descended upon them, killing the two horses, the carriage man and the bridegroom. We took the bride back to the cave. My great-great-granny knew that we needed to kill her outright but my great-great-granddaddy had a hard time with this. She didn't make it any easier.

"Please," said the bride. "I will do anything. Anything."

Weakness took over my great-great-grandfather in that moment. She stared at him with her big brown eyes that were damp with tears in her white wedding dress. She looked terribly beautiful in her suffering and she was going to suffer more. Besides, Agnes wasn't able to give him any more children at that point. He let her live after, well, after having what he wanted from her given to him. I don't know how she was able to run away, but she did and got herself to the closest village.

That bitch told them everything.

Not only did that English bitch get everyone riled up, she was able to get word to her father-in-law about the death of his son. He was angry enough to tell his cousin who turned out to be James the VI of England. The next thing that happened was a mob that marched towards our cave. The family was gone during that time. We were hunting when the mob arrived. There were thousands of people. My great-great-granddaddy was too old to go off on the hunt and my great-great-grandmother and her oldest daughter were taking care of the wee folk when they were dragged out of the cave.

Shoat are funny, ain't they. They love their parades and their justice when it's them but when they get all scared all that goes out the window. There was no trial. There was no jury or the like. No, they hung them at the Hairy Oak tree that still stands at our first home, all three of them. I don't know what happen to the youngins. They ain't our family anymore, anyway. Probably mixed in and gone to the ages. I will hate the English for this forever but it had to happen. It should have killed us off but it didn't.

We started to thrive.

All of the family decided to spread through the world. My great-granddaddy looked to the New World. Those who weren't wanted in the Old World were being forced off to the New World. If there was going to be a life for us it wasn't going deeper into Europe. It was going to be in the New World.

We went to Virginia.

It was the dumbest place for the shoat to have ever settled. There ain't nothing to hunt if you're shoat. The water is bad and not drinkable. If it hadn't been for the red shoat they would have died. Ain't they funny animals, ain't they though? I'll give you dogs credit. You learned not to trust them English shoat pretty early on. Don't let them get too close. The red shoat didn't think about that. They thought about them being some sort of friends. You know, the idea of keeping as friends. I think there is something wrong with white shoat. They put the black shoat in chains and treated them worse than cows. It wouldn't have worked out if it wasn't for the quick thinking of the head of the pack of red shoat. Nothing lasts like that. I mean...them shoat always fight. When their boy became injured they got a new president. He was tortured to death. This was bad cuz it got cold and people started to stave. The Shoat started to starve.

We didn't.

I think it was a pity that caught my great-granddaddy when it came to Jamestown. They had fought so hard to get here and it was time to make a new place. I don't know if it was that or he thought that he could be king of the New World. This was a land that could be for our kind and a place for the Smiling God. There was something else. You know it, there was a power that was somewhere on this continent. You know what we're talking about there, little dog. We ain't never seen it, but I can smell that it's gone. Soon, there was a congregation for the Smiling God that would track for food. There were some people who went off trail. I think there was one who ate his pregnant wife. That don't seem right. You want to produce heirs. We always told them to hunt the Red Shoat. That's what we did.

It was how we got the Curse.

I don't know who the bitch was that they killed or at least related to them. I don't care to understand how the shoat organize themselves since it don't mean anything to us. I will be happy if we take down a buck over a doe and it's sort of more honorable that way. I don't know who she was, though. Maybe she was their medicine woman. I don't think you need to read anything into this. We kilt her. I suppose we should have been aware that she wasn't alone. They took our family hostage.

The next thing that happened was my great-granddaddy being dragged out into the woods. There were fires in the trees as faces were around him and my ancestors. They were bound naked as there was chanting that filled the air and buzzed around his ears. A tall man stood over my great-granddaddy with a long black knife. He thought that the man would kill my great-granddaddy. It wasn't death that he was given. With the long black knife, the man took out every bit of our soul from him. He was cursed. Because of his greed, he would be forced to feed on the flesh of shoat, never being able to die and we'd live in torment. I suspect that it would be a death sentence for anyone else but we're hunters of shoat and have been for years. We ain't cursed.

We got more powerful.

At the end of the Starving Time, we hung on the edge of the colony. It didn't matter to us. The English would bring new colonists and then we'd pick off the ones dumb enough to wander into the woods. It did well until Lord De La War come over with his religious mission. The reason I say that is because they brought something with them.

They brought your kind.

I don't know if I should ever be angry at y'all for being their attack dogs. I guess if you didn't find your own way to survive they probably would have burned you out. They love dogs and always hated wolves. Dogs make them feel safe so they brought your kind there. I can remember stories of people talking about the black dogs that walked in the woods with those glowing eyes. That's your kind, ain't it? My oldest said that y'all were black as night. Makes sense, it's what the word Crowe means. I've been angry at your family since I heard that name. We could have runned together, but that ain't what happened. Your kind chased us. You chased us so far into the woods that we ain't ever coming back out.

It's why y'all have to die.

I'm gonna let them kill you first, little dog. I promised my boys that you'd die first because, well, it seems you already took one of mine and your fella here. I promised him that he'd get to watch as they tore you apart. Then, we're gonna kill the rest of your pack.

It's time.

Come on, little dog.

42.

He'd unbound Jodell from the table first before throwing a choke chain around her neck. To this day, she couldn't tell you why she didn't pounce on him then. Maybe it was too much to take in. Maybe she was still thinking about the story that she'd been subjected to and that had taken her aback. Maybe it was the fear that he could easily just snap one part of Bill and he'd be dead and that, Jodell decided, was not something that she could ever live with on her mind. Instead, she allowed herself to be dragged outside. She had tried to walk before she stumbled to her hands and knees. She had never thought that this was more fitting than now. She was a dog being led on her knees.

She hated that.

Out of the corner of her eye she saw Bill. He was mostly limp with his head to one side as he watched her with half opened eyes. He wasn't going to last much longer before he either died or was consumed by the curse. She had no fear of him turning from the curse. He was going to die first and that was noble of him.

She was going to die before him though.

The sky lit up as flames started to ignite around her. Jodell felt her stomach turn as the heat from the flaming torches around her bellowed out a thick black smoke. She knew that smell. She supposed that she could be thankful that whoever made the torches had rendered fat away from the rest of the person. It only left that strange bacony smell that would usually be welcome. Here, it was a sick white fear stabbing at her stomach. She heard the slow steps around her as he tilted her head back and petted her head. She cast a glance back at him before she looked up. It shouldn't have surprised her to see the skulls bellowing black smoke. It didn't. None of this was going to be surprising, she told herself. She did not have time to be surprised.

"Is that her?" said a voice beyond her field of vision. "That's the bitch who killed our kid brother. I'm going to fuck her up."

Her eyes went wider as she looked at the moving faces in the shadows. She saw the pale faces staring at her the same as they did two nights ago when they charged into the homestead and ripped her family apart. More than that, it was like all the times that Huston looked at her before he was about to hit her or worse. There was so much worse. She looked at them carefully, watching as they walked around the torches looking more and more like snarling monsters than people. She watched one of them approach her. He had a limp. If anything, Jodell had hoped that she'd been able to get a swing in.

He stared down at Jodell with a light smirk. She watched as flames flickered, showing a line of teeth that started to protrude from his lips. She tried to back up away from the men standing up only to be pulled into a choke. She fell back before she felt Milo on top of her. He gripped the back of her head.

"I'm going to fucking rip you apart," he whispered in her ear.

Pa pulled Milo off of Jodell almost violently. She wasn't sure if she should have been relieved or terrified. She tried to back up again, knowing that the chain wasn't going to allow her to go anywhere. Pa shook his head.

"Ain't time yet," he said. "We're going to do this; this is going to be a sacrifice to the Smiling God."

Then, she was alone in the circle. Shadows moved in the thick cloud of black smoke shifting from what she could only assume was bare feet to the dusty sound of cloven hooves stomping into the dry dirt. She hesitated as she felt the ground shake with the rhythm of the hooves stomping. She knew that sound of drums. Her kin would do the same when they felt that they needed some sort of music. Jodell felt her body get pushed over. Pa planted his boot on her back. He turned his hands up as he looked at the sky through the black smoke.

"Oh God of Death who smiles on us.

That with black reaches and chokes out all that is good in this world.

We offer you now this dog in sacrifice for the blood that has been shed.

Give us the strength to reap the blessings that you have given us in this new place.

Help our family grow in strength and power that we were once given.

Let our Curse choke out those who would see us harmed."

Pa took his foot off of her back as he let out a low snarl.

"Don't be gentle. She ain't shoat. She'll not break too easy."

Jodell's breath came out in a hard groan as she looked up. Before her, she could see the long twisting antlers that looked like broken branches twisting in the fall night. Below them was the skull of something that looked like a deer completely devoid of flesh with razor sharp teeth hanging over each other. All of that led a large black body covered in coarse fur. The creature that ran before her was running on what looked like its hind legs with powerful hooves, its hands reaching down for her. She tried to brace for impact but was left without any sort of protection. Clawed hands picked her up and then threw her down. Jodell coughed as she tried to find her feet in this fight. She felt her body crack as hooves struck out from behind, shoved through her body and pushed her forward. Black teeth tore into her front, ripping flesh clean from her body. She choked back a scream. It didn't matter how bad that she was going to be hurt, she wasn't planning on screaming. Screaming was weakness.

She wasn't going to show them weakness.

As her flesh tore from her body, she balled her hands into tight fists. She finally let out a scream, but it wasn't keyed to something that could be called pain. Jodell knew what the sound of pain was and this wasn't even close to pain. This was something far more primal. She would call it some sort of powerful totem or battle cry to try to get her body to push forth a final effort. She swung her fist down on the skull of the dead face that had been biting into her face and neck. Jodell's fist immediately went into the wide socket of the monster's eye and pushed down as hard as she could. If she thought hard about it, there would be something completely disgusting to her in this action. She wasn't thinking. Thinking would be reserved for a time later when feelings of disgust were more appropriate. Right now, she was going to survive.

You had to wade through shit before you could get to the other side.

The monster that was ripping at her bloody chest closed down harder as he let out a terrifying yowl of pain. Jodell did not let go. If anything, she dug harder into the flesh she could find and started to scratch at everything she could make contact with. She could do nothing but rip out every piece of tissue, trying to pull it through the socket. The monster then stopped. He finally fell to the ground. Jodell let out a quick sigh of relief. If there was nothing else gained, she was going to get a moment to breathe. Then she looked around. She wasn't exactly sure what she was expecting but there they were. Around her she could see dozens of eyes staring at her with the same hungry expression as Milo and Pa. One was down, sure, but that meant there were more waiting. Jodell had a moment before they'd be on her.

And they were on her.

Before she could even catch her breath, Jodell found herself swarmed by at least six different large beasts each of them ripping at her body as they tossed her between them. Jodell couldn't focus as the claws, teeth and hooves were tearing at her body. She could have let out a scream, but she couldn't get her body to do so.

Then, it stopped.

43.

The first thing that Jodell became aware of was the sound. It wasn't the sound of the hooves or flesh being ripped from her skin, but it was a new sound. It was a bright purple hum that echoed literally on six vastly different frequencies that was both jarring and comforting at the same time. Jodell felt her ears ache with the threat of her eardrums bleeding. She knew that it was beyond weird when she covered her ears rather than yanking the chain from her neck or something similarly sensible. The beasts let out a howl as they also heard the frequency. Jodell looked up, watching them pause in their attack.

She saw it.

Just as the sound hit the pitch to shake the trees, she saw a bright purple light roll through the woods. She wasn't exactly sure what she could call it. It wasn't exactly a fire though there was a bright heat starting to work through her that gave her a sense of hope. If there was a way to explain it, it was like some sort of bomb went off and threw out a shockwave, shaking the woods. It was a weird bomb that ended up being a very bright purple and glitter that blew out all the black smoke and terrible smell. It was magic and powerful magic at that. Jodell didn't pick up on it at first.

Pa did.

Pa's lip curled as a low growl rumbled through his chest and he tilted his head up to the sky. He sniffed the air in a direction that he thought the wave had started, baring his teeth. It did nothing to deter whoever threw that powerful wave. He raised his hand, holding back the other beasts as he turned towards Jodell. For the first time, Jodell yelped as he pulled her up by her hair, staring at her with eyes glowing viciously.

"Where is she?" he demanded from Jodell spitting on her face with disgust. "Where is the god damned witch?"

Jodell didn't fully understand what he was saying to her for a full minute. She stared at him almost dumbly, swaying under his grip as she thought. He wasn't talking about Tilly. Tilly was not someone who went into the woods. She, instead, directed things from the comfort of her shop. While werewolves and witches were more likely to hang out, there wasn't a witch that Jodell knew. Not immediately.

"I don't know no witch," Jodell said stupidly.

"Don't lie to me girl!" Pa yelled. "Where is the god damn witch that just threw that spell?"

Then it occurred to her, there was a powerful being in the woods who was wielding purple energy like a weapon. It dawned on her. What had happened had to be a psychic energy attack. There was only one person that Jodell knew who wielded psychic energy like that: Norvita. Jodell's heartbeat quickly with a small amount of hope. Norvita wasn't stupid enough to come into the woods alone. Either she brought the pack of the Crowes or the Department of the Arcane. Regardless of who Norvita was with, it meant that the cavalry was on its way. Jodell just needed to do one thing.

Hold on.

"I said tell me about the fucking witch!" Pa yelled shaking Jodell like she was a half-dead ferret.

Jodell couldn't put her head together to figure out exactly what he wanted. Was he asking her questions about Norvita? Karl had talked about her frequently, but she didn't know that much about her. She wasn't exactly sure that she could call her a witch. She didn't think that witches were near as obnoxious as Norvita. She was also pretty sure that Norvita didn't draw her power from an altar.

"I don't know no witch," she muttered again.

Jodell was almost certain that she was going to be beaten by a large hand until the wave happened again.

It was louder than the first time -- a wave of sound and purple light. Jodell was beyond sure that the sound had ruptured one of her eardrums, if not both. She knew that Pa had let go of her, dropping her body to the ground. The earth shook, almost breaking the sod apart. Jodell watched as torches dropped. Pa turned around with a scowl.

"Sniping from far away like that," he yelled. "That don't make things a fair fight."

"I get a feeling that you aren't a big fan of a fair fight!" Norvita yelled back from her sniper's nest.

"Bless your heart, you think you're pretty smart," he yelled, putting his boot on top of Jodell's skull. "Get out here or I'll crush her head."

Why that was the motivating factor to bring Norvita out, Jodell wouldn't be completely sure. That being said, the next thing that happened was the leaves on the low hanging bushes shook at Norvita seemed to wander out of them. Her eyes flashed as the purple light still haloed around her. She tossed her hair back looking at them while assuming her usual jaunty hands-on hips posture. Pa put a hand upholding off his boys while he laughed at her.

"You come up here like that?" he said with a low bellow. "Who do you think you are, little girl?"

"My name is Norvita Patel," Norvita said with an otherworldly confidence that was disproportionate to her own small frame. "I'm with the Department of Arcane. You are under arrest."

"By you?" Pa laughed. "You came here alone; that ain't smart."

"Bless your heart," Norvita said. "You think that I was dumb enough to come alone."

44.

It echoed. Whatever the sound was pouring into the farm, it echoed in the most disturbing way that she'd ever heard. Jodell panted as she listened. She realized why the sound echoed throughout the woods. On one side of the trees was the sound and then around her were also the sounds of howling. That was when Jodell realized that she recognized the sound. I have already told you about the times that wolves howl. One of the reasons that wolves will allow a howl is when the faster members of the pack have found the object of their hunt or if a pack member had gotten lost. No one was lost.

They had found their prey.

Jodell's eyes went immediately to the woods surrounding the farmhouse. In the trees, she could see the flickering light bouncing off of dozens of eyes staring at her, Pa and the farmhouse. It felt like it was taking forever for anyone to move. Jodell could have easily assumed that this was an effect of her own adrenaline. Her head was pounding and creating a strange sense of things being very, very slow. She knew what the pack would be doing really. They were starting to assess and make a plan. Under normal circumstances, this would have been reasonable to Jodell. She would have never asked for an attack without a plan. This had been far from the normal circumstances. As the unseen seconds ticked past, Jodell was starting to become impatient. She was terrified that there was nothing to be done to save her. Pa paced as he raised his hand. There was the sound of pounding hooves as one of the monsters ran into the woods.

There was a dreamlike quality to her perceptions when the first one of her kin raced towards Milo. Instantly Jodell recognized him to be Vaughn which was something that she almost expected. She had never realized how big the full form was. Of course, she hadn't seen it before. Most of the time, family members preferred to run on all fours as the black dogs in the woods. She watched as his long back stretched back as his snout extended, teeth starting to tear at flesh. Jodell sat up and watched as black wolves ran on, each engaging in the forceful fight of claws, fangs, and flesh that danced in the blackness. Wolf pack style, when one fell back, another leapt in, using their numerical advantage to prevent the enemy from regrouping, rallying, or taking a brief rest. She glanced around her. Someone was missing.

Norvita.

Jodell looked around as she loosened the collar from her throat. Just as she did, she caught a glance of Norvita backing away from Pa's looming frame as it twisted into something that was far more terrible than she had previously seen. Norvita thrust her hands forward trying to push him back with a bright purple blast. Pa raised a clawed hand. He grabbed Norvita's face ripping into her skin and shoving down. She struggled to get her feet beneath her before she felt the man on top of her. His clawed hands were around her throat, squeezing as his mouth opened to reveal rotting teeth.

"You die here witch," Pa hissed at her. "I am Wendigo. I am Curse."

Norvita's eyes started to roll back in her head as her body started to twitch. The starving heat burned through her body as air was being denied to her lungs. Blood coursed down her face and over Pa's hands. Jodell paused, watching. She should have been able to get Bill away and to somewhere that would make her life better. Norvita wasn't her family, but she was here for Jodell's family. She was going to die here.

That wasn't right.

"Let go of her!" Jodell bellowed.

That was the last time she was going to be able to say anything for a while. Pa turned his head to look at Jodell to utter some sort of taunt or threat. Jodell started a run, bringing herself down to all fours. Her footsteps became more and more powerful, shaking the ground under her feet. Pa quickly started to run towards Jodell, pounding along as his body twisted into the large form of a distorted and terrible monster. He tilted his head down, charging towards Jodell. Jodell finally stood up on her hind legs and it was impressive how big she was.

She was quite large.

As she stood on what had become her back paws, she was almost ten feet tall. Her front paws were up in the air and spread nearly six feet across. She was bigger than her family members that were wolves. Jodell was no sort of werewolf.

Jodell was some kind of bear.

She brought her large arms down on top of Pa's head, batting down the horns before they could come in contact with her body. Her large jaws opened and snapped down on the wendigo's neck, biting into his flesh. Her paws continued to bat at any part of him she could, as the sound of pained snarling pitched higher. Pa dug into Jodell's side, trying to push the massive bear off of him.

Norvita watched as she sat up. Her brain was starting to snap back to reality as she observed what she could only describe as an image that she'd seen once air sprayed on the side of her boarding school roommate's boyfriend's van. It was sort of stupid looking on a vehicle but watching these mere inches from her face in person, it was sort of cool.

It just needed a giant bald eagle swooping down between the pair of them.

After she got over the shock of what exactly she was seeing, Norvita realized that there could have been a need for some sort of assistance between the pair of them. The rest of the pack had handled the other wendigos and that was fine but, she was sure that they had to kill Pa. Norvita knew that she should easily do this. She couldn't figure the how out exactly. Then, it dawned on her. He was curse.

You can counter a curse with a prayer.

Norvita brought her hands up to her forehead as she pulled herself to her knees. She bowed her head. Her lips pursed as she slowly started letting out a prayer that repeated on a rhythm that she'd never heard before. I would love to tell you the prayer itself but there are two problems with it. The first problem would be the fact that writing this prayer down in any sort of way or form would diminish the prayer the next time that it needs to be used. The second would be after it was uttered, the prayer was gone. However, as Norvita spoke the prayer, she tilted her head forward, feeling a power grow inside of her. Her eyes went wide, filling with a great purple light. Her hands separated as she stood up. A large ball of purple started to form at her forehead as she pulled her hands apart. With one great yell, she pushed out, hitting right through the Pa-wendigo-thing, throwing both him and Jodell back as hard as is possible short of a major explosion. The brawling pair were blasted apart and fell away from Norvita. Or Jodell fell somewhere beyond the trees, but Pa wasn't so lucky. Between Jodell's fight and Norvita's blast, parts of Pa fell in a strange path. The black blood oozed from the open parts seeping into the ground. Norvita stood up slowly just as the ground shook more violently than before. Then, it stopped.

Norvita wasn't sure how long it took Vaughn to find her in the quiet and death. He looked around before she glanced back at him.

"Is it done?" he asked her.

"No," Norvita said breathlessly. "Not even close."

45.

For the first time that year, snow was starting to fall on Gaiman Heights. Before that it was just starting to become colder and now the world had finally frozen over. After the third day of the cold snap, the furnace in Twillinghast Asylum finally turned on. It made a strange bellowing noise and a loud creak which made Nurse Catherine jump. She was a jumpy person or had been in the last few months. She paused as she heard someone screaming in manic terror and her body finally calmed as she turned down a hallway and up the steps to the staff offices. She paused at the one at the end of the hall and quietly knocked.

No answer.

After the second knock, she opened the door. On the other side of the door was the office of Jacob Farris. Dr. Farris had joined the staff sometime in late November. It was a miracle to find a young doctor after the surprise murder of his predecessor and the disappearance of a pair of patients. He was a handsome man who had lined the walls of his office with several different diplomas from a very, very prestigious university. They both hoped that no one would ever look at them very closely.

One of them said that he had a doctorate of defective head meat.

If I told you that they were lying to most people, then I would be correct. I won't tell you exactly all of the Master Plan because there is far too much to reveal about either one of them. I would hope that you might be able put two points together and glean some information about both Doctor Farris and Nurse Catherine.

When she walked into his office, Dr. Farris had his back to the door. He was hunched over his desk. She watched as he opened a small bird cage, taking a little bird out. The other ones were bouncing around fanatically with mild terror as he held their brother down with one hand. He reached for a small hammer. Nurse Catherine jumped as she heard the small bones in the bird's neck and skull break.

"Jesus, that is never comfortable," she whispered.

He paused as he brought his head up. He turned his head to one side.

"What do you want?" Dr. Farris said. "I'm busy."

"The woman in 6-G," she said quietly. "She's awake."

"Oh good. I wonder if she's hungry."

****

Snow was spitting from the gray sky as they drove down one the major highways from Hamptons towards Kingsport. She wasn't exactly sure what that would mean, but Norvita was terrified that it meant she would have to be stuck there one more day and she was not prepared for that. She didn't hate the region in particular, but she had other problems. When she wasn't looking out of the passenger side window, she was looking at her hands. Norvita hadn't been positively sure that she would be powerful enough to blast something with her mind. It meant that she wanted to talk to a couple of people. She'd need to make a visit to Exposition Jones and then she'd have to call her grandfather. None of those things could be discussed in a hotel room. It was something that she needed to do on her own turf and where she knew that her fake ID would get her a stiff drink at Pitch's afterwards.

You let go.

Was that the whole point? She didn't want to think that's how you let go, but she supposed that was exactly what she did. It meant that things had changed, and she wasn't sure what that meant. It probably wasn't like that. Somewhere in the back of her mind she wondered if this meant that things were going to start to return. Maybe she'd see Asher return to the land of the living like Aslan the lion bringing on a new age. She quickly dismissed that. Things like that didn't happen irl (- in real life. Yes, Norvita is on her phone so much, she often thinks in text message shorthand). Life wasn't laid out neatly at the end of a story.

There were untied threads that would dangle. She'd done her best. It was time to go home.

Ever so often, she would glance over at Jodell who was in the driver's seat. Her hands were almost white knuckled as they drove over what would be otherwise a straight road. She was insisting on driving Norvita to the airport in some sort of weird sense of loyalty. Norvita had come to respect the woman, but she wanted to distance herself. There were things that they would have to both talk about and neither one of them wanted to share what was on their mind. Norvita even tried to get a ride share, but it was too expensive and hard to catch so here they were. They were fine with each other.

It didn't mean that they were going to be talking.

She was thrilled that there was nothing but the dull sound of some oldies station that buzzed between them. They didn't have anything that they could say to each other. No doubt, Jodell had questions about herself, but was smart enough to not bring it up to Norvita. Norvita didn't know a single thing about the world Jodell lived in and probably needed to speak to someone else about it. What she did appreciate was that Jodell was willing to drive her to a big box store first. It had taken some roundabout talking, before getting to the point of what she needed. It had been the only conversation.

"For what you need? You'll need Shop Mart," Jodell said quietly. "It's got the best selection of feminine needs and self-checkout."

Norvita couldn't ask for more than that.

Jodell quickly pulled into the parking lot of a Shop Mart in the fire lane. It wasn't that big of a deal. She wasn't going to be there that long and if there was a fire then, well, she'd move the vehicle. Norvita rolled out of the car as quickly as she possibly could and into the store. Jodell watched before she leaned back.

The third member of this car ride was Bill.

Somehow, he'd survived. Admittedly, it had taken some of the best healers that could be found and even then, it wasn't certain that he'd make it through the night. He had though, and over the course of the next couple of weeks, he'd get his strength back. Explaining that one to his work was going to be hard, but the less said the better.

The mystery made him look more like a stoic badass. He thought that was funny.

One day, he'd probably be able to return to work, but that wasn't today. Jodell wasn't prepared to leave him alone. She watched as he tensed at her gentle touch before he opened his unswollen eye. He offered her a smile to promise that he was fine.

She didn't believe him but she appreciated that he'd made the effort to lie to her.

"Hey," he said weakly.

"Hey yourself," Jodell replied. "How you feelin'?"

"Like I got mauled." Bill coughed hard. "Is it time to talk about the thing?"

She turned away to cover up her falling face. She wasn't as good at lying to him as he was at lying to her. He was bringing it up again. After the fight on the farm, there had been an offer made by Dr. Duke to Jodell to join the central office in Gaiman Heights. She'd been flattered even if she thought it was more to keep an eye on her than for her skills as a law enforcement officer in the hidden world. She also had no intention of taking the job itself. She was just now starting to understand herself and, more importantly, reconnecting with her family. She couldn't just give it all up.

She also didn't want to talk to Bill about it.

"We'll talk about it when you're feeling better," Jodell said quickly. "It ain't the time."

"I don't know if you care for my opinion or not, but I think you should take it."

"They're offering it to me for the wrong reasons."

"Fuck their reasons for giving it to you. You earned it. You're the best damn agent down here."

"I think you should take it," he said again. "You're good at your job. Take the promotion."

She was about to tell him a flat out no but was interrupted by the slamming sound of her passenger side door. She turned quickly to look at Norvita. Norvita sat with an expression that she'd only seen on wild animals that were staring down the barrel of a gun or the muzzle of one of her cousins.

Jodell wasn't sure if she was ready for another fight.

"Norvita?" asked Jodell. "What's wrong? You look like you've seen a ghost."

"I think I have," Norvita said as she collected herself. "Can I ask you to come in with me? I want you to see my ghost."

She expected to be a little more hesitant, but there was Jodell following Norvita into the Shop Mart before she really stopped to think about it. She almost ran as she followed the other woman through the store before they made it to housewares. Norvita pointed.

Jodell wouldn't have believed it herself if she didn't see him.

He stood staring at a security camera with a furrowed brow that they both knew was his expression when he was thinking too hard. His hands were on his hips with his sleeves rolled up to his elbows. She knew that it would only last for a moment before he remembered the tattoo on his left wrist and shoved his sleeves back down. She should have stopped Norvita who was picking up a plastic soap dish that she was preparing to throw at the spectre. She couldn't move though. Jodell was just as surprised as Norvita had been.

"Karl?" she whispered.